Cue the DEAD Guy

H. Mel Malton

RENDEZVOUS
PRESS

Cover art: Christopher Chuckry

Le Conseil des Arts du Canada DEPUIS 1957 | The Canada Council for the Arts SINCE 1957

Rendezvous Press gratefully acknowledges the support of the Canada Council for the Arts for our publishing program.

Napoleon Publishing/RendezVous Press
Imprints of TransMedia Enterprises Inc.
Toronto, Ontario, Canada

Printed in Canada

05 04 03 02 01 00 99   5 4 3 2 1

Canadian Cataloguing in Publication Data

Malton, H. Mel , date-
    Cue the dead guy: a Polly Deacon Murder mystery

ISBN 0-929141-66-0

I. Title.

PS8576.A5362C83 1999   C813'.54   C99-931190-5
PR9199.3.M34C83 1999

The support of several generous friends and colleagues helped in the making of this book. I am indebted to Teri Souter and Karen Hood-Caddy, who provided insightful and friendly feedback, often rather late at night. Thanks also to Cathy Glass for keeping tabs on Becker, and to Anne, Peter and Mary for making sure I ate occasionally. Special thanks are due to my publisher Sylvia McConnell and editor Allister Thompson, whose sensitive handling of author and material is very much appreciated.

One

SERPENT: *Beauty potheteth a dangerouth punch / She will make you her thlave and then have you for lunch.*
-The Glass Flute, Scene vii

Rico Amato makes a great woman. When he's in drag, he looks like a twenty-ish university student—an ultra-hip babe studying environmental science, with a minor in theatre arts. His look is purely classy. No flashy jewellery, no blue eyeshadow or platform heels. He has better taste in clothes than I do.

When he's decked out, he likes to call himself Ricki, and because he's a friend of mine, I play along with it. That's how I ended up with a broken nose at the tail end of Steamboat Theatre's "meet the cast" masquerade party.

My name is Pauline Deacon, and I'm a puppet-maker by trade. You may think that's a ridiculous thing to be doing for a living these days, but actually, the puppet market is booming. Perhaps it's because the current political and economic climate has made us all search desperately for something we can control. There's nothing like pulling a few strings to make you feel powerful. Lately, there's been a run on police marionettes and Prime Minister hand puppets.

I have a fair amount of experience building big, theatrical pieces, and that's what got me involved with Steamboat Theatre.

They're a small children's touring company based in Sikwan, a town in the Ontario cottage-country District of Kuskawa. Just north of Sikwan is Cedar Falls, the village I call home.

Steamboat was remounting a guaranteed moneymaker called *The Glass Flute*, a black-light production in which puppeteers, dressed from head to toe in black (so they can't be seen) manipulate large, glow-in-the-dark puppets under ultra-violet light. Kids really love black-light theatre. Watching it is like watching a live cartoon, except that it's bigger than a TV screen, and when you throw stuff at the actors, they throw it back.

The theatre was reeling with the shock of a ninety percent cut in government funding, and needed a sure-fire hit. *The Glass Flute* was it—the kind of show that schools and library associations book faster than a Sharon, Lois and Bram concert.

It was an old show, written in 1980 by Juliet Keating, the company's founder and artistic director. It had been re-vamped and remounted so many times that the theatre's staff groaned at the mention of it. They called it "The Glass Fluke" or "The Fluke", for short, but the truth was that it had saved Steamboat's ass more than once, and Juliet had decided to trot it out again. That's where I came in.

The props, larger-than-life foam-constructed animals, people, trees and flowers, had taken a battering over the years and their original designer had moved to L.A. to work in film. So, Juliet called me and asked me to re-design everything.

I jumped at the offer. What I said before about the puppet-business booming? I lied. I was broke and starving. So there. I'd done well at Christmas with my patented Jean Chrétien sock-puppets, but the rest of the winter had been very, very lean, made worse by the fact that I was nursing a wounded ego following a stupid affair with a cop. When Juliet called on the first of April, I was drinking the last of my home-made dandelion wine and going quietly bonkers. She offered me the gig, four weeks of puppet-making followed by an intense, one-week rehearsal period, teaching the actors how to be puppeteers. I made sure it wasn't a sick April Fool's joke, then got so excited I danced around like an idiot, which made Lug-Nut (my dog—an idiot too) so hyper he peed on the rug.

The masquerade party was Juliet's idea. It was a sort of "get acquainted" thing on the eve of the first rehearsal. Maybe she thought that the cast and crew, many of them fresh from Toronto and suffering from culture shock, would be more at ease if everyone dressed up funny the night before and got howling drunk. Juliet's an odd one. Raised in an old-money Boston family, she spat out the silver spoon at the age of seventeen, ran away and joined a Vegas-style touring show as a chorus girl. She immigrated to Toronto in the mid-sixties and co-wrote and produced a series of naughty musicals that shocked the straight-laced Canadian audiences, who, nonetheless, flocked to the theatre to be outraged. Juliet and her business partner, Dennis Gold, made pots of money, particularly with their last one, *Hogtown Hooker*. When Dennis died of a sudden heart attack, Juliet closed up shop and moved north, settled in Sikwan and started Steamboat.

What Juliet doesn't know about life on the road would fit comfortably on the back of a pack of piano-lounge matches. She's in her late fifties, favours short skirts and tight, low cut T-shirts, and has a smoking habit that makes me look like a nun. She's good at what she does, though, and while she might scare some of the more staid Sikwan-ites, she is generally respected.

I invited Rico to Juliet's party because he's my new best friend. My old best friend, Francy, is resting peacefully in the Temple of the Holy Lamb cemetery and I haven't forgotten her, but Rico helped me through some rough times after she died, so he gets the dubious honour of replacing her in my affections.

The transvestite community up here in Kuskawa is somewhat limited, and I knew Rico would enjoy the opportunity to dress up. He always struts his stuff at Hallowe'en, whooping it up at a nearby resort that's gay-positive, but once a year is not enough when you've got a hobby you really like. Juliet and Rico know each other because they're both on the board of the local AIDS foundation, but I had to ask if I could bring him as a guest, because Steamboat parties are known to be somewhat exclusive.

When I arrived to pick Rico up outside his antique store by the highway leading into Cedar Falls, I hunkered low in the cab of the truck, which I had borrowed from my neighbour and landlord, goat-farmer George Hoito. I was rigged out as a goat (a costume I'd made three years before for a mascot-gig at a dairy-farming conference) and I felt a little goofy, because it wasn't Hallowe'en, and the costume had enormous goat ears that flopped around a bit.

I felt even goofier when I saw the pretty young woman standing by the phone booth outside the Tiquery, presumably waiting for her boyfriend to come out of the Quick-Mart next door. She was pretty hot, and made me feel frumpy and old. I'm only in my mid-thirties, but still. She was dark-haired, about twenty-four, with large flashing eyes and a red mouth, sulky-looking but very sexy. I remember thinking that she wasn't from around here—that she must be from the city. She wore black jeans, red Doc Martens and a tight red sweater. She was, as they say, stacked. A black leather biker jacket was draped casually over her shoulders. I looked around for the Harley. When she waltzed over to the truck and got in, I almost screamed aloud.

"Er…can I help you?" I said.

"Boy, is it ever cold for May," Rico said. I waited until my heart had stopped doing push-ups in my throat.

"Jesus, Rico. That you?" Duhh.

He giggled. "Fooled ya, huh?" Fooled was not the word. Bowled me over was more like it.

"Rico, you are amazing," I said. Even his voice was different. Sort of Demi Moore-ish. It was going to be an interesting evening.

When we got to the theatre, the place was ablaze with light and we could hear the music from the parking lot. I'd taken the back roads, not because it was faster, but because George's truck, born a year before I was, didn't like modern speed limits.

We were a little late.

Most of the cast had arrived that day from the city. (After all, very few professional actors live in cottage-country.) They were all staying in hotels or B&Bs in Sikwan, prior to the road-tour, where they would all be staying together in whatever accommodation presented itself. Juliet had made Kim Lee, Steamboat's general manager, include an invitation to the party when she sent their contracts. The invitation said something like "We're glad you're coming aboard Steamboat, and if you know what's good for you, you'll come to the party and provide your own costume as well!"

An actor-friend from way back, Simon Wolfe, once told me that he would never, ever wear a costume unless he was being paid to wear it, and I wondered how many cast members might share his views. It was pretty unusual, and not, I dare say, a terribly professional request. Typical Juliet. People who act for a living, even those poor souls who have to take badly-paid, under-rehearsed gigs in the boonies, have some pride.

Juliet met us at the door dressed as Snow White. She was carrying a martini glass in one hand and a lit cigarette in the other. Her Snow White outfit was close to the Disney original in colour and design, but the cut was tweaked high and low to show off her ample physical features. The effect was startlingly soft-porn, as if old Walt had overdosed on Viagra before dreaming up the character.

"Darlings!" Juliet said, transferring her smoke to the martini hand and pulling each of us towards her with an iron grip to deliver a couple of air-kisses. Her raven hair was helmeted to her head with spray, and the makeup was laid on with a trowel.

"Ricki, you look divine," Juliet said. "Absolutely delicious. A triumph." Rico glowed.

"Polly, dear, are you dressed as a cow?" she said to me. She was referring, I think, to the coy pink udder that was part of my costume. Nothing outrageous, but it was there because I'm a stickler for detail.

"A goat, Juliet."

"Oh. A goat. That would make Ricki…I know, Heidi!" She howled with laughter, and Rico joined in. I chuckled to be polite, but my heart wasn't in it.

"Oh, lighten up, Polly. You look sweet. Go in and get a drink," Juliet said.

I hate costume parties, and I hate being told to lighten up. We waded into the crowd.

"I haven't met the cast yet, but I've seen their head-shots," I said. "I think that's Amber Thackeray over there. She's playing the Princess and the Serpent."

"Didn't I see her in that new McDonald's commercial?" Rico said.

"That's her. Juliet said she's fresh out of theatre school. She's done some commercial and modelling work, but I don't know if she can act."

"She probably doesn't have to," Rico said. Amber was cover-girl gorgeous. She had a long, luxurious mane of real, honest-to-God red hair, her teeth were white and even, her skin was flawless, sprinkled with cinnamon freckles, and her body positively vibrated with sexual energy. She was dressed in a Greek-goddess toga, but she could have been wearing sack-cloth and ashes and she still would have had every eye in the room. I just hoped that her beauty hadn't made her mean. It can do that sometimes.

She bounced over to us.

"Well, hello there," she chirped. Her voice was lightweight, and I knew instantly that she was going to have trouble projecting through the black hood she would have to wear in *The Glass Flute*. I wondered if she had been told that she would have to be masked from the audience, swathed in black velvet.

"I'm Amber Thackeray. Are you in the cast, too?"

"Polly Deacon," I said and held out my hand. "I'm the puppet designer." She shook hands by clasping mine in both of hers and squeezing. A large diamond ring glittered on her left hand.

"Oh, I just saw your stuff upstairs. All those cool props. Pleased to meet you, Polly." She smiled with a warmth which was almost tactile. People would be falling in love with Amber all over the place. Maybe the ring on her finger was a talisman to ward off unwelcome suitors.

"This is my friend, Ricki," I said, putting my hand on Rico's shoulder. "She's not in the show, just came for the party."

Amber shook his hand, too. "How come you didn't wear a costume?" she said.

Rico smiled a secret smile. "Short notice," he said. "I loved your McDonald's commercial."

"Oh, thanks. I'm trying to avoid that stuff now, though," Amber said. "I want to work at Stratford one day."

A Steamboat Theatre children's puppet show was a long way from doing Shakespeare, I thought. Amber read my mind and grinned bashfully. The effect was adorable.

"Yeah, I know. But you gotta start somewhere. I'm taking voice with Bob Green in Toronto, and he told me to audition for this to build up my stamina. I almost died when I got it. You're teaching us puppetry, right?"

"Yep," I said.

"Who's doing voice?"

"Well, I don't think anyone's actually hired to coach in that department, Amber. Ruth Glass is the music director, and she'll be working with all of you on the singing numbers, but I don't know if she'll have time for individual coaching. I guess you're on your own."

Amber squealed and hopped up and down, in a cute way. "Ruth Glass? You mean, the Ruth Glass? Of Shepherd's Pie?"

"Uh huh," I said. "She lives around here. Taking a break from touring."

"Oh my God," Amber breathed. "Like, oh, my God." She was in full Valley-girl mode, but it was still cute. I began to find her annoying. "Oh, God. I hope I can do it. I'm so nervous," Amber said and rushed away to greet someone else who was just arriving.

"She's a bit eager, isn't she?" Rico said.

"Positively puppyish," I said. "I hope she survives. Touring kids' theatre is the worst kind of trial by ordeal. If you haven't got the chops for it, you sink real quick."

"You've done it?"

"In spades. I was a touring stage-manager and performer with a company out east for years. Even kept my Equity standing, although I haven't been on stage for a long time. Touring is murder, Rico. There's no way I'd ever do it again."

"Never say never," Rico said, shaking a manicured finger in my face. "Anyway, good thing you don't have to tour with that one. She looks like she may be a sinker. Mind if I mingle? I've got to see if the bartender recognizes me." He gave me a pert wave and pushed into the crowd.

"What did Amber just say to you?" said a voice in my ear. I turned to find Jason McMaster, the stage manager, gazing intensely at Amber's retreating form. He was dressed in stage-crew black, the uniform of stage managers everywhere, and carried an arm-load of audio cable. Black was not his colour. I swallowed my preferred response, which would have been to raise an eyebrow and say in a chilly voice: "You are her keeper, yes?"

"Excuse me?" I said, instead.

"What did she say to you?" he repeated.

"She introduced herself," I said. "Does she need your permission for that?" Jason and I had enjoyed a couple of run-ins already and weren't destined to become bosom buddies.

He shook himself like a wet whippet and glared at me. "Of course not. It's just that she seems to be avoiding me, and I can't figure out why."

"I think she just wants to meet everyone," I said, carefully. I could at least make an effort to be friendly, I figured. "You know her, I take it?" I had known Jason for less than a week. He came up in advance of the cast, as per his Equity contract, to do the stage-manager's organizational thing. He was originally from Kuskawa and a graduate of the Laingford High drama club. I'd heard that he'd been through the theatre tech program at Kingsway

Theatre School in Toronto, and he took his job seriously.

He'd never mentioned a connection with any of the cast-members.

"Amber's my fiancée," he said.

TWO

MOTHER: *You'll meet with strangers on the path, take care / Be wary, but polite, and comb your hair.*
-The Glass Flute, Scene ii

Jason's eyes started flickering around the room. He'd lost sight of Amber, and he was panicking.

"Have you been engaged for long?" I said.

Jason looked at his watch. "Three and a half hours," he said, then grinned. "And six minutes." The smile perked up his face, lending it a kind of basset-hound sweetness. I'd never seen him smile before. He usually looked as if a timber wolf had just bitten his butt. The smile was the first warm moment we had shared.

I grinned back. "Congratulations," I said. "You work fast."

His face immediately soured. "We've been going out for three years," he said. "Both of us getting this contract was a fluke, and it speeded things up, that's all."

"I was kidding," I said, backtracking. Golly. Touchy. "Well, congratulations, Jason. Why don't you let me buy you a drink?"

"I'm working," Jason said. "Setting up the rehearsal space for tomorrow."

"Oh, relax. Take a minute to celebrate. You don't get engaged every day. One drink isn't going to hurt." He thought about it, shrugged and followed me over to the bar.

Sam Ruttles, the theatre accountant, was in charge of the drinks. Short and bald, with a horrible taste for practical jokes, Sam was known as the Don Juan of Sikwan. Women were drawn to him like flies to a Vapona strip, for reasons which they thankfully kept to themselves. He was surrounded by his usual harem, which included Rico, who gave me the thumbs-up sign. That meant that Sam hadn't recognized him, I supposed.

"Scotch on the rocks, please, Sam. And something for my friend Jason, here, who has just gotten engaged."

"What would you want to get engaged for, Jase?" Sam said, grabbing a bottle of generic Liquor Control Board of Ontario mystery scotch. "Marriage takes all the fun out of it." He handed me my drink—a quarter inch of pale yellow liquid with too much ice. Jason asked for a beer, which was wise, because Sam couldn't be stingy with that.

"We're engaged because we're in love," Jason said, simply. All Sam's ladies said "Awww," including Rico.

"Love'll get you through the first month, tops," Sam said. "I should know. Been married six times."

"He's the only guy I know who owns his own tux," I said. We all looked at Sam. He was wearing it.

"What are you dressed as, Sam? The robber bridegroom?"

"No, Polly," Sam said, "just a wicked bachelor." He made a lunge at Rico, who swooped away, shrieking. I chuckled. Sam would just poo when he found out.

Jason took his beer and audio cables and melted away. I winked at Rico and moved off into the crowd. Listening to Jason talking about Amber had reminded me that I was very single, with no prospects on the horizon.

My last affair, back in the fall, had ended miserably. I had lived in the District of Kuskawa for almost four years, and all I had to show for it in the relationship department was a failed flirtation with one of Kuskawa's finest, an Ontario Provincial Police officer called Mark Becker. We had been overcome by a roaring chemical attraction, which turned into one admittedly wonderful date, which turned into chaos after I offered him a post-coital joint. We hadn't spoken much since, other than to exchange polite greetings in town.

One night of passion in the last forty-eight months. I think I had the right to be a little depressed.

"Why the long face?" It was Tobin Boone, the technical director, with whom I'd been working for the past four weeks in the shop downstairs. Nice guy. Very married.

"Oh, you know, Tobin. The kissy-face thing. Singlehood. Jason just got engaged."

"Oh yeah, I'd heard that. Guy plays close to the chest, eh?" Tobin said. "But you, Polly? You don't strike me as the marrying type." He flashed his pearly-whites at me. Tobin was dressed up as a black-face minstrel, white gloves and all. He's black to begin with, so it was okay.

"I'm not," I said. "Maybe I should make more of an effort, though. I could take lessons from our fearless leader." We both glanced over at Juliet, who was flirting madly with Jason. The young stage manager looked annoyed and defensive.

"She should know better than to hit on the kid," Tobin said. "We'll be dealing with a sexual harassment suit before you know it."

"Why is he setting up the rehearsal space now?" I asked.

"He said he wanted to. I swear, I've never met a more obsessive SM in my life," Tobin said. "Never quits."

Jason was handsome in a petulant, underfed way. He had a flop of dark hair that fell romantically over his brow, and he was always flicking it back impatiently. I had vowed a week earlier to tie him down and hack it off with a pair of shop scissors. Tobin had promised to help.

In the theatre, there's a long-standing tradition that all stage crew people wear black. The idea is that if you wear black, you can't be easily seen onstage or in the wings as you go about your job. Most of the stage managers I've known have a wardrobe almost entirely made up of black stuff. Jason was no exception, but he took it to extremes. Every time I'd seen him, he was wearing the same trademark black leather vest, with multiple pockets for notebook, keys, pens and tiny flashlight, the tools of the trade. He wore black boots, black socks and black T-shirts. It was likely he wore black underwear as well. The vest clanked and jingled when he walked, and I would bet he wore it to bed. The vest was his authority, and without it, he'd be diminished.

He was the kind of stage manager that we used to call a stage-mangler when I was in the touring biz—the officious kind who gave everybody folders at the first rehearsal, with schedules and contact sheets with everybody's home phone number on them. He would read the company rules aloud and make sure everybody had a copy. He would call Equity coffee breaks in the middle of an important moment in a rehearsal, then get huffy if the actors said they wanted to continue to the end of a scene. He would be a pain—well, he already was. He had already been in my face downstairs in the shop, criticizing my work, which is why, as I said, we weren't destined for lifelong friendship.

"That's going to be too heavy for Amber," he'd said, just as I put the finishing touches on the serpent puppet.

"There's a waist-belt inside, Jason," I'd said. "The weight's carefully balanced."

"If you have to rebuild it, don't come crying to me," he'd replied. His face told me that if the puppet turned out to be too much for the actress to manage, he would be secretly delighted. This power-tripping was not uncommon in young stage managers, but it was obnoxious nonetheless.

"I'd better go over and interrupt," Tobin said, "before Juliet hauls him into her office for a private audition."

As Tobin moved away, he squeezed my elbow. "Go downstairs," he said. "The party's better in the shop."

Steamboat Theatre is housed in an old marina on the shores of Sikwan Bay, next to the falls. On the main level are the offices and lobby, the rehearsal space is upstairs in the attic, and downstairs, where the boats used to be, is the shop.

Steamboat doesn't have a performance space. There's no point, because Steamboat's a touring company. Their performance spaces are wherever there's an audience; school gymnasiums, libraries, community centres, whatever.

The workshop is a wonderful space, but cold. They never got around to boarding up the open water, so the paint-tables and storage racks surround a square pool where several boats would be moored if the place were still a marina. It's great in the summer, but awful in winter. They have space-heaters, but there's still frigid water in the middle of the room, no matter what you do.

In the spring, when the smelt are running, you can dip a net into the pool, scoop up a bunch of flashing silver fish and fry them up right there on the workshop hotplate. In the summer, you can stop what you're doing, strip off and have a swim. In the winter, your fingers freeze. The only good thing about the workshop in winter is that the cold temperatures make the contact cement dry really, really fast. I had been working in the shop since early April, and in Kuskawa, you never discount the possibility of snow until mid-June. It was May 7, and there was still a little snow on the ground, in the shady places.

It was jeezly cold down there that May evening. You could

see your breath. A bunch of people were standing in a circle at the bottom of the stairs, and they all glanced up furtively when I opened the shop door. That could only mean one thing. Something of an illegal nature was being passed around. Goody.

Closest to the stairs was Meredith Forbes, the Belleville-based actress hired to play the Mother and the Cat characters. She had toured *The Glass Flute* before, twice—a Steamboat Theatre veteran. She was a moody-looking woman in her late twenties with dark smudges under her eyes. She wore crimson lipstick and was aggressively muscular and fit. She probably jogged every morning. On tour, she'd inevitably be the first person up in the mornings, the one to hog the motel-room shower. Rooming with her would be awful. She probably went to bed at nine. She wore a cat-costume which I had seen hanging in the wardrobe room, and she didn't look very pleased about it. It was too small for her, and made her look like a lion that has eaten too much zebra.

Next to Meredith was Bradley Hoskins, the Toronto actor playing the Woodsman and the Dragon, an older man whose presence in the cast was unusual. Touring kids' theatre is normally considered "paying one's dues," something every young actor has to do. It's not a job that's readily accepted by the more mature members of the theatre community. Maybe Hoskins really needed the money. I'd heard he was recently divorced and had a kid. I didn't know for sure, but the tour would probably be a stretch for him. The job isn't just about acting. It's about loading and unloading sets and costumes and performing a show twice a day with a half-hour lunch break. It's about sharing a room with several other actors and sitting in a cramped van on the road when you're not performing. It's not easy, and Bradley was kind of pudgy.

I didn't envy Jason. It would be his job to drive the van

and keep the peace. The cast, it seemed to me, was a bit oddly-matched.

Ruth Glass was down there, too. Ruth is the lead singer for Shepherd's Pie, a folk band that's pretty hot right now. Her partner, Rose, was in Seattle with her dying brother, so the band decided to take a six-month break. Ruth, never one to sit around, took on the Steamboat gig to keep her mind off Rose's absence. She was officially the music director, and we were all pretty excited about it. Her job would be to work with the actors on the musical numbers in the show and to record the show tapes. She'd probably end up doing a lot of voice coaching as well, seeing as Amber Thackeray likely couldn't project her way out of a wet paper bag.

When I joined the circle, Bradley was just sparking up a joint. I immediately imagined Detective Constable Mark Becker coming down the stairs and arresting all of us. I tensed up. Meredith pointedly didn't partake, which made me wonder why she was down there. Maybe she was afraid she'd miss something, or perhaps she was secretly in league with Becker. When Meredith passed the doob to me (at least she wasn't afraid to touch the stuff), I took the sweet smoke into my lungs, held on and wiped Becker from my thoughts. Take that, Officer. We started talking about the play.

"It's not a bad script," Bradley said, "but I'm not looking forward to sweating through two shows a day wearing those hoods. How are we going to breathe?"

"Through your mouth, as usual," Meredith said. "You'll get used to it. And you'll sweat off a couple of pounds per show, guaranteed."

"What do you mean by that?" Bradley said, bristling.

"I mean that the *Flute* is demanding, physically, Brad," Meredith said. "That's all."

"You don't think I'm up to it, is that it?"

"You said it, I didn't."

These two would be a delight cooped up in a van together, I thought.

"Anyway, who cares about that stuff?" Brad went on. "We won't be seen, anyway, right?"

"You'll be in black from head to toe," I said. "In the *Flute*, the actors are secondary to the puppets. You'll get to take your hoods off for the bows at the end."

"Guaranteed to bug Amber," Meredith said. "She won't like not being seen."

"That's not fair, Meredith," Ruth said. "The kid's enthusiastic as hell, and she doesn't seem the type to worry about hood-hair."

"You just wait," Meredith said, darkly.

Tobin had joined us, and I wondered if anyone upstairs had noticed that the crowd in the lobby was getting thin. Everybody seemed to be in the "smoking room".

"Thing I'm worried about is the lights," Tobin said. "I've rigged up a new system that's supposed to be easier to tour— lighter, more compact. But if more than one of the bulbs goes, we're in trouble, 'cause I could only get two spares from Techtronics and they said they couldn't get any more from the States until mid-June."

"I've heard that UV lights are bad for you," Brad said. "Like they're radioactive or something."

"Can you hit a high B-flat, Brad?" Ruth said. Shop talk, all of it. It bonded us.

There were footsteps on the stairs and Meredith, who was holding what was left of the joint, flicked it into the pool in the middle of the room. We all straightened up, just in case it was Juliet, who knew that people sometimes toked in the shop, but was known to throw tantrums if she caught them at it. It was dark down there. The lights were off, and we were all suddenly very quiet.

Down the stairs came two figures, Rico, or Ricki, I suppose, and a good-looking young man with short blonde hair and smooth, tanned skin, whose arm was around my friend's shoulders. This must be Shane Pacey, I thought. The actor had been hired at the absolute last minute to play the lead character, Kevin, after Juliet's first choice got a movie gig and backed out of his contract.

He was having a hard time with the stairs, and Rico was giggling like a school girl. Pacey was not wearing a costume. He had on a tight pair of jeans and a heartbreakingly lovely white wool sweater, which made his skin glow like a Mediterranean sunset in the dim light. He was as lovely as Amber was, but very male. I felt my mouth go dry, but it could have been the joint. Yay for Rico, I thought.

Neither of the men had seen the circle of dope-smokers. They thought they were alone. The blonde man suddenly stopped trying to stumble down the stairs. He straightened and pulled Rico towards him.

"That's far enough, babe," he said in a husky voice. Ruth Glass coughed, delicately, just before Pacey thrust his hand between Rico's legs.

"Holy fuck!"

It all happened very fast. I was watching, not out of prurience, I swear, but grinning to myself, thinking that Rico had, you know, found someone he could have some fun with—God knows he doesn't get much fun in Cedar Falls. I saw the lust on Shane Pacey's face turn to utter disgust and horror. I saw that horror turn ugly in a fraction of a second, before it became something I hope I'll never see again. He grabbed Rico by the shoulders and with all of his strength, threw him down the stairs towards the open pool of freezing water.

I stepped in the way, as did Tobin and Ruth, all at the same time. It was weird, all slow-motion arms and legs. I don't know whose arm or leg hit my nose—it doesn't matter, anyway. We ended up in a tangle at the bottom of the stairs, just inches from the black water. Pacey was screaming filth and scrambling down the stairs to get a second chance at Rico, and Tobin disentangled himself from the bodies to hold on to him. I was hugging Rico, and my face was inches from Rose's, which was perched oddly on top of Rico's shoulder.

"You're bleeding on me," Rose said to me.

"You fuckin', fuckin' faggot. Come on to me like a bitch in heat. Whaddya think, I'm a fuckin' queer? You fuckin' make me sick!" Pacey's words washed over all of us in a stream of abuse. Rico's eyes fluttered open.

"Polly, take me home, please," he said in a small, frightened voice.

Three

CAT: *It's just a scratch, young man, but don't you see? / It's safer to stay out of it, like me.*

-The Glass Flute, Scene v

The Sikwan District Hospital admissions nurse just missed getting nominated for the Tactful-Locals Award. She didn't bat an eyelash when the big black guy in blackface, accompanied by a blood-spattered goat, staggered up to the admissions desk after midnight, May 13. She did, however, display mild shock when she saw Rico, tagging along behind us. Rico had refused to remain at the party after Tobin offered to drive me to the hospital to have my nose looked at.

"I'm not staying in the same building as that animal," Rico had said. He meant Shane, who had been escorted forcibly up the stairs and into the lobby by Ruth.

Rico had been crying, and his careful eye makeup was plastered all over his cheeks. His wig was askew, and one of his breasts (water balloons, I found out later) had burst, leaving a wet patch on his nice red sweater. The harsh fluorescent hospital lighting did not help. Rico looked dreadful. So did I, I realized, catching my reflection in the glass separating me from the admissions nurse.

Both hospitals in Kuskawa had been renovated in the late eighties, thanks to a burst of pre-election spending by a provincial government trying to convince us that rural health-care was high on their list of "Important Issues". Someone had seen fit to replace the homey, country hospital atmosphere with a design scheme that had all the ambience of a Manhattan bank. There was bullet-proof glass all around the reception area, and the nurse's face gleamed eerily green in the light from her computer screen. As I handed my health card through the little hole at the bottom of the window, I saw my swollen schnozz outlined right before my eyes, framed by the floppy brown velvet ears of my goat-costume. I snatched off the headpiece quickly and held it by one ear at my side. Tobin snorted.

"You're lucky you can snort, buddy," I muttered. My voice sounded muffled, as if I had a thundering great cold, and my head ached abominably.

Luckily, there was no-one else in the waiting room, so the doctor on duty could see me right away, which meant a thirty-minute wait while the nurse paged him. I guess if I had been bleeding to death with a severed artery, the service might have been a bit faster—at least I hope so. I had been triaged, and had factored in at less than critical. When I was ushered into an examining room by a cheerful young intern with coffee breath and muffin crumbs on his tie, I tried not to feel resentful.

"Well, what have we here?" he said. I swallowed an urge to tell him that the baby was due any second and instead pointed wearily at the purple turnip in the middle of my face.

He examined my nose gently, which hurt, sent me for an x-ray (although I figured that if any splinters of bone had slipped up to lodge in my brain, I would have been blowing spit-bubbles at that point), and then he packed my nostrils with cotton, gave me a couple of pain-killers and washed his hands.

"It's broken all right," he said, "but we can't put a cast on it, ha-ha-ha, and it's not bad enough for surgery." He seemed to be quite taken with his little nose-cast joke and I tried to smile to show my appreciation, but every time I stretched my mouth in that direction, the cotton up my nose shifted weirdly. I compromised by offering a hoof and muttering my thanks. It seemed to surprise him. I guess doctors don't get thanked much these days.

"When the swelling goes down, you'll find the shape has changed a bit," he said. "Not drastically, though."

I was resigned. I've never been particularly vain about my looks, which aren't anything to write home about anyway. My nose was, before this, just a blameless blob. It might have been a bit long, perhaps, but not out of proportion with the rest of my face. I wondered what the Doc meant by "the shape will change a bit," but I figured I'd just have to wait and see. In the meantime, I'd avoid mirrors.

The cotton stuffing in my nose felt strange, but oddly comforting. The bleeding seemed to have stopped, and I'd taken one of the painkillers as soon as they were handed to me. It worked fast, dissolving like a double scotch under my tongue. I was grimacing (the closest I could get to a grin) as I emerged from the examining room, to find Rico and Tobin sitting side-by-side in the waiting room, having what appeared to be a serious conversation about a recipe in Canadian Living.

"Hi, guys. The vet says I'll be okay."

Tobin looked at Rico.

"You're okay to drive her home?"

"I don't drive standard," Rico said.

"I'm fine," I said. "We'll take the back roads route, and I'll go slowly, don't you worry."

"You sure you're fine?" Tobin gazed with concern into my face. "You look like hell."

"Thanks, chum. Listen, I had a watery scotch about three

hours ago, which has certainly worn off. The tiny pill I just took has erased my headache, but it's not like I'm seeing kangaroos on the ceiling or anything."

"Promise?"

"Promise. Look, we've got to get you back to the theatre, anyway." Tobin had driven us to the hospital in George's truck, because his own Neon was hemmed in by cars in the Steamboat parking lot. "I'll drive back," I said. "If I start weaving or nodding off, you can take the keys away and we'll crash in the lobby."

"I'd rather be set on fire," Rico muttered, but I ignored him.

The party was still going on when we got back. The music was still blaring out into the parking lot, and through the windows of the old boathouse, you could see the outlines of people dancing, like Balinese shadow-puppets. It would apparently take more than a little accident on the shop stairs to dampen the partying instinct of a bunch of theatre people.

I pulled up to the front door to let Tobin out.

"Do we see you at rehearsal tomorrow?" he asked. "Juliet will probably understand if you can't make it."

"I'll probably be in better shape than most of the cast," I said. "At least I'll get some sleep."

"And no hangover," Tobin said. "Maybe Juliet will take pity on everybody and show the video first, although I seem to remember Jason saying something about a music rehearsal. God help the actors if that's the case."

"We can only hope it's the video," I said. *The Glass Flute* is sort of like a ballet, in that all the puppet manipulation is precisely choreographed to music. Juliet liked to make her actors study the old videotapes of past productions in order to get the hang of how it was supposed to look. Most performers really hated this method, as it left absolutely no room for original interpretation. ("No, no, sweetheart. It's always been done like this..."). However, I would be willing to bet that nobody would complain about sitting quietly in a darkened room nursing a cup of coffee the morning after a party that had still been rocking at two a.m.

On the way out of town, I discovered that I was out of smokes. There was an all-night convenience store on the corner just before the Old Rock Cut Road, which was our route back home, and as we neared it, I tried to decide whether or not I was up to the embarrassment of letting Lori Pinkerton, the night cashier, see me like this.

Lori and I had attended Laingford High together, and we had been rivals of sorts. She had been one of the fluffy, cheerleader types with perfect clothes who dated grade twelve boys. Everybody wanted to be seen with her and to be her friend. I, on the other hand, had been a charter member of the "out-crowd", a browner who got high marks, spazzed out in gym class and listened to classical music on purpose. I also didn't sprout breasts until I was sixteen. Bad move. I had been the butt of most of her clique's jokes, an object to be pitied, and in Grade Nine, I would gladly have murdered her.

Of course, getting over my adolescent hatred of Lori was made easier by the fact that she was the night clerk in a convenience store and the mother of several small, smelly, squealing humans, but she still had the power to make me feel inadequate. I knew that showing up in her store at two-fifteen a.m. with a broken nose stuffed with cotton, while wearing a blood-stained goat costume, might possibly draw comment. Still, I had a nicotine habit to cater to, and I couldn't send poor Rico in there to do my dirty work.

"I'll be right back," I said, and left the engine running. Lori was not as tactful as the admissions nurse had been. She burst out laughing.

"What the hell happened to you?" she said, reaching automatically for my tobacco brand of choice. I grabbed a chocolate bar from the rack in front of the counter and tried to smile. It hurt.

"I got mugged," I said.

"No kidding. Somebody tried to milk you, eh?" She was referring to my udder. I blushed, feeling a lot of blood rushing to my battered nose. We must suffer for our vices. I was overwhelmed by the need to explain. Lori always made me feel like that.

"Actually, I fell down some stairs at a costume party, Lori. Broke my nose. It feels like hell."

"Hey, that's too bad, eh? Sorry for laughing, Polly, but you do look sorta weird."

"I know. It'll pass." I paid and went out, almost bumping into a tall figure in blue who was coming in.

"Polly?"

Oh, God. "Hi, Mark." Mark Becker, police officer, looked me up and down and whistled. It was not an admiring whistle —not the kind you get on a sunny summer day when you're wearing shorts and a tank top and you walk by a construction site. This was the kind of whistle people make when they've just been told that you, an upstanding member of the community, have been hauled away to the loony bin after running down the street bare-ass naked singing a Bobby Gimby song.

I felt very angry suddenly, seeing the next few weeks stretch ahead of me in a never-ending stream of questions, explanations and pitying shakes of the head.

"I was at a party, okay?" I said, belligerently. "I fell down

26

the stairs and hit my nose on the bannister. It's broken. My nose, I mean. It'll probably be crooked forever. I'm wearing this because it was a costume party, and I bled all over it, and I'll probably never get the stains out. Lori was just laughing at me. If you say one word about my udder, I'll kill you." Then I burst into tears.

Four

WOODSMAN: *When you chop down a tree, don't believe that it's dead / For the spirit inside will take root in your head.*
-The Glass Flute, Scene vi

He wrapped me in his *arms and let me sob on his shoulder, stroking my back with a sure, safe hand. He lifted my chin gently and wiped the tears from my cheek, then he said very softly...*

"How much have you had to drink?" He grabbed my arm and led me out to the cruiser where his partner, Earlie Morrison, was sitting waiting for him, sipping a Tim Horton's cappuccino.

"Hey! Let go of me!" I said, and he did. I was humiliated. I could see Lori standing in the doorway of the convenience store, gloating. I glanced over at the truck, whose motor was still running, and noticed that Rico had scrunched down in his seat so that just the tangled top of his wig was showing. Good move, I thought. Becker wasn't all that positive towards persons with alternative lifestyles.

"Hey, Polly. What's going on?" That was Constable Morrison, giving me a big, sympathetic smile, which made the tears prick again at the corners of my eyes. When you've been crying, a friendly voice and a bit of sympathy will start you up again much more efficiently than harsh words will.

Morrison looked good—better than he had in a long time. He'd dropped some weight, definitely. When I first met him, he'd weighed close to three hundred pounds. I knew he'd been hanging around my Aunt Susan a lot lately, because he was doing the Big Brother thing with Susan's ward, Eddie Schreier. Maybe she'd dragooned him into helping load feed at her agristore in Laingford, a job that had been mine when I was a teenager. Anyway, he looked good, and I was glad he was there, because Becker was being a jerk.

"Ms. Deacon has been at a party where she fell down and hurt herself," Becker said, speaking for me, which I hate. "I just want to give her an opportunity to blow into a little machine before we let her drive home."

"I don't believe this," I said, letting fury overcome all the other emotions I was currently wearing on the sleeve of my goat get-up. "Do you really think that I, of all people, would be driving drunk?"

Mark Becker knew, because I had told him about it when we were getting to know each other, that my parents had been killed by a drunk driver. It had happened a long time ago, but that didn't mean that I had forgotten, or that I was the kind of person to risk doing the same thing myself.

"No, I don't think you would, normally, Polly," Becker said. "But you're acting in an erratic fashion, and you don't look good, and you just burst into tears for no reason, so I wouldn't be doing my job if I didn't check it out."

"Why not just ask me, then?"

"Ask you what?"

"Ask me if I've been drinking."

"Would you tell me the truth if I did?"

I just glared at him.

"Okay, okay. Ms. Deacon, have you taken a drink tonight?"

29

"Yes, officer, I have." That surprised him. "I had a small, watery scotch at about midnight, but I didn't finish it because halfway through it, I broke my nose. Satisfied?"

He made me do the breathalyzer anyway. It didn't register. He seemed disappointed and shook the machine a couple of times, like it was a watch that had stopped. I think he was stalling, trying to think of another way he could get my goat, so to speak. Geez. Ex-boyfriends can be so vindictive. Whatever you do, don't go to bed with a cop. You'll never live it down.

He escorted me back to my vehicle and watched me get in. I made a show of doing up my seatbelt and checking the mirrors.

"Who's that?" Becker said, peering in the window. Not that it was any of his business. Rico was pretending to be fast asleep in the seat beside me.

"A friend from the party."

"Drunk?"

"Geez, Becker. You never give up, do you? So what if he is? He's not driving."

"He?"

Oops.

"Yes, he. It was a costume party, like I said."

Becker backed away from the truck, shaking his head.

"Drive safe," he said. At that moment, I didn't know what I had ever seen in him, really, I didn't.

The light rain had turned to fog, and it was a long drive home. The Old Rock Cut Road is much better than the highway, because when the weather's bad, you can creep along without some idiot coming up on your tail doing a hundred and thirty, trying to get past. I drove carefully, but Rico displayed an annoying tendency to cringe at every corner and apply the phantom brake at every opportunity.

"So, Rico," I said, "what exactly did happen back there with Shane Pacey—before the stairs incident?" It was a nosy question, I know, but he was hanging onto the strap above the door with a white-knuckled hand, and I thought that getting him to talk about the evening would relax him.

"Oh, God, Polly, it was so embarrassing. I'll never be able to go back there."

"It wasn't your fault, you know."

"Well, it was, in a way. I suppose I led him on."

"He really thought you were a woman, didn't he?"

"He must have. Did you hear what he said after he...after he found out I wasn't?"

"I could hardly miss it. Not a nice boy, our Shane. But it's weird. Guys like that aren't usually so easily taken in. He must have been plastered."

Rico didn't say anything.

"Not that you weren't totally convincing, Rico, but usually you can tell, really up close, you know?"

"Well, that's what I thought," Rico said, finally. "I mean, when he made a pass at me upstairs, I thought, oh goody, a kindred spirit. Someone to—you know—flirt with a little. He kissed me on the way downstairs, you know. You'd think he would have figured me out by then, eh?"

"Did he come on to you just out of the blue?"

"I was talking to that lovely girl, Amber, when he arrived. Pacey was already drunk then, I think. He met Juliet at the door and made a big show of complimenting her and so on. He bowed and then swept her into one of those ballroom dips and kissed her on the mouth. Everybody laughed."

"I see. So why did you think he might be a kindred spirit?"

"No straight guy would take a risk like that, would they? Juliet would swallow him whole."

"True."

"That's what I thought. Then he came over to the bar, where we were standing. He knew Amber, you could see that right off, but it was obvious that they didn't like each other much. She seemed really surprised to see him. They said hi, but they were sort of stiff. Anyway, seeing as every other male up there was drooling whenever they looked at her, I figured that Shane was more my type than hers. Then she introduced me and I saw his eyes light up. It was wonderful."

"She know, do you think? That you were a guy, I mean?"

"Oh, yes. She had already said that she thought I looked incredible. She was fooled at the beginning, but it didn't take her long to figure it out once we got talking. She's smarter than she makes herself out to be, I think."

We had just taken the last corner before the rock cut, and a car behind us passed, flashing its lights. Rico didn't even notice.

"Anyway, when he looked me over, she smiled. It was a match-maker smile, like she'd done us both a favour and maybe would be collecting on it later. I was planning to thank her, but I've changed my mind."

"She set you up, you mean?"

"Could be. If she knew him, then she must have known how he felt about girls like me. Men with that attitude don't generally make a secret of it."

"Maybe she didn't know him that well," I said. It was hard to imagine the puppyish Amber deliberately being cruel.

"Or maybe she sicked Pacey on me, then stepped back to watch the fun. You keep an eye on her, Polly. Pacey, too. If you guys hadn't been at the bottom of those stairs tonight, I'd probably be dead."

"I'm glad we were there, Rico."

"Sorry about your nose, eh."

I knew my nose would be a conversation piece for the next couple of weeks, and I was already tired of it. I just nodded.

"I'll never be able to show my face at Steamboat again," Rico said for the millionth time. "They'll all be laughing at me. And I've got to go in tomorrow to meet with Kim Lee about the AIDS benefit. I can't cancel. We've had this set up for weeks."

"It'll blow over, Rico," I said. "You know how self-absorbed theatre people are. As soon as they get into rehearsal, they'll forget it ever happened. Anyway, tomorrow, you'll be Rico, not Ricki. They won't even know you."

We were almost home. Crossing the highway from the Old Rock Cut Road to our concession road was usually a nightmare, but it was nearly three at that point, and there was nothing coming either way. I gunned it and pulled into the strip mall where Rico's antique store sat sandwiched between the hardware store and the Quick-Mart. He lived upstairs in an apartment cluttered with his favourite pieces, the ones he "simply couldn't give up", and the tools of his trade—sanders, cans of paint, varnish and polish, ledgers and reference books, and a fat old cat called Oscar. We could see Oscar sitting in the upstairs window, waiting. Rico had left a light burning, and the apartment looked cosy and inviting.

"You want to come in?" Rico asked. Usually, I would have, but I had chores to do at home in less than four hours, and my own pet, Lug-nut, would be waiting for me, too.

"Not this time, thanks. I need to grab a couple of hours' sleep before rehearsal tomorrow. You want a lift in for your meeting with Kim?"

"Thanks. I'll be ready. I'll dress butch. Maybe Pacey won't recognize me."

"He'll have forgotten the whole thing, guaranteed," I said. One could only hope.

I don't even remember driving the last two kilometres home. My nose throbbed and I was utterly bagged. I had to work with the cast the next day—well, the same day, really, and I wasn't going to get much sleep. Still, I figured that everybody else would be in more or less the same shape.

I parked George's truck next to the farm house and staggered up the trail to my cabin. Half-way up, Lug-nut met me on the path and gave me a hero's welcome, jumping up and licking my face and wagging his butt-end as if he hadn't seen me in years. Once home, I lit an oil-lamp (I don't have hydro) and shucked my goat-costume (ruined forever by blood-stains and bad karma). Then I set the alarm for seven-thirty and flumped down on my futon. Just before I fell asleep, I reflected on why I love my dog so much: he was the only one who had made absolutely no comment about my damned broken nose.

Five

PRINCESS: *Our castle's built with bricks of gold / but one-by-one they're being sold.*
-The Glass Flute, Scene viii

Early mornings in Cedar Falls in the District of Kuskawa are always beautiful, even if it's pouring rain, which it wasn't. The air was soft, full of moisture, and there was a mist rising off the hayfield, mingling with the pale lavender of the sunrise. It was a little chilly, though, and my breath was visible as I shivered on the porch in my long underwear and mukluks while Luggy had his morning whizz. Over at the far end of the field, a small herd of creatures was grazing. It surprised me to see them. George couldn't possibly have milked the goats already and let them out, could he? Then I noticed the rack of antlers on the largest one. Deer are very like goats—same delicate necks and curved lines. Same colour, too. I felt myself grinning with delight until a peculiar pain in my nose caused me to lift a hand to touch it. Oh yeah. Reality.

The cabin where I live is not mine, although I've called it home now for several years. I had moved in after fleeing from a bad affair with a bad actor back in Toronto, and somehow I had become a permanent fixture. I was introduced to George by my aunt, Susan Kennedy, who runs the feed store in Laingford, the town to the north of Cedar Falls. She had arranged for me to stay in George's old homestead cabin on the edge of his property for as long as I wanted, to make my puppets in peace and nurse my wounded pride. George Hoito, the septuagenarian Finnish farmer who is now my landlord, runs a modest dairy-goat operation, and in lieu of rent, I help out with the chores.

It's my job to do the morning milking, which explains why, despite my late night, I tugged on a pair of overalls, which covered longjohns, workpants, undershirt, sweater and plaid Kuskawa dinner-jacket at seven-forty a.m. I was late.

I can't say I hurried down the hill to the barn, though. The morning was perfect and the deer were still peacefully browsing, as motionless as OPP deer-decoys, the kind they use along the local highways to entrap drive-by poachers.

The goats yelled, as usual, as soon as they heard me outside the door. The noise they make, if you've not heard it before, would make you think that none of them had been fed, watered or milked for a year and a half. Goats are good at sounding desperate, but it's all a ploy. Actually, contrary to popular belief, it takes a lot to rile a goat.

I was greeted inside the door by a tumble of goat-kids, the first spring crop, all ears and legs and too cute for their own good. George's goats are Nubians, with long, floppy ears and Roman noses. They're gentle, loving animals, they don't stink (well, the females don't) and they're very finicky about what they eat. No tin cans or shirts off the laundry line for them. Only the very best hay and molasses-fortified grain will pass Nubian inspection. If there's even a tiny bit of dust in the hay, or a touch of mould in the grain, they'll look at you with their weird, lozenge-pupilled eyes, curl their fuzzy lips and sneeze in your face.

The kids weren't hungry, because they were still small

enough to be nursing off their mother, Donna Summer, the herd leader. She was going on eleven, but still producing triplets every spring, predictable as tax time. I fed her first, because those were the rules and she would have made her displeasure known if I hadn't. I cleaned her manger, doled out her grain ration for the day and watched her gobble it up, scratching her ears as she chewed. She moaned with pleasure, a curiously human sound, like someone who has just finished an enormous Italian meal and is contemplating a plate of fresh, perfect cannoli.

The kids climbed into the manger too. The slats are too wide-apart to keep them from going wherever the heck they want, but it doesn't matter. Goats are pretty relaxed about whose kids are where, although a milking doe won't let someone else's kid steal a quick drink unless she's too busy to notice. The only problem arises when, as sometimes happens, a female kid with no sense of decency happens to slip into the breeding buck's pen and gets pregnant prematurely. It doesn't hurt the doe any, but pre-teen goats have teats like plastic drinking-straws and milking them is a pain in the butt.

Donna Summer's kids were too small to worry about that yet, though. They were about the size of long-legged retriever puppies, and primarily interested in things that looked like they might produce milk. As I scratched Donna Summer's ears, one kid already in the manger put its forefeet up on my back and started sucking on my left earlobe, while another grabbed my thumb.

Next in line was Julian of Norwich, a patient old girl whose milk production was down a little, on account of the fact that she was fifteen years old and getting a bit creaky in the joints. Most of the goats had no trouble leaping up onto the milking stand, but Julian executed the manoeuvre in several stages, fixing me with a reproachful eye, as if I were somehow responsible. I sang as I milked her (which often coaxes an extra ounce or two of milk into the pail—don't ask me why). I noticed right away that my voice had a curiously nasal quality to it. Great, I thought. It probably meant that my speaking voice sounded stupid, too, which meant that not only would I be dealing with nose-comments during every single face-to-face encounter in the foreseeable future, I would also have to deal with it on the phone.

Good thing Juliet had given me a cellular. I could take the batteries out whenever I got home. There, at least, safe in the cabin, I could be miserable in peace.

My nose throbbed as soon as I thought about it. Up until then, the pain had remained in the back of my mind. With both my nostrils stuffed with cotton, I could hardly miss the bulging, which insinuated itself into my normally clear peripheral vision, but hadn't taken centre-stage as yet. It did, though, not long afterwards. I finished the milking, let the goats out to browse and frolic in the early spring air and headed up to the farmhouse to join George for breakfast.

I hadn't actually seen a reflection of myself yet that morning. There was only one mirror in the cabin, and I must have forgotten to stop by for a pre-dawn primp before heading to the barn. I should have checked, I guess. I should have prepared myself.

"Jesus, Mary and Joseph, what happened to you?" George positively yelped as I walked in the door. I explained.

"You poor child," he said gently, which made tears well up in my eyes again. I realized I would have to get a grip on that if I was to get through the day. "You look," he said, "like a raccoon."

"I beg your pardon?" I said. The remark effectively dispelled the weepiness. He probably said it to have precisely that effect. George is not a cruel man, normally.

"Your eyes, Polly. Have you seen your eyes this morning?"

Oh, God. Spare me. I went to peer at myself in George's hall mirror. Shiners. Two of them. One on each side of my pathetic nose, which, I was glad to see, had shrunk a little from the bloated root vegetable it had been at the hospital. But the two black eyes were there to stay for a while. I smiled in a friendly way at my reflection. The effect was horrible.

"At least I'm not actually performing in the show," I said, returning to the kitchen table, where George had poured me a big steaming mug of fresh-ground coffee. "At least I won't have to go on stage looking like this."

"Didn't you say the actors have to wear masks anyway?"

"That's true. Of course. Black hoods, actually. Maybe I should ask Juliet to give me a part. I could wear the hood all the time until my face gets back to normal."

"It is not that bad," George said, soothingly. Then he ruined it by asking if I had any makeup up at the cabin.

He put together a wonderful fry-up of bacon, eggs, fried green tomatoes and fried bread. I had three cups of coffee with cream and sugar, and in the last cup, George tossed in a capful of scotch (Glen impossible-to-pronounce) to chase the chill away. He is a lovely man and I want him to be my wife.

We took our plates outside for Lug-nut to lick, and then we smoked on the porch, me a cigarette and George a pipe full of new tobacco he was trying out because it was on sale at the Quick-Mart. It didn't smell as good as his usual cherry-scented stuff, but he soldiered on with it because he is a Finn, and Finns never give up.

"It's Canadian," he said, coughing. "Susan says it's additive-free and politically correct. I must give it a chance."

George's pet raven, Poe, who was watching George struggle

with brand-loyalty issues, croaked in disgust. Poe was perched on his old friend's shoulder, but as the tobacco began invading his space, he shook his black, sleek head, did his usual inelegant flapping hop and landed with a thump on mine, instead. I didn't mind. In fact, when Poe sat on me, I felt blessed. Poe seemed to like cigarette smoke.

"You're right, my friend," George said, nodding at the bird. He dumped the smouldering mass into the bay tree that sat in a pot on the porch, refilled the pipe with the old brand, lit it and sighed in satisfaction.

"You can't teach an old dog new vices," he said. He sent a perfect smoke ring into the morning sky. "Peaceful," he murmured. "Perfect."

That was when the Neighbours From Hell kicked in.

A week or two previously, the abandoned tar-paper Kuskawa shack adjacent to George's farm had been invaded. For years, we had assumed that it would crumble into the ground, as it was destined to do. It backed on to a useless piece of swampland (well, useful to frogs and marsh creatures, but no good for farming) and the shack itself was hideous and needed pulling down.

The deed (George checked) was in the name of an old Kuskawa family that no longer lived in the area. George had been keeping tabs on it at the municipal office, preparing to put an offer in when it came up for back-taxes, so he could buy it and ensure his privacy. No such luck. In late April, the Neighbours From Hell had moved in.

We had never been formally introduced and were only vaguely aware of what they looked like, having stolen sly glances sideways when we drove by. Finns and old British stock share this trait. Never stare at people you want to kill. The racket they produced, however, was prodigious. We didn't need to see them to know they were there.

There were three adults. The older man was Grandpa, or, as he was more frequently called, in voices that were too loud to be real, "You Stupid Old Fuck." The younger woman, pregnant (this much became obvious during a drive-by) was Stacey. The younger man, according to the Cedar Falls grapevine queen, Donna-Lou Dermott, who knew everything, was an ex-con called Randy.

There were two boys, one, a shrill-voiced toddler called Tyler and the other an older boy called Wade. We knew their names because they were screamed at, frequently. There were several dogs, too. Tied up behind the shack and miserable enough to howl.

It was eight-thirty, and they all seemed to boil out of the house next door at once, shrieking.

"Wade, get your fucking shoes on!"

"Come here right now, you bitch, and help me with this!"

"Maaaa!!!" The dogs began a frenzied barking.

Then the chainsaw started.

George shook his head slowly and sadly.

"I have work to do," he said and went indoors.

Six

PRINCESS: *Without my crown, I'm incomplete.*
CAT: *You're still a princess, though, my sweet.*
-The Glass Flute, Scene vi

At nine o'clock, I stopped outside Rico's and honked the horn. He poked his head out the door, waved, then emerged holding two tiny cups. He had, as he promised, dressed "butch," in a Hydro coat, denim shirt, green work-pants and boots. He looked like a downtown Toronto construction worker. He hadn't shaved.

"A little pick-me-up," he said. "Espresso—fresh-made. I bet you didn't get enough sleep. I didn't, anyway. The whole thing kept going around and around in my mind like a bad Madonna video."

"There's no other kind," I said and thanked him. I didn't really need the caffeine jolt, but it was welcome nonetheless.

"Nose looks good," he said. "Hey. You're wearing makeup." I blushed. George's remark had been meant as a joke, because I never use the stuff normally, but when I was back up at the cabin, I'd accidentally looked in the mirror again. It was too much. I'd given in and searched out a crusty old tube of Max Factor foundation, left over from my fashion-conscious days in the city. I'd started out using only a little bit, just to hide the raccoon eyes, but that had made the rest of my face look pasty, so I'd gone the whole hog, slathering on the foundation, powdering it down, then using blush (sparingly, you understand) and topping the whole mess off with a coat of mascara that made my eyes look like two spiders. Actually, I looked okay. I'd unpacked my nose, and the swelling had gone down enough that I didn't look like George Chuvalo any more, at any rate. I felt shy about the makeup, but by then it was too late to wash it all off again, so I just thought the hell with it, dressed to match in a decent pair of jeans and a new Mexican vest that Aunt Susan had given me for Christmas, and hit the road.

Rehearsal had been called for ten o'clock, and it's a theatre rule that even if you're dying, you get to rehearsal on time.

People trickled into the lobby slowly, and it took a while for me to realize that just about everybody in the cast and crew was wearing makeup that morning, so I didn't feel so out of place. It wasn't just the women, either.

Rico usually wore a tiny bit of eyeliner, applied discreetly so you didn't notice it unless you'd seen him without it. Although he's dark-complexioned, his eyelashes are sparse and his eyes are blue, so the eyeliner just makes up for what nature forgot. He may have been dressed "butch," but the eyeliner was in place.

Juliet wore full daytime facial camouflage. She was seriously hung over, and when she came in moments after we did, she brushed past us with a grunt, went into her office and shut the door—very gently.

Kim Lee, the general manager, always wore a bit of makeup and today was no exception. She looked fresh and positively perky (she doesn't drink). After one look at Rico and me, she steered us over to the coffee-maker in the lobby, handed us both a cup and then took one in to Juliet.

"She's brave," Rico muttered. I nodded. Juliet in a bad mood was worse than a pregnant crocodile.

Meredith and Bradley came in together, talking in low voices. Meredith, who had done the show before and knew how physically taxing it was, was wearing sweats. Bradley had on a tight pair of pants that would make him a soprano before the day was out. They said polite good-mornings (not forgetting to ask kindly about my nose), served themselves coffee and retired to a low sofa near the front desk to continue their conversation. At best, they were mildly hung-over, and Bradley had crimson lipstick on his neck, more or less the same colour as the stuff Meredith had on her lips.

Tobin came in next, looking ill. He sat with us, sighing as his large frame settled in the easy chair next to the coffee table. His bunch of keys, the badge of office for every Technical Director in the world, jingled heavily from a loop on his belt.

"Just plug me in," he said and held out a muscular arm, veins up, in front of the percolator. "I closed up the place last night. This morning, I mean. Can you believe it? Four-thirty. I'm too old for this." His eyes were bloodshot, and he, too, had not escaped the makeup epidemic. His lips, which had been cartoon-white the night before, still held a ghost of greasepaint. He caught me looking.

"I know," he said, wiping at his mouth with his sleeve. "Serves me right for mocking a mockery, I guess. I tried everything. Vaseline. Cold cream. I'm marked for life. Just call me honky-lips. Nice nose, by the way."

Ruth Glass arrived in a hurry, clutching a folder crammed with sheet music. Her eyebrows were still clogged with green goo from her Martian outfit of the night before. She headed for the stairs which led up to the rehearsal hall.

"Sorry I'm late," she said, and stopped in mid-stride.

"Hey. Why isn't everybody upstairs?"

"Rehearsal doesn't start for another fifteen minutes, Ruth," Tobin said. "Our fearless leader is still in her office." He pointed and we all looked. The door was still ominously shut.

"She's being nursed into wakefulness by Kim," I said.

"I'm going up, " Ruth said. "Juliet wants to do a sing-through this morning—told me last night, at two a.m."

"A sing-through?" I said. "After last night, nobody's going to be able to sing a note."

"I know. It's Jason's fault," Tobin said. "Spurned her advances and made her cranky. Then he started fussing around up in the rehearsal room and kept coming down to ask her tech questions in the middle of the party. Pissed her off enough for her to get vindictive."

"Yay, Jason. Where is he, by the way?"

"Probably up there now, getting ready to take attendance," Tobin said, gloomily. "He's a real hard-liner, that one. Don't know where Juliet found him."

"He's a local boy who made good," I said. "You know how she is. Anyway, I think he came as a package deal with Amber."

Ruth walked over to Meredith and Bradley to tell them about the morning schedule. Tobin lifted himself out of his chair, poured another coffee, put three sugars in it and headed for the basement. "Anyone needs me, I'll be in my office," he said. I knew he was going down for a last minute smoke, and I wondered if I had time to join him.

"A sing-through? Is she crazy?" Meredith said loudly. Her voice was hoarse. Everyone's voice was hoarse, come to that. "You don't do a sing-through the night after a party when everybody's been whooping it up. Does she want to damage us for life?"

"Easy, girl," Bradley said. "She won't be able to stand the

noise, anyway. She'll call it off as soon as we're halfway through the opening number."

"Well, I should damn well hope so," Meredith said. "I'm not straining my chords just so Juliet bloody Keating can sit back on the first day of rehearsal and do dick-all."

Outside, a very large car purred up to the front of the building. We all stared through the glass doors of the entrance, mesmerized by the sheer luxury of the automobile. None of us drove anything like that. We heard a door slam with an expensive clunk, and Amber Thackeray and Shane Pacey made an entrance.

"I can't believe you said that," Amber was saying, almost in tears. "You are such an ignorant pig, Shane."

"I was joking, for Chrissakes, Amber. It's not my fault that wimp you call your fiancé is too stupid to take a joke, is it?"

"That was not a joke. It was an insult to me and to Jason. Why can't you just let bygones be bygones?"

"Amber, he's an idiot. You know it and I know it and I don't understand why you…" They both stopped and stared at the group gathered in the lobby. We stared back. A pause.

"Top o' the mornin' to yez," Shane said, with a fake Irish accent, lifting an imaginary hat. He smiled radiantly, a beautiful smile. He really was a most disturbingly gorgeous man, in spite of being an obvious dink. Amber emitted a peep and scurried over to the coffee, avoiding the eyes of the group. We all muttered hellos and let the moment pass.

Shane came straight up to me and put a hand on my arm.

"You're Polly Deacon, right?" I nodded. "Listen, Polly, I'm really, really sorry about last night. I had way too much to drink and acted like a complete asshole. I'm sorry about your nose. You okay?" His charm was unnerving. I responded immediately, against all logic, gazing deeply into his dark-lashed, makeup free eyes. Something stirred deep inside me. An octopus, aroused.

"I'm fine, Shane," I said. "Thanks for asking." He squeezed my arm once, warmly, then let go. Then he turned to Rico. I could feel my friend stiffen beside me.

"You're the person I should really apologize to," Shane said, quietly. "I don't remember a lot of it, but Amber filled me in. I'm not supposed to drink. Shit happens when I do. Can you forgive me?" Rico was flabbergasted. So was I.

"Well, yeah, I guess," Rico stammered. "It was, you know, a…misunderstanding, I guess."

"Sure was," Shane said, bathing us both in that impossible smile. "You make a terrific woman, eh? Just warn me next time." Then he turned away and made a beeline for the coffee. Rico looked at me.

"Close your mouth, Rico," I whispered.

"Is he real?" Rico whispered back.

"Hey, where's Jason?" Ruth said, hurrying down the stairs. "He's been messing around with my keyboard and the amp cables are gone."

"Haven't seen him," I said.

"He wasn't around when we got here," Rico added.

Juliet's door opened and she stepped out, followed by Kim, who had an armload of scripts. "Well, kiddies, shall we go up?" Juliet said. "Where's that little stage manager?"

We heard heavy, running footsteps on the basement stairs and Tobin burst into the lobby. His face was so pale it was grey.

"Jason's vest is floating in the workshop pool," he said.

Seven

WOODSMAN: *The job is hard, the days are long / but forest work will make you strong.*
-The Glass Flute, Scene vii

We all went to look, thundering down the stairs like a bunch of kids let out of school.

It was Jason's leather vest, all right, tangled in rope and floating at the edge of the black square of frigid water. Without Jason in it, it was just a piece of clothing, but the implication was horrible, nonetheless. It was like seeing Jason's persona, drowned.

"Jesus," Rico said.

"You think he's down there?" Amber whispered. A rush of blood rocketed to my head, which made my battered nose throb. One thump like a drumbeat. I'd seen a dead body before—two, actually—and I wasn't keen on seeing another one. We all stared at the water in silence, expecting to see a dim, pale shape bobbing just below the surface.

Nobody ran forward to fish around. After all, it was just a vest, but there was an uncomfortable, final sort of feeling in the air. Meredith crouched at the edge and reached down to untangle the garment from its tether. She laid the sodden vest on the shop floor, where it oozed water like a dead seal. It's just a vest, I kept telling myself. It doesn't mean anything.

"I suppose he could have, you know, taken it off down here and it fell in, and he just didn't bother to pull it out," Tobin said, doubtfully.

"He never took it off," Amber said.

"Except to shower," Shane said and snickered. There was a nasty little pause and we all stared at Shane, shocked. "Sorry. Joking," he said, lifting his hands in a gesture of apology.

"Even if he did take it off, and it fell in somehow, he'd rather have died than lose it," Amber said. We all let that one hang in the air.

"Did Jason know how to swim?" someone asked. Amber burst into tears.

Kim and Juliet went upstairs to call the cops, and the rest of us just stood there until someone noticed that Amber was making the transition from tears to hysterics. Shane put his arm around her and led her up the stairs.

"Let's go to the lobby, kid," he said. "You don't need to be here. It's nice and warm up there. C'mon, you'll be okay."

"Hope he doesn't try to jump her," I heard Meredith mutter.

Ruth was gazing intently at the mass of black cord that had prevented Jason's vest, if not his body, from disappearing into the icy, swiftly running depths of the Kuskawa river. The spring run-off was at its peak, and the edges of the pool foamed with the movement underneath. One end of the rope had somehow caught on one of the old brass mooring cleats and the tip flashed silver. "Those are my missing amp cables," she said. Not rope. Audio cable. Weird. "They'll have my fingerprints all over them. They'll think I did it."

"Did what?" Bradley said. "Killed him? It was obviously an accident, Ruth."

"What kind of accident?" I said.

"Well, he probably fell down those treacherous stairs,

49

like your friend did last night," Bradley said, pointing at Rico, who cringed.

"Yeah, that's possible, I guess," Ruth said, thoughtfully. "He fell down the stairs with his arms full of amp cables and went straight into the water. Bumped his head, maybe, going down."

"What would he be doing coming down here with amp cables at four-thirty in the morning?" Tobin said. "That's when I locked up. He wasn't here then."

"He was obsessive," Bradley said. "You know he was setting up the rehearsal space last night. Didn't you check upstairs?"

"Sure I did. Like always. Lights were off. Nobody home."

"Maybe he was in the bathroom."

"You don't turn the lights off in the room you're working in if you're just stepping out to go to the can," Tobin said.

"So maybe he was conserving energy."

"Anyway, he wouldn't come down here if he was setting up sound equipment. That's all stored upstairs," Tobin said.

"Polly," Rico said.

"What?"

"I want to go home."

"I know, Rico. Me too, but we'll have to stay. The police, eh? Oh, man. I bet they send Becker."

Rico shot me a look that was pure sympathy.

"Look, guys," I said, "we can't do much good down here, and the more people that hang around, the more mess we'll make of the scene, whether it was an accident or not. We probably shouldn't have pulled the vest out of the water. Tampering with the evidence, you know?"

"Well, excuse me for living," Meredith said.

"I didn't mean you did it on purpose or anything," I said, but Meredith was already making her exit.

"Come on, Bradley," she said. "Let's leave Nancy Drew to

collect clues." She stomped up the stairs, and Brad followed meekly behind.

"Oops," I said.

"Touchy," Ruth said.

"You did sound kind of bossy," Tobin said. I stuck my tongue out at him. "You guys can go up, but I'll stay down here," he said. "Someone should, in case, you know, the killer comes back or something. They'll want to talk to me first, anyway. I was the last person here last night, and I found Jason's vest."

"The killer? You don't think it was an accident?" Ruth said.

"Look at the cables," Tobin said. "That's not an accidental tangle. Someone's wrapped the cable around the cleat like they were mooring a boat." We looked. It was true. The nautical knot at the end of the cable couldn't possibly have happened by chance.

"Yikes," Ruth said. "You haven't handled the amp cables, have you, Tobin? You two get along okay?"

"Just go upstairs."

The cast wasn't in the lobby. There was only Kim Lee, working calmly at her computer, wearing that blank, expert-keyboard-person expression which meant that her brain was directly connected to her fingers.

"Where is everybody?" I said.

"They're upstairs. Juliet said they might as well get started with the video, instead of sitting around worrying."

"How sensitive," Rico said. Kim smiled slightly and kept on typing.

"No sing-through?" I said. "Meredith'll be pleased."

"Juliet wanted one, but Ruth said her amp cables are otherwise occupied, so there's no sound system." Oh yeah.

Tobin would have to go out and buy new ones. Usually, it was the stage-manager's job to purchase tech supplies, but Jason was "otherwise occupied", too.

"Are the cops on the way?" I asked.

"They said they'd send somebody over," Kim said, "but they didn't seem overly concerned. They said Jason's vest didn't sound like enough to warrant a river search. Usually they wait for twenty-four hours in the case of a missing person."

"Typical," I said. "Kuskawa's finest, responding with speed and alacrity. Jason's body'll be washed out to Port Mortimer by the time they decide the missing person is missing for good."

"Well, that's what they told us," Kim said and shrugged. "Anyway, they did say someone would come, but it didn't sound like they'd drop everything and scream in here with the flashers on. Juliet told me to wait for them."

"What about our AIDS benefit meeting?" Rico said.

"We could have it now, I guess," she said. "Polly, you should go on up to the rehearsal space. Juliet's not in the best of moods." Rico told me he would find his own way home after the meeting.

I went. The cops would send Becker, I knew they would, and I'd rather sit though the *Flute* video for the thousandth time than have to deal with him.

The Glass Flute is a simple, lovely story, extolling the virtues of bravery, self-sacrifice and love, all of the things currently lacking in children's television programming, which is why the show is such a hit. While the production itself is reasonably hi-tech, with ultraviolet light, glow-in-the-dark effects and several actual explosions, the story is not set in cyber-space.

The plot revolves around a young boy called Kevin (played by Shane). Kevin's mother (Meredith) is in bed, wasting away from a romantic, fatal disease that makes her weak and soft-voiced but doesn't have any visible nasty stuff. (Rico once said that the *Flute* would be more timely if the Mother puppet was actually covered in purple sores. He can be bitter sometimes.) The only thing that can save Mother is to have a bite of the Fruit of Life, which grows on a tree at the top of the mountain nearby. Mother is, of course, a widow, and therefore the only answer is for Kevin to go get it himself.

Brave little Kevin decides he's up to the job, in spite of the fact that the mountain is full of evil characters.

"Take this for protection," Mother says and gives him a glass flute, which has been in the family for generations. Kevin is gently derisive, saying he'd rather have a gun, but takes it, dutifully. We all know the flute is magic, because whenever it's taken out of its leather sheath, weird unearthly music comes from nowhere.

Kevin's adventure begins. On the way up the mountain, he meets a Cat (Meredith again) who tries to convince him that his quest is futile, and that lying around all day is much more sensible. He meets a Princess (Amber) who needs rescuing, a Woodsman (Bradley) who does the father-figure thing, and a serpent (Amber) who does Biblical temptation-acting. The flute helps Kevin make the right decisions, the Dragon (Bradley) defending the fruit is vanquished, the apple is plucked and Mother is saved. The Woodsman and Mother end up completing the requisite nuclear family, much to the delight of the Christian schools that book the show.

The *Flute* may sound mawkish and sentimental, but it was written by Juliet—a master. If Juliet can get reviews like "Heartwarming, a tear-jerker" out of her 1973 hit *Barmaids on Parade*, then a show like the *Flute* is, well, child's play.

When I got upstairs, the lights were dimmed and the cast

huddled on the floor like kids watching Saturday morning cartoons. They were paired off, Shane with his arm around Amber, and Bradley and Meredith snuggled together like conspirators. The blue light from the TV screen, set up in front of the "black box" of the portable stage, cast an eerie glow over their faces, which were intent and serious. Amber's face was tear-streaked, which may have been the effects of Juliet's script, but was more likely due to the Jason-thing. Juliet sat at the SM's/director's table at the back of the hall with Ruth, going over some notes.

"Police here yet?" Juliet asked quietly, as I tiptoed over and pulled up a chair.

"Nope. Tobin's down there keeping an eye on the evidence until they get here."

"Evidence? Polly, dear, you are too *Grand Guignol* for words. If the kid has drowned, it's a tragedy, but let's not jump to conclusions."

"Amber said he never takes that vest off," I whispered back. "What's your explanation?"

Juliet made a significant grimace towards Shane and Amber.

"I'd say there was some history with those two and young Jason couldn't handle it," she said. "I think he threw his little SM's vest in the water as some sort of defiant gesture and made tracks. Which," she added, "leaves us with no stage manager." She fixed me with a stare that made the hair on the back of my neck stand straight up.

"You've kept up your Equity membership, haven't you, dear?"

I shivered. What had I said to Rico the night before? Touring is murder. There's no way I'd ever do it again. Still, I blush when I lie, and Juliet knows it.

"Ummm…yeah. I'm still in good standing."

"Puppet business booming, is it?"

"Not as such."

"You'll get two months at production stage manager rates, with a per diem and use of the Steamboat van. Now, let's talk about the rehearsal schedule," she said, pushing Jason's prompt script binder towards me.

I sighed. PSMs make big bucks. The cast would hate me for taking Jason's job when his body wasn't even a body yet, and anyway, I hate stage management. But I had a dependent now. A mutt called Lug-Nut whose vet bills were climbing (a recent run-in with a porcupine) and whose per-month food bill was more than I get for a marionette commission.

"Write it into my contract," I said. "My dog comes with us on tour, and I get my own room."

"Whatever, dear," Juliet said. "Now, perhaps you'll go out and pick up some amp cables so we can do a sing-through this afternoon. Keys are in the van."

Eight

MOTHER: *A single note will soothe the breast / when evil puts you to the test.*
-The Glass Flute, Scene ii

The interior of Fish Gundy's Musical Emporium is very dark. There are lava lamps in every corner, though, and once your eyes get used to it, the atmosphere is quite soothing. Fish usually sits at the back in an ancient leather bean bag chair, which is elevated on a platform behind the counter so he can lounge there and still be able to reach the cash register. It gives him a Godlike aspect, which is possibly deliberate. If you buy something from him, you sort of have to look up, but if you were standing on the floor next to him, his nose would reach your sternum.

Fish hasn't changed much since high school. When we were in Grade Nine at Laingford High together, he came to class dressed in striped bell-bottoms, a Nehru shirt and sandals. This was at a time in the late seventies when all that hippie stuff was recent enough to be excruciatingly uncool. People laughed at him, partly because of his size, but mostly because of his style. He didn't alter it, though, which lent him a kind of weird mystique, as if he had become stuck against his will in an era the rest of us wanted to forget.

We became friends because we were both charter members

of the out-crowd (Lori Pinkerton wouldn't even acknowledge Fish Gundy—she looked right through him) and he was an incredible guitar player. Ruth and Fish and I used to hang out together in the school greenhouse at lunch and write songs. Fish's tragedy was compounded by a terrible case of adolescent acne, which he finally overcame in Grade 13, but by then the damage had been done. Once nerd-hood is established, you can't escape it unless you change schools. Ruth, Fish and I shared the burden of the label with all the dignity we could muster. It was only later that we were able to acknowledge that being in the out-crowd was a good thing. All the really interesting people were members.

Fish went away to university, earned a PhD in medieval music history and learned to play the shawm and sackbut. Later, he travelled, took up the sitar and mastered various unpronounceable Japanese instruments, then came back to Kuskawa and opened up his emporium in Sikwan. He's married to a Japanese woman called Mako, and they have twins, child prodigies, both of them.

"Hey, Polly. Peace," Fish said from his beanbag throne as I made my way through the murky interior to the back of the store. The walls of Fish's place are studded with guitars, from ancient Rickenbackers to shiny new Fenders. He does a brisk trade-in business, and the bands that come through town on tour often re-fuel there, so there's a collection of wildly custom-fitted electric guitars, some of them autographed by their former owners. The rest of the place is crammed with instruments from around the world. There are Bolivian rainsticks and pan pipes, a whole collection of African drums, some beat-up coronets and baritones, a bunch of Quebec-made violins (plus an old European one that he keeps locked up), a Celtic harp and a set of bagpipes. Collectors from

Toronto often come up to Sikwan just to see Fish.

"How are things up in Cedar Falls?" Fish said.

"Looking up, Fish," I said. "Spring's in the air and I just got a paying gig with Steamboat Theatre."

"Good for you," he said. "Doing what?"

"Well, I was the puppet designer until about ten minutes ago. Now I've been promoted to stage manager."

"Cool. I thought you hated stage management."

"Yup. But somebody bumped off the other one, so I'm filling in."

"Seriously?"

"Well, we think so. He's vanished, anyway."

"Bummer," Fish said. That's all he said, which is one of the reasons I like him. He knew that if I wanted to talk about it, I would. I didn't.

"I need amp cables."

"Right this way," he said. I followed him into the back of the shop, where he kept accessories and sheet music. We spent a half hour discussing techie-stuff, and as we were comparing the relative merits of the brands of cable available, he stopped mid-sentence and gazed up at my face.

"You do something to your hair?" he said.

"No, Fish."

"Huh. You look different, somehow."

"My nose. I got a nose job."

"Oh. Cool. Suits you." That was that. There are plenty of fish in the sea, but there was only one Fish for me. I left with the requisite gear carried in a loop over my shoulder. I would have liked to have stayed and gabbed some more, but I had a rehearsal to run. I was sure that I had wasted enough time at least to have missed Becker's visit to the theatre, which was the whole point of the exercise. The other music shop in town was closer to Steamboat, a place down in mall-land that specialized in Hammond organs and ukuleles, but that trip would've taken me less than fifteen minutes.

The Steamboat Theatre van is a big Ford with one bench seat in the back and eight feet of storage behind it. This is the classic children's theatre touring vehicle, with just enough seating space for four actors (who traditionally fight like five-year-olds about who gets to ride shotgun) and the stage-manager, who gets to drive. The set, lighting, costumes and props are packed in, wedged roof-high behind the bench seat.

Loading up the van at the end of every show means following a pattern. If you pack the gear in the wrong order, or put it in the wrong place, you can end up with a few pieces at the end that simply won't fit. If that happens, you have to pull everything out and start over, which can be disastrous if you've got half an hour for lunch and another show at a school twenty kilometres away. Sometimes the technical director will issue a kind of floor-plan, like the "what's where" directions in a box of chocolates, which gets taped to the back door of the van. After a week, the cast learns the order of the pack, and things go smoothly. The first few days, it's hell.

If there's a lot of travelling involved on tour, the cast quickly learns to establish ground rules for van-time. Being stuck like a thespic sardine in a five-foot by three-foot space for several hours a day is no picnic. Personal hygiene, for example, becomes very important, as does music etiquette (if you like listening to rap music, you bloody well wear a portable CD player and you keep the volume turned way down). When I told Rico that touring was murder, I was remembering vaguely how uncomfortable it could get. Now, driving the empty Steamboat van back to the theatre, it struck me full-force that I had agreed to do it again.

"I must be completely insane," I muttered. I tuned the radio to CBC, knowing full well that once we hit the road, there would be arguments over which station to listen to and battles over volume control. Mid-tour, a fog of depression would permeate the van, as the five adults cooped up inside came to terms with the fact that they were doomed to spend another month in each other's company. Touring is like being in a marriage with four other people. If the chemistry's right, it can be a blast. In my experience, that happens on one out of every six shows. Long odds.

The van bounced and rattled its way along the shore road leading to the theatre. It was designed to run best with a couple of thousand pounds of equipment in the back and seemed to resent being taken out with an empty belly. I passed a couple of kids walking a dog along the shoreline, and they gave me a friendly wave. I waved back, realizing that driving the Steamboat van was sort of like wearing a clown costume. It was painted to resemble (not surprisingly) a steamboat, and there was a fake smokestack on the roof. Very cute, in an ice-cream-truck kind of way. Every school-aged kid in Kuskawa had seen a Steamboat show. The company began each tour with a local performance or two, to test the waters.

I parked the van in the Steamboat lot, killed the engine and reached over to grab the new amp cables, just as the OPP cruiser pulled in beside me. It was Becker and Morrison, of course.

"What are you doing here?" Becker said. This was not an unusual question, coming from him. We had enjoyed several similar encounters last fall, when my best friend, Francy Travers, had been the prime suspect in a murder case in Cedar Falls. I'd done a fair bit of meddling, and I always seemed to turn up just a little bit before the OPP did. It made Becker fratchetty.

"I work here, Mark," I said, as pleasantly as I could.

"Oh. So it was you who called in the missing person report?"

"No. That was probably the artistic director, Juliet. Our stage manager's disappeared, and we found his vest floating in the pool in the basement. We think he might have fallen in the river."

"How do you know he hasn't just gone out for coffee?" Morrison asked, coming around the side of the cruiser to stand beside his partner.

"He's a stage manager. He's not at rehearsal. In the theatre biz, that's a cardinal sin. It just doesn't happen. That's how I know, Earlie," I said.

Becker sighed. "That's all we need," he said, "a bunch of flaky theatre people."

I smiled sweetly. "We're not all flaky, Officer. Some of us are actually quite normal, with mortgages, morals and a healthy respect for authority. Follow me, and we'll see if we can find one."

We headed inside, Becker muttering behind me all the way as if I were leading him into hell. Turns out, I was.

Nine

KEVIN: *Everybody tells you when you're young how to behave/ Like 'wipe your nose, say thank you, save the world, kid, and be brave.'*
-The Glass Flute, Scene iii

"You'll probably find this useful," I said, pulling the cast and crew contact list off the callboard and handing it to Becker on our way through the lobby. He gazed at it suspiciously, as if I'd just typed it up for him as a kind of step-by-step guide to who might've dunnit.

"It's standard procedure," I explained. "When you've suddenly got twenty or so new people to deal with, it helps to have a list. This is everybody who works here, what they do and where they're staying. If you need to talk to the cast, we're upstairs in the rehearsal space." I introduced the policemen to Kim Lee, whose calm efficiency seemed to reassure Becker.

"You're the one who called us?" he said.

"Yes, I did. I'm Steamboat's general manager. Jason McMaster, our stage-manager, is pretty conscientious, and his disappearance is odd, so we thought you'd appreciate a call. You'll want to see the shop, I expect. Polly, why don't you go upstairs and tell Juliet the OPP is here and keep the cast occupied." She turned to Becker with an apologetic grin. "They're all a bit freaked out by this, officer. You know theatre people." Well, Becker didn't, actually, but her attitude was right in line with his own, and he grinned back at her. I felt a twinge of jealousy, which was patently ridiculous, as I wasn't the slightest bit interested in him any more; I suppressed it as soon as I recognized it for what it was.

"Lead the way, Ms. Lee," he said, and followed Kim to the shop stairs. Morrison rolled his eyes at me and fell into step behind Becker, doing a hunch-backed, Igor-impression. I turned my snort of laughter into a sneeze, but I needn't have bothered. Becker didn't even turn around.

"The cops are here," I said, walking into the rehearsal space. Ruth was the only one there, leafing idly through Jason's prompt book.

"Good," she said. "The video's over and Juliet's got them in the wardrobe room trying on their costumes. We've wasted the whole morning and they're getting antsy. Let's send our fearless leader downstairs and get some work done." I handed her the amp cables and left her to get her equipment set up for the sing-through.

There would probably be no complaints about a music rehearsal at this point. The first rehearsal day is generally a full one, scheduled to the hilt, with non-stop business and a feeling of suppressed excitement and anticipation. With only one frantic week of rehearsal before the first performance, it was essential that the first day set the tone for the rehearsal period. Wasting a morning lolling around watching videos and playing dress-up would not be good for cast morale in the long run.

"Geez, these are attractive," Bradley was saying, surveying his rotund figure in a full length mirror. The outfits worn by the puppeteers in the *Flute* couldn't exactly be called costumes. The gear was known as "blacks," which is what they are. The idea was to cover every inch of skin, so that the actors in the black playbox would disappear completely under the ultra-violet light, and the puppets and props would spring magically into view, glowing. Both men and women wore skin-tight black body stockings and tights, with black cotton turtlenecks over top. To cover their arms and hands, they wore tight black wool gloves with elbow-length velour cuffs. The lower extremities were masked with black socks and dance slippers, and their heads were covered with black velour hoods. The hoods were the worst part. Like the rest of the outfit, the hoods left no skin exposed, and visibility was poor through the square of black screening that fell from the peak of the baseball cap around which the hood was built. The hems of the hoods were fitted with snap fasteners, which corresponded to snaps around the collars of the turtlenecks to keep the headgear securely in place. After a few minutes in full blacks, the cast of the *Flute* would sweat buckets.

"There's no doubt about it," Bradley said, sadly. "Dance tights are not my best look." The turtleneck stretched over his belly and stopped just short of modesty, an inch or two above his crotch.

"Dancewear only looks good on dancers, darling," Juliet said. "If you like, we can have someone sew an extra length of velour around the bottom of your shirt so it falls lower."

"Don't bother, Brad," Meredith said. "More material will just be hotter. As long as it covers your skin, that's all you want."

"You will, however, need a dance belt," Juliet said, leering. "A size large, it looks like." A dance belt is the arts-world equivalent of an athletic supporter. Required gear for men in tights, believe me. Bradley went very red but leered back, which was the only way to deal with Juliet at times like these. "Come and help me pick one out, Juliet," he said.

I told the director that the police were downstairs, so she said "carry on" in a breezy way and swooped out.

"Good save, chum," Meredith said to Brad. "But you will need a dance belt, you know. Don't know where you'll get one around here, though. I'm going to need an extra pair of tights as well. The backups they gave me have holes in them."

"There's a dance supply place in Laingford," I said. "If you guys can figure out what extras you're going to need, I'll order them tomorrow." Everyone would need two sets of everything, in order to be able to get through two shows a day without stinking up the playing area.

Meredith, having done the show before, had brought her own body leotards, top-quality cotton things that would be a lot more comfortable than the cheapo synthetic ones the rest of the cast had to wear.

"How come she gets to wear cotton?" Shane said, reaching out a hand to pinch Meredith's sleeve. She jerked away.

"Because I have seniority," she said. It was close to a snarl. Our Meredith was obviously underwhelmed by Shane's charm. He had come out from behind the changing screen, looking manly, somehow, in the bizarre get-up. He was wearing a dance belt. I checked.

Amber made her entrance timidly. She held the turtleneck in one hand and the hood in the other, perplexed. The leotard was a bit too small for her, producing a décolletage of magnificent proportions.

"You'll have to cover those up, kid," Meredith said. "They'll glow in the dark."

Amber, to her credit, just smiled. "I can't figure out how this stuff goes," she said and handed Meredith the hood and shirt. Faced with such direct acceptance of what was plainly her need to be top dog, the older actress became motherly. She helped Amber get togged up, snapping the hood fasteners down and then getting into her own hood. They trooped out into the rehearsal space, Meredith leading, like a broody hen with her chicks.

"You can't see much, eh?" Shane said. There they were, four black-clad figures, ranged in a row, gazing at themselves in the studio mirrors that lined the walls. Now that they were all dressed the same, you could hardly tell them apart.

"We won't rehearse in costume till later," I said, "but you should know what you're up against. We'll put you in the box and kill the lights so you have some idea."

"I *have* done this before, Polly," Meredith said. "I'll sit this one out."

"Solidarity, Meredith. I know it's torture. You might as well get back into the habit, so to speak, and you can help the others get their bearings," I said. "We've only got a week, remember."

The cast made their way backstage, into the black box puppet theatre which was their performance space. The box was about sixteen feet wide, nine feet high and five feet deep. The frame was made out of steel pipes, held together with key clamps (the kind of fittings that require an Allen key to tighten and loosen them), over which were draped several acres of black velour curtains, or masking. At the front of the playing area was a shelf about three feet high and two feet deep, which was essentially the "stage" where the puppets would strut their stuff. Extending out from the sides of the box were two curtains, which served to mask the backstage area from the audience.

Suspended on a pipe above the playing shelf were the "magic" lights, six full-strength ultraviolet tubes that cast what appeared to be no light at all, until one of the fluorescent puppets or props came into view.

The whole contraption was designed to break down into dozens of portable bundles, for ease of loading and unloading them from the van, and for carrying them up and down school staircases. Once the cast got good at it, the stage could be ready to go in about forty minutes. I explained this to the cast, who, with the exception of Meredith, refused to believe me.

The props and puppets themselves were stored under the shelf, behind the masking curtains and littering the backstage area. Every single item had a specific place to be, part of the "pre-set," which was crucial to the smooth running of the show. If you've got to make a flower appear at a precise musical moment, two minutes into the show, the flower had better be where you expect it to be, because the backstage area is very dark and you're squinting through black netting. All this stuff would become obvious to the cast as we rehearsed, but I could hear Meredith telling them anyway, issuing dire warnings, as if they were all entering enemy territory.

Once they were standing in the playing area, Ruth turned out the rehearsal room overheads, and I flipped the switch on the UV lights. Immediately, the cast disappeared. If you were standing close, you could see the faint blue outline of each figure, but from five feet back, the playing area was empty.

"Meredith, can you bring up the flute, so we can see how this works?" I said. Meredith reached under the shelf and brought out the glass flute, a larger-than-life prop made of clear plastic, painted with a wash of fluorescent pink to make it glow. All the props were equipped with black handles or dowel sticks, so that they appeared to be floating in mid air. Meredith made the flute float around and everybody went "oooh, aaaah." It really is a cool effect, even if you're a grown-up.

"To make it disappear," Meredith said, obviously getting into her Vanna White role, "you take one of these black flags, and just move it in front, like this." A square of black velour mounted on a dowel, the flag was one of the "tricks" that made audiences gasp. She shooed the rest of the cast out of the box to watch the effect from an audience perspective.

"I wondered how that was done when we were watching the video," Shane said.

"This is going to be fun," Amber said.

"Can we take these off now?" Shane said. "I'm cooking."

"Just wait till you're halfway through the second show and you can hardly breathe," Meredith said primly from the box. "Don't think you can stop just because you're hot."

"Meredith, we knew what we were getting into when we signed our contracts," Shane said, losing his cool with alarming speed. "You don't get any extra medals just because you did it before, so stop acting like such an asshole." To be honest, I agreed with him. Meredith's know-it-all attitude was bugging me, too.

Meredith tore off her hood, and her face appeared out of the darkness, disembodied and distorted with anger. Her teeth were bared and gleamed blue under the UV light.

"Listen, you little shit," she hissed, "I'm trying to give you the benefit of my experience, and if you don't like it, then why don't you go back to turning tricks on Church Street?" There was a little gasp from Amber, Shane drew in his breath, and suddenly Meredith's face disappeared.

"Is this part of the play?" said Becker, from the door.

Ten

SERPENT: *What you believe ith true ith an imaginary notion / The thingth you thee and touch are real, the retht ith jutht emotion.*

-The Glass Flute, Scene vii

When the overhead lights came on, Meredith could be seen in the box, struggling to remove the black flag that was draped over her head. A tubby figure stood next to her, with its arms crossed. Since Shane and Amber were out front, Meredith's flag-man had to be Brad. He was still wearing his hood, but I swear I could feel him grinning.

Meredith was in full hissy-fit mode. "You think that's funny, Brad? Dicking around with the props? These aren't toys, dammit. I thought you were a professional."

"Merry, dear, you are taking yourself way too seriously. This is the first day of rehearsal. If you keep this up, you'll blow an artery before we open," Brad said.

"Uh, folks," I said, "police're here." Nobody but me seemed to have heard Becker's remark. He stood in the doorway, wearing that baffled expression you see sometimes on non-theatre people who interrupt a rehearsal and can't figure out what's real and what's not. Meredith's remark about Shane would definitely bear checking out later, but it struck me that an in-house investigation might be more diplomatic.

Becker, I figured, could be kept in the dark for now. Theatre people do sometimes over-dramatize things—I admit to that tendency myself—and if you take everything they say at face-value, you could wind up reaching the wrong conclusions.

"I have a few questions I'd like to ask," Becker said. "Can you take a break for a few minutes?"

I suggested that the cast go and change back into their street clothes first. "We'll work in full blacks later in the week," I said. There was no point in making the actors endure an interview with an OPP officer while they were dressed like dorks.

While they were changing, Becker sat down at the SM's table and took out his notebook.

"Did you check out the scene downstairs?" I asked, trying to make light conversation.

"No, Polly, I thought I'd just come up here and ask questions without knowing what the hell was going on. Of course we've checked downstairs." Boy, Becker was touchy.

"I was just asking," I said.

"Are you going to be able to get fingerprints from the amp cables?" Ruth said.

"And you are…?" Becker asked, flipping to a new page in his notebook. Ruth introduced herself as Becker unfolded the contact list I'd given him in the lobby and made a little check mark next to Ruth's name. I looked over his shoulder and saw that he'd checked off Tobin already. At the bottom he'd added "Rico Amato, antique dealer and hanger-on" and there was a check mark beside that, too. Yay, I thought, with some satisfaction. I knew that list would be useful.

"Now why would you think we'd need to check the cables for prints, Ms. Glass?" he said.

"Well, somebody obviously tied the vest to the side of the pool…don't you think?" she said.

"Never mind what we think. Right now I'm just trying to get some details down," he said. "How well do you know Jason McMaster, Ms. Glass?"

"Hardly at all," she said. "He came up here, when, Polly? About a week before the cast did?"

"Yup. The SM—that's stage manager, Becker—is usually contracted for a week before rehearsals start. It's called pre-week. That's when they do all their paperwork and stuff. He came up last Monday."

"I gather he lives in Toronto," Becker said.

"You kind of have to if you're an SM or an actor," I said. "There's not a lot of professional theatre work around here—except for Steamboat."

"Where do people stay?" Becker asked.

"Sometimes they're billeted with local staff, or they get rooms in B&Bs. Some of them stay in motels until the show hits the road. I think Jason was at the Falls Motel. The address and number are right there on the contact sheet."

"Mr. ah…Boone said that McMaster is from around here originally, though," Becker said. "Doesn't he have family he could stay with?"

I shrugged. "You'll have to ask someone who knew him better, Becker. He wasn't exactly forthcoming about his background."

"Well, we'll have to get in touch with his family and find out if they've seen him," Becker said. "He could have gone back to Toronto."

"You mean you don't think he's in the river?" I said. "I thought that was obvious."

"Look, Polly, we've got one wet leather vest and no body. I know you love to get involved in a good murder, but there's no indication at present that we're dealing with a death here.

Right now, according to you folks, Jason McMaster has gone missing for a few hours. That's all. It's hardly worth investigating at this point."

"But he's a stage manager. An obsessive one. Obsessive SMs don't just blow off a rehearsal. That's why we called you in the first place," I said.

"I know, and we appreciate that," Becker said. "But until he's been missing at least 24 hours, this is just a courtesy call."

The cast filed in from the wardrobe room.

"But what about the vest?" I said.

"I'm not convinced that a vest in a pool of water necessarily means murder, Polly," he said, in a tone that was so condescending, I wanted to smack him. "Now, you folks are the actors, I take it? Take a seat, everyone, and we'll have a chat."

"Oooh. Just like in an Agatha Christie book," Bradley said. He pointed to Shane in mock accusation. "He did it. He did it."

"Cut it out, Brad," Meredith said, pulling up a chair. "Jason is missing after all, even if we don't all think he was drowned on purpose." She glared at me as she said it, as if she thought I was responsible for the whole thing.

"So you all think he was drowned?" Becker said. "Your director thinks that Mr. McMaster just left because of personal reasons." He stared at Amber. "You're his fiancée, aren't you?"

Amber nodded.

"Amber Thackeray, right?" He consulted his list. "You're staying in the Falls Motel, but in a different room from your intended. That's unusual nowadays, isn't it?"

Amber turned pink and fiddled with the ring on her finger. "We only just got engaged, Officer," she said. "We didn't, you know, live together or anything."

"Ah, I see," Becker said. "So everything's fine between you?"

"Y-yes," Amber said. "I mean, like, I didn't see him at the

motel after the party because he was working late, but everything was okay. We said we'd see each other here this morning. He kissed me goodnight." Her lower lip trembled at the memory.

"And Mr. Pacey. Which is Mr. Pacey?" Shane raised his hand slightly. "You're staying at the motel too?"

"Guilty," Shane said.

"You and Ms. Thackeray know each other? Before here, I mean?"

"What's that got to do with anything?" Shane said.

"According to Ms. Keating, a lot. Your director said that Jason McMaster was unhappy about you coming up to do this little play, Mr. Pacey. Now why would that be?"

"You tell me," Shane said. We were all staring back and forth between Becker and Shane, trying to figure out where this was going. I knew that Shane was a last-minute casting decision, but nobody had mentioned that Jason had a problem with it. Usually, information like that whips round the theatre faster than a company cold.

"Weren't you two an item at one time?" Becker said. Amber looked like she wanted to hide under the table. Shane looked like thunder.

"Amber and I dated in theatre school for a while, if that's what you're talking about," Shane said, through his teeth. "Not since."

"You were engaged?" Becker said.

"I don't know where you're getting this from, but it's none of your goddamn business," Shane said. That would explain why Juliet had told me earlier that she thought "there was some history" between Shane and Amber. Would that make Jason insecure enough to ditch the show and ditch his brand-new fiancée? It seemed unlikely to me. Jason was the kind of

73

guy who would get all scrappy and confrontational with a rival. He wouldn't run away.

"Ms. Thackeray?" Becker said, turning to her. She stared at him for a moment like a bunny caught in the headlights, then began to cry. There are some people who are like that. Amber had been weepy all day, understandably, I might add, but most of us would try to control it. Amber was the kind of woman whose distress sets up an immediate chemical reaction in those around her. She cried beautifully, big, clear teardrops that didn't redden her eyes, just poured artistically down her cheeks without taking a side-trip to her nose, the way they do with the rest of us. No snot, no hiccups. Just Hollywood tears. She made next to no noise when she cried, just little tiny puppy whimpers. Instantly, the whole lot of us got all protective.

Meredith put an arm around her, and Bradley passed her a handkerchief. Ruth made a little "tsk" sound and Shane growled low in his throat.

"I thought so," Becker said, getting up. "I think we'll find that Mr. McMaster is back in Toronto, dealing with a few jealousy issues."

"This is ridiculous," I said, speaking, I thought, for the group. "The fact is that Jason's vest, the one that he never, ever takes off, was found floating in the pool downstairs this morning. We've told you that he was an obsessive stage-manager, absolutely dedicated to his job. He wouldn't just leave the company in the lurch. Whether he drowned by accident, or for some other reason, you won't find him in Toronto, you'll find him at the bottom of the Kuskawa River."

"This is not a Stephen King movie," Becker said, "and I've wasted enough time trying to explain to you people that the police need more than a discarded piece of clothing to start an investigation. We'll get in touch with his family and check out the Toronto angle, but I'll bet that you'll hear from him before the day is out." We all stared at him.

"When you do," he added, "we'd appreciate a phone call." He left, taking his notebook (in which he'd written nothing) and the cast-list with him.

"Nice guy," Bradley said. "Real thorough."

Eleven

MOTHER: *I know that you'll succeed, my son, it's written on your heart / you'll vanquish fear, your fame will spread, you'll play a noble part.*
-The Glass Flute, Scene i

We listened to Becker's regulation boots clomp back down the wooden staircase to the main floor. None of us said a word for a few moments, and I think we all felt a bit silly. After all, what had we based our assumptions on? A leather vest in the shop pool, that was all. Becker had been pretty convincing, and now that we knew about the Shane and Amber thing, whether or not it was still going on, it seemed entirely plausible that Jason had skipped out because he couldn't face the competition. Why not? Jason was a peculiar little man, and several of us had wondered what Amber saw in him. Shane, on the other hand, was a walking, talking version of Michelangelo's David, and Amber was Venus on the half-shell. They were perfect for each other, and what aesthetics has brought together, let no man (or woman) put asunder.

"I guess he thinks that Jason's okay," Amber said in a shaky, relieved little voice.

"Seems he does," Ruth said. "Whether he's right or not is another question, though."

"So Jason didn't come back to the motel last night?" Bradley asked.

"I don't know," Amber said. "He didn't come back with us, and he said he was planning to come in at six this morning, so we didn't expect to see him until rehearsal."

"Us?" said Meredith. "We?"

"Yes, us—we," Shane said. "We're all staying in the same place. So big deal. I was too drunk to drive last night and Amber drove my car, okay?" He looked round defiantly. "I know what everybody's thinking, and I can understand that after what that cop said, but listen. There's nothing going on between Amber and me. Okay? Okay? We're just old friends, that's all. Jason knew that."

"If he knew that, then why did he disappear?" Meredith said.

"Maybe he got a call to say his mom's sick or something," Brad said.

"His Mom lives in Laingford," Amber said. "I was supposed to meet the McMasters this weekend. We were supposed to have dinner there."

"You haven't met his parents yet?" Meredith said. "How long have you been going out with him?"

"Three years. He didn't get along with them, eh? It was a big thing, us going there."

"Is that why he was staying at the motel and not with them?" I asked.

"I guess. And Laingford's a half-hour drive from here."

"So why don't we just call them and ask if he's there? Maybe his Mom is sick," Brad said.

"He would have left a note, you'd think," Amber said.

That's when Juliet came back, bustling in full of business and energy.

"Right, kiddies, that's sorted out." She was rubbing her hands, Pilate-like.

"You found him?" Amber said, leaping up.

77

"Found him? Of course not, child, but the police agree with me that the boy's probably just gone off in a snit somewhere and he'll turn up eventually. Not," she added heavily, "as if I'd ever think of hiring him again after this fiasco, but I really don't think we need to worry about it any more. We've got work to do."

"We thought we might call his parents," I said. "See if he's there."

"Good idea," Juliet said. "We probably should have done that in the first place, instead of bothering that disturbingly handsome policeman. Why don't you call them in the break, dear, and put our minds at rest?"

"We're taking a wait-and-see attitude with this, then?" I asked, innocently. I had other ideas, but I wasn't about to discuss them with our fearless leader.

"Exactly, Polly. Now. Have you done the Equity business yet? We should have done that at the beginning, but things were just crazy this morning, so we have an excuse." She smiled widely and rubbed her hands together again.

The rehearsal day had finally begun.

The Canadian professional theatre business is governed by an organization called the Canadian Actors' Equity Association, or Equity. Virtually every professional theatre company in the country is an Equity company, which means that all the contracts they enter into with actors, dancers, directors and stage management personnel are drawn up according to Equity rules. Equity puts out a handbook of those rules, called "the Purple Book" or "the Red Book" or whatever colour they've chosen for the cover of the most recent edition.

You're not allowed to work for an Equity company unless you're a member, but you can't become a member unless you've done a certain number of Equity shows. This, of course, doesn't make a lot of sense. That's why there are a lot of really frustrated actors out there, saying "Hi, my name is Buffy and I'll be your server for tonight." To become a member, you have to accumulate Equity credits. To do that, you work as an apprentice, making less than full-member salary in an Equity company. After you collect the requisite number of apprentice credits, you get to become a full member, after paying the registration fee.

Kid's touring theatre is the most common way to collect credits. That's where the expression "Paying one's dues" comes in. Amber, being fresh out of theatre school, was an apprentice. Usually, after a couple of years of touring theatre, an actor becomes a full member and moves on to theatre for grown-ups. In grown-up theatre, there are dressing rooms, a callboard, a wardrobe department, a decent rehearsal period and the chance to get your teeth into a meaty role. Also, in theatre for grown-ups, you don't have to lug the sets around with you in a van and perform in school gyms.

However, there are times when an interesting kids' show comes along and an experienced actor will take it on, for the fun of it. That's what they'll tell you, anyway. The truth is more likely that they've auditioned for Stratford, Shaw, Factory, Passe Muraille, and everything in between from coast to coast and they're still being Buffy, your server. They're desperate for work, and if they get a contract under the Theatre for Young Audiences Agreement (which means the hours are brutal, and overtime payments are a figment of your imagination), they'll jump at it.

Bradley was in that category. His résumé listed a number of fairly prestigious roles in good plays in the 80s. In the nineties, the roles thinned out and became walk-ons in CBC dramas and commercials. He'd done a few summer stock seasons in Newfoundland, playing Officer Krupke in *West Side Story* and Second Husband in *Chicago*. His most recent gig was a Toronto Fringe Festival production of an original one-act play by someone called Gregory Pecker. Bradley Hoskins had taken *The Glass Flute* role at Steamboat Theatre in Kuskawa because he needed the job, no question.

Shane's situation was a little different. He was a full member of Equity, and his résumé showed that his career was ticking along nicely, thank you very much. He had graduated from the Kingsway Polytechnic Theatre School in the spring of 1997 and immediately landed a summer theatre gig in Gananoque, playing Gilbert in *Anne of Green Gables*. From there he went on to juvenile leads in a couple of high-profile Toronto productions and had performed a supporting role in a LiveShow mega-musical that had gone on to Broadway. This guy was no waiter. Juliet had told me that she got him to do the *Flute* because he owed her a favour (whatever that meant) and that he wanted a rest from the grind of big-theatre schedules. I knew what kind of money a LiveShow job paid out. That would explain Shane's car.

Meredith, unlike the others, was a dyed-in-the-wool touring performer. She'd worked for every children's touring company in Ontario, several times over. Her résumé revealed that she'd done at least three productions a year for the last decade, and she'd never had more than a month off. She was a trouper in the truest sense of the word. While I admire that kind of tenacity, it makes me nervous. It would mean that she knew more about touring than anybody in the whole wide world, including me, her stage manager. This would make her either a very useful ally in inter-cast disputes, or a royal pain. I suspected the latter.

I got all this information in secret, after the rehearsal day was over, and everybody had gone home. While it wasn't exactly classified information, it was in a file in Juliet's office, and I had to hunt around for it. I had help—but more on that later.

The Equity business Juliet was talking about was a formality. Every company was supposed to elect an Equity deputy, who would liase with the stage manager and the administration with regard to working conditions, touring reports and the like. Every time the company put in for overtime on the road, for example, the sheet was supposed to be signed by the deputy and the SM before being submitted. If a cast member had a problem, he or she was supposed to be able to go to the deputy for help. It was a teacher's pet job, the kind that you got elected to if you happened to step out for a moment to go to the bathroom. Nobody ever volunteered for it.

Meredith volunteered for it.

I had shooed Juliet out of the room (artistic directors aren't allowed in on Equity meetings), pulled the deputy package out of Jason's paperwork box under the desk, tossed it on the table and called the meeting to order.

"Let's get this over with, then," I'd said. "Time to elect the dep. Who's in?" I said it in the usual, jokey, don't-all-shout-at-once kind of way.

"I'd be glad to do it," Meredith said, evenly. "I've been looking at the schedule, and I think there may be a couple of overtime difficulties where we're supposed to travel over our lunch-break. I'm also worried about the size of the set, not to mention the short rehearsal period." There was a funny little pause.

"Er, anybody else interested?" I said. Nobody was.

"Right, then. All in favour?"

"Yeah, sure," Bradley said. "You go, girl."

"I can't be deputy if I'm an apprentice, right?" Amber said.

"No, you can't," said Meredith. "You couldn't handle it anyway."

"It's not rocket science," Shane said. "Do it if you want to. I don't care." Meredith smiled—a Cheshire cat smile that would have stayed even if her face had disappeared.

"Carried," I said, without enthusiasm, and pushed the package over to her. She opened it immediately, pulled out the Green Book (its current colour), and wrote her name on the cover. Golly, I thought. I guess I'd better find my copy and re-read it. I had a feeling there would be a quiz on it later.

Twelve

PRINCESS: *It's hard to be a princess when you're lost and cold and scared / I'd ask that stranger over there to help me, if I dared.*
-The Glass Flute, Scene iv

Working a puppet convincingly requires the same kind of brain-hand coordination that you need to be able to pat your head, rub your belly, tap-dance and sing the alphabet backwards, all at the same time.

The puppet gods who manipulate the Muppets make it look easy. It isn't. Anyone can stick a sock on their hand and wave it about, of course. Anyone can speak in a funny squeaky voice and wiggle Bozo the fluffy dog while they're speaking, to let the audience know that Bozo has the floor. In the world of puppet manipulation, we call this "jiggling dolls." Jiggling dolls is about as far removed from true puppeteering as a Sunday school nativity tableau is from a full-scale production at the Canadian Opera Company. The only thing these two kinds of productions have in common is the temperament of the performers.

True puppeteering talent is immediately recognizable. The techniques can be learned, just as the rudiments of singing or painting can, but when there's natural talent, the puppeteer simply disappears and the puppet transcends its inanimate state.

In rehearsal, it was my job (as puppetmaster, not as SM) to assess the abilities of each performer, introduce each of them to the puppets they would be manipulating, and let them loose in front of the studio mirrors to work. When the *Flute* was in performance, they wouldn't be able to see what they were doing, so mirror practice was useful.

In addition to the handles and black dowels attached to each of the objects that appeared in the *Flute*, the speaking characters each had a mouth-mechanism that had to be co-ordinated with the speech of the performer. In Muppet-like puppets, you work the mouth by opening and closing your hand inside the puppet's head. In the puppets we were using, the mouth-mechanism was a complicated series of wires and pulleys built into the frame of the head. The mouth was opened by a squeezable trigger at the back, like those spring-loaded exercise devices that muscle-men use to increase the strength of their grip. By the end of the tour, the actors would have forearms like Hulk Hogan's.

The trick of co-ordinating speech and puppet-mouth movement is best practiced at home, when there's no-one around to worry that you're losing your mind. First, locate some lipstick. (This aids in the effect.) Make a loose fist and draw a set of lips on your hand, with the thumb as the lower lip and your knuckle and forefinger as the upper. If you want, draw eyes on your knuckles as well. Then start talking to yourself, making the lips outline every syllable. Go slowly at first, or you'll get a thumb-cramp. Later, find a four-year-old and see if you can keep her attention for more than two minutes. If she talks back to your hand, you've got the idea. If she starts crying and reports you to the authorities, you need more practice.

None of the cast was a hopeless case, thank God. The

audition process involved a "Here's a puppet; see what you can do with it" section, and the inveterate doll-jigglers were weeded out.

Meredith, having worked with Steamboat puppets on many occasions, was quite adept at the trick of co-ordinating speech and mouth-movement, but the puppet was wooden in her hands and probably always would be. It was as if her puppet-manipulation were the stage version of low-budget animation. There was no spark, but she was competent.

She was, however, impossible to teach, and I shouldn't have even tried. She was working with the pale and languid Mother puppet-head, which was attached to a fake body in the bed. Throughout the show, the mother-head is attached to various floating objects in dream-sequences. Later, at the end of the show when Mother revives and actually gets up, the mother-puppet is attached to the mother-body waiting backstage.

"Meredith, why not try a sort of full-body sigh with your arm under the blanket while she's in the bed?" I suggested, demonstrating by slipping my hand under the covers of the small, prop bed and creating a lump there which moved with breath.

"Lift it up with the in-breath, and down on the sigh. Wiggle your fingers, and that's her toes stretching. Then you can make her do that smack-smack mouth thing, like she's about to go to sleep."

Shane was working next to her with the Kevin puppet. He was a natural, the kind of puppeteer who can make a ketchup bottle come to life just by picking it up, walking it across the table and making it stare at you with Heinz-label eyes. He'd never done puppetry before—a director's dream. He moved the Kevin-puppet over to watch.

"Hey, cool," Kevin the puppet said.

"Polly, I don't need any coaching from you. I have done this show before. I'm going over old material here, and I'd appreciate it if you'd just let me work." Meredith said. Out of the corner of my eye, I could see the Kevin puppet staring at Meredith. Instinctively, Shane was living through the puppet, gazing intently at Kevin's terrycloth, fluorescent-painted face. It's a symbiotic thing; the focus of the puppet's eyes is the key to the magic. If the puppet is looking at something, and the puppeteer is looking at the puppet, the puppeteer no longer exists.

"Who's she?" Kevin the puppet said, giving his woolly head a little twitch to indicate Meredith. I couldn't help myself. I chuckled and gazed deeply into his ping-pong ball eyes, which I'd painted with my own hands not two weeks before.

"Well, Kevin, she's an actor who doesn't want my help," I said to the puppet. Kevin nodded slowly, sadly. Using the dowel attached to Kevin's arms, Shane made Kevin's foam-rubber and terrycloth hand reach out and pat my hand, still under the covers of Mother's bed.

"Too bad. That breath-thing was a nice bit," Kevin-the-puppet said. Shaking his head, Kevin moved away to join the others, pulled by Shane, who was smiling a little.

"Show-off," the Mother puppet said, woodenly.

Amber was wrestling with the snake puppet, which is large and rather awkward. In order to make it move properly, its thirteen-foot, foam-rubber body is strapped to the puppeteer with a waist-belt. Its mouth is worked with a Brobdignagian version of the spring trigger, which takes both hands. During the show, the body is manipulated with the help of another performer, Brad in this case.

Neither Amber nor Brad had missed the Mother/Kevin/me exchange. Straining to coordinate the snake's mouth, Amber commented with a somewhat-adapted line from the script.

"You're brave and true and strong of heart," the serpent said, "But what you seek...will make Mom fart." Brad twirled the snake's tail and blew a raspberry. They dissolved into giggles and Juliet lifted her head from her script, where she was making notes.

"Actually, that's not a bad line, dear. Kids love fart jokes."

"Oh sure, let's put it in," Meredith said loudly. "And while we're at it, we could add a scene from Beavis and Butthead and make the whole show more accessible to our audience." She tossed the Mother puppet to the floor and stalked out.

"Good time for an Equity break," I said.

Equity rules state that performers are entitled to five minutes of break per hour of rehearsal. Generally, the breaks are loosely adhered to—say ten or fifteen minutes every two and a half hours. Finding a good moment to break is part of the stage manager's art.

For many, the Equity break is synonymous with "smoke break". If the SM is a non-smoker, she can make herself very popular with the cast if she remembers that the need for a cigarette tends to surface in the addicted mind every half-hour or so, and if it isn't indulged every two hours, the work suffers. Being a smoker and an SM at the same time, this was not a problem for me. In every show I've ever done, the smokers share a special bond, as if they're in a separate show called "Smoke Break". On the *Flute*, the smoke break cast included me, Amber and Shane.

"That was weird," Amber said, sucking mightily on a DuMaurier Ultra Light in the basement shop. Shane lit a full-strength Du Maurier regular and lit my Extra Light for me with an engraved, gold-plated lighter.

I don't know why it is that so many theatre-type smokers

choose this particular brand. It could be because the company is known for big time arts funding, but more likely, it's just the monkey-see, monkey-do principle in action. My dating history can be traced by the brands I've smoked over the years. Get a new boyfriend; switch to his brand. Makes the sharing of smokes easier. The heroin addict hangs out with the heroin addict, after all; the cocaine snorter with fellow snorters, and the smoker likewise. Gotta quit, one day.

"What was weird?" I asked Amber.

"That thing with Meredith. She doesn't like you much, eh?"

"I think she's just trying to establish that she has experience," I said, carefully. "She wants to be treated with the respect that comes from seniority."

"Huh," said Shane. "And she gives the rest of us the respect that she'd give a babbling toddler. Still, I'm glad it's you SMing, Polly, and not Jason. Sorry, Amber. Had to be said." Amber seemed to take this remark in stride, blowing out a cloud of smoke and gazing contemplatively off into the middle distance.

"You're right, Shane. Like, he is my boyfriend and everything, but he wouldn't have been able to handle Meredith. She would have taken over." I noted that Amber was speaking about Jason in the present tense.

"Meredith's a high-maintenance puppy, definitely," Shane said. It was a joke-label, not very complimentary but quite accurate.

"Which reminds me," I said. "I should call Jason's parents and find out if they've seen him. We're going to look really dumb if he's gone home to Mommy. Where did you say they lived, Amber? Laingford?"

"Yeah. They've got one of those monster homes on a lake up there. It was supposed to be a summer cottage, but Dr.

McMaster—that's his Dad—moved his practice up here from the city when Jason was ten. I've never been to the house, but Jason showed me a picture. It's like Kurt and Goldie's place. Huge."

Kurt Russell and Goldie Hawn, the American movie stars, had built a palace on one of the lakes in Ontario cottage country some years ago. They sold it eventually, saying that the locals were bothering them. The local papers retaliated by saying that if Kurt and Goldie had wanted privacy, they shouldn't have built a mansion on the waterfront of one of the busiest, most tourist-infested lakes in the region.

Amber rummaged through the bulging purse she always carried with her and produced a personal daytimer. "Here it is," she said, handing me the diary. Sunday, which was our official day off, was marked with stars. "Important" was written on that day's page in a childish scrawl. "Visit the Gorgons." I copied down the telephone number.

"Jason called them that. Like I said, they weren't close. We were supposed to go there for dinner and a spring cruise on Dr. McMaster's antique motorboat. I bought a new outfit and everything."

"For the doctor's benefit, or for Jason's?" Shane said.

"Ha-ha, very funny," Amber said. "I just wanted to make a good impression, that's all."

"Dr. McMaster used to take young girls out on the boat all the time," Shane said. "Trust me, if the new outfit is skimpy, it would've made an impression."

"You know them?" I asked, surprised.

"Jason and I went to Laingford High together," he said, with a wry smile. "I'm a local boy, too, you know."

"Holy Toledo," I said. "When were you there?"

"About ten years ago," he said. Something passed across his face like a grey shadow, and he extinguished his cigarette, along with the subject. "I gotta take a leak before we start. Excuse me, ladies."

"High school can do that to some people," I said. "Bad memories. I should go make that phone call."

"Polly?" Amber said, "if Jason's not there—at his parents' place, I mean—where do you think he is?"

I was going to say "at the bottom of the river", but thought better of it. Amber was hard to read, and she was, after all, wearing a honking huge diamond that Jason had apparently trothed his plight with.

"He'll turn up," I said vaguely. "Ummm…Jason didn't know that Shane was going to be in the cast, did he?"

"No. It was a last minute thing. After he found out, just after I got up here from Toronto, he burst into my motel room and asked me to marry him."

"May I ask why you said yes?"

"Polly, we have a show to do. It's my first big break, and I didn't want to ruin it by pissing off the stage manager."

"You accepted an offer of marriage because of a puppet show?"

"Well, that's not the only reason. We have been going out for three years. We get along okay. Also, I'm pregnant."

Thirteen

CAT: *Deeds done in the dark are much more fun / than prissy Boy-scout stuff under the sun.*
-The Glass Flute, Scene vii

"Are you happy about that?" I said. Amber looked at me thoughtfully, a tiny frown creasing her flawless forehead.

"I'm not sure," she said. "I haven't told Jason, although I think he probably guessed, but I'm not really sure it's his." She didn't wait to hear my reply, which was just as well, as I hadn't the faintest idea what to say.

"See ya upstairs, Polly," she said and threw her cigarette into the shop pool. It went out with a faint hiss, like the voice of a tiny serpent.

I went to phone Jason's parents.

Mrs. McMaster told me that the police had already called her and she hadn't heard from Jason since he arrived in Sikwan the week before. She didn't sound particularly worried.

"He used to go off in a sulk by himself all the time as a boy," she said. "The police asked us to let them know if Jason got in touch, and I suppose it's all we can do."

"Did they tell you why we were concerned about him?" I asked.

"Well, they said that he hadn't shown up for work, and there was some garment of his left in the theatre," she said.

"Yes. His vest. The black leather one he always wears," I said. There was a silence on the other end of the line. An empty one, as if Jason's mother wanted to say "So? What's your point?", but was too polite to do so.

"Amber says he would never take it off, you see, and in the theatre business, stage managers always show up for work, no matter what. I don't want to distress you, but we think something's happened to him."

"Well, that's not what the police told us," Mrs. McMaster said. "Frankly, Ms. Deacon, they warned us you might be calling, and said not to let you put ideas into our heads."

Damn Becker. I should sue him for defamation of character. Still, my gut feelings about Jason's disappearance sounded as lame when explaining them to his mother as they had when I had told them to the police. Maybe I was just making a murder out of a molehill, so to speak.

I was due back in rehearsal, but I knew I wouldn't be comfortable about things until I'd spoken to Jason myself. Tobin was out somewhere, and the shop was empty. I stared at the pool, envisioning the various possible scenarios, all of them ending in Jason's headlong splash into the pool, the struggles and grunts of a non-swimmer followed by a gurgle as he went under.

On my way back upstairs, Kim handed me a note from Rico.

"Polly," it said. "Tobin had to go to Laingford, so I got a ride with him. He said to tell you that he called Jason's Toronto number. No answer but he left a message on the machine. Can I get a ride in with you tomorrow? Drop by for coffee after rehearsal. Rico."

The rest of the rehearsal day was relatively uneventful. The sing-through revealed that Amber, whose speaking voice was as light as popcorn, had a rock belt that could rattle the windows. Shane and Brad had fine, strong singing voices and Meredith sounded like Maureen Forrester in her prime. The four-part harmony they produced sent shivers up my spine, and Ruth at the keyboard was smiling from ear to ear.

"Well, even if you just stood there and jiggled dolls all through the show, you'd still have their little bottoms pinned to their seats," Juliet said with satisfaction. "We'll cut it short for the day, I think. We've had a lot of excitement, and I imagine that Polly needs some time to go over her paperwork. Jason left a certain number of matters unfinished."

"We'll start at ten tomorrow morning," I said, using my official "I am a stage manager whether I like it or not" voice. Meredith approached me as the others headed out.

"I gather that you're officially taking over as SM, even if Jason shows up again," she said.

"Yep."

"Well then, I brought this up with him last night, and I was hoping he'd speak with Juliet. I don't think the stage manager should do all the driving."

"Excuse me?"

"Look, I know that there's an extra ten bucks a day for driving, once we're on the road. It's in the Green Book. I think we should share the wealth around," she said.

"That's not company policy," I said. It's not an expression I've ever used in my life, but it just popped out. Meredith, I was discovering, brought out the mingy bureaucrat in me.

"We did it on the last tour I was on with Theatre on the Road," she said. "It worked very well. Besides, some people are better drivers than others."

I don't know if she was trying to imply that I wasn't a good driver (she could hardly know one way or another, as we'd never shared space in a vehicle), but my hackles went up immediately.

"All the more reason to stick to one driver who knows what she's doing," I said. "Besides, the insurance allows for one principal driver and a back-up. The Equity deputy is usually the back-up driver, so you'll get a bonus on the days you drive."

"That's not good enough," Meredith said. "I'd like you to talk to Juliet about it. Jason said he would."

"Oh, I will too, Meredith. Believe me," I said.

"And I hope you know that company policy forbids smoking in the van," she said, on her way out.

Ruth had been puttering around with her equipment, and looked up in surprise at Meredith's last remark, which had been unnecessarily loud.

"She's going to be trouble," Ruth said.

"Got that right. Ruth, tell me again why I didn't tell Juliet to take a flying leap this morning when she told me I was taking over Jason's job."

"You need the money," Ruth said.

"Oh."

"And you're just a girl who cain't say no," she sang, accompanying herself on the keyboard. "You're in a terrible fix/ You always say C'mon, let's go…"

"…just when I outta say shit," I finished. We'd both been in a production of Oklahoma in high school, and had made up naughty words to most of the songs. Suddenly we were back there, goofing around like seventeen-year-olds. It was a good place to be, and I realized that the job stage-managing would have its benefits. I'd be spending a lot of time with Ruth.

"You going home right away?" Ruth said.

"Nope. I want to collect up Jason's SM stuff first and update the cast list. There's no computer in Polly-land."

"When are you going to enter the twenty-first century, girl?" Ruth said.

"Hey. Juliet gave me a cellphone. I'm getting there."

"And one day you'll have hydro and running water in your home, just like the uppity rich folks."

"Naah. Then I'd be like everybody else," I said.

"Speaking of which, what was it like seeing Becker again?" I'd told Ruth about my short-lived relationship with the clean-cut cop and admitted that, while he drove me crazy, he also drove me crazy, if you know what I mean. In other words, I still liked him. More than a bit. Bummer.

"Oh, you know. Chalk and cheese. Fire and ice. Same old thing."

"Anything there still?"

"I don't know, Ruth. Probably not. Anyway, I'm still smoking dope and he's still a cop, so there's not much chance of a reconciliation."

"Too bad," Ruth said. "Well, I have to get back. Rose is calling me at seven, and phone sex is better than nothing."

"Play safe," I said. After she left, I restored the puppets to their proper pre-set positions backstage, as per Jason's diagram. He had been efficient, I'd give him that. Then I gathered up all the paperwork, stuffed it into the cardboard box marked "*Flute* stuff" and headed downstairs to the office area behind the lobby.

Tobin was pouring a cup of incredibly thick coffee into his mug and going over a list of technical supplies for the show.

"Juliet's gone," he said. "She wants a production meeting at nine, if that's okay with you."

"Charming," I said. "From lazy, late-rising puppet-maker to early-bird stage manager in one swell foop."

"I'm glad you're doing it, Polly. Couldn't stand that little bastard Jason."

"Gosh," I said. "I didn't know you felt so strongly."

"Not enough to do him harm, if that's what you mean," Tobin said. "He just got up my nose, that's all. Attitude."

"So do you think he's holed up somewhere, licking his wounded heart?"

"Nope. I think he's feeding the smelt," Tobin said. "But the police don't think so, and they didn't even bother to take his vest away."

"Really? Where is it?"

"Hanging in Juliet's office, dripping onto the carpet," he said.

"Did they search the pockets?"

"I don't think so. They just kind of looked at it, wrote some stuff down and left," Tobin said. "Juliet picked it up and said she'd keep it for him until he shows up."

"He'd have to ransom it," I said.

"I think that's the idea."

"Rico said you called his Toronto number."

"Yeah. I gave it to the cops, but I thought I'd call it myself, on the off-chance he was there. Told him to call us."

"He won't, though."

"No. Doubt it." We looked at each other for a moment, and then without speaking, turned and headed for Juliet's office.

Juliet never locked the door. Any valuables were kept in the safe near Kim's desk, but walking through the portals felt like burglary anyway. With the exception of Kim Lee and a few chosen men friends, her office was strictly off limits. If she conducted interviews, they were done in the place where the prospective employee would be working.

The room was Victorian in the extreme. Thick, crimson curtains festooned the windows, a fully stocked bar outfitted with heavy cut-glass goblets lurked in a corner, an honest-to-

God crystal chandelier hung from the ceiling, and an inviting, overstuffed sofa, complete with lace antimacassars, had pride of place in front of an enormous desk. Show posters covered the walls, many of them advertising the old Toronto revues that had made Juliet Keating a famous name in the sixties. In amongst them were playbills from the Royal Alex and what used to be the O'Keefe Centre (now named for a new corporate benefactor, proving that theatrical prostitution is alive and well in Toronto). There were posters from obscure summer stock companies in rural Ontario, Nova Scotia and Vancouver, and several from New York. There were autographed headshots of famous and not-so-famous performers, photos of Juliet kissing or being kissed by various members of the glitterati, and one stunning shot of Juliet in full chorus girl gear, looking like a million bucks. I could've spent hours in there, just checking out the walls.

Jason's vest was on a hanger suspended next to the radiator near the door, dripping water onto a newspaper spread carefully underneath it. Again, I was hit by how the vest seemed to represent Jason's personality, how lost he would be without it. The pockets bulged. Nobody had even bothered to rescue the mini-Maglite that was slung through a loop over the breast pocket.

"As if he would go anywhere without his Mag," I said, sadly, but left it where it was. I reached into the bulgy right-hand pocket and extracted a swollen, soggy notebook.

There's a stage manager's expression which goes "If it's not on the page, it's not on the stage." Knowing how hyper-efficient Jason was, every chore, every moment of his working day would be recorded in the book. It amazed me that the cops hadn't even bothered to look. Still, they thought he was alive, which would make the notebook irrelevant, I suppose.

If he were dead, though, the book might contain some hint as to why.

"I'll take this, if you don't mind," I said to Tobin. "If nothing else, there may be some show-stuff in it I need to know about."

Jason's keys weren't there, but that was no surprise. Like Tobin, he carried his in a jingling mass on his belt-loop. They would be with Jason, wherever he was. A few drowned pens and pencils completed the inventory.

Outside, the evening had descended, but we didn't want to turn on the lights in the office, both very being aware that snooping in Juliet's inner sanctum would not be considered an acceptable after-rehearsal pastime.

"Do you have a copy of his résumé?" I said. "If he was pushed, as they say, and is actually dead, we'll need to know more about him if we're going to find out who did it."

"I don't, but Juliet's got 'em all on file somewhere."

"Shall we?"

We started to search. Most of Juliet's paperwork was kept in an ancient four-drawer filing cabinet pushed against one wall, which was masked slightly by a lace cloth and a revolting collection of china shepherdesses.

It didn't take us long to find the personnel file. Every production of *The Glass Flute* was filed according to year, and the thick, green folders bulged with headshots, résumés, production reports and profit breakdowns. I took a moment to snoop at the folder marked 1995. I'm not much of a money person, but it was quite obvious why Juliet liked to trot out the *Flute* when times were tough. The show truly raked in the bucks, according to the Steamboat Theatre bottom line. There was a five-year-old eight-by-ten of Meredith in the folder. She'd aged quite a bit in a short period, I noticed. At least here was proof, if one needed it, that she had indeed done the show before and therefore had a right to lord it over the rest of us.

In the folder for the current production, the résumés of the entire cast and crew were included, along with a sheaf of notes written in what looked like shorthand. The study of Pitman shorthand died out in Ontario schools in the early 70s, and I never had a chance to learn it. Actually, I'd rather have been set on fire than taken shorthand in high school, same with home-ec or typing, which is why I'm a perennially unemployed puppetmaker with no marketable skills. If I'd taken typing, for example, I could have risen in the ranks and been a wealthy Microserf by now. Still, at that moment I would have given anything to be able to translate Juliet's notes, which were written on steno paper, one sheet per résumé, and I'll bet they contained secret messages about each employee.

I scanned the other résumés quickly, out of sheer snoopiness, before I found Jason's. It was quite dark by then, and I used my own Maglite, feeling like a cat burglar.

"Here it is," I whispered to Tobin. When I got no reply, I looked up to see him standing in the middle of the room, his ears pricked like a terrier on full-alert. He put his finger to his lips, and then I heard it too. Someone was making their way down the hall, very quietly.

In an overstuffed Victorian office-space, there are plenty of places to hide. We could have dived under the big oak desk, which was surrounded by a coy, frilly thing that would have hidden us nicely. We could have thrown ourselves onto the sofa, which I swear would have swallowed us. We chose, however, in true Polonius-fashion, to head for the heavy velvet curtains. I chose the left one, Tobin the right. As soon as we were safely hidden behind the arras, someone came into the office.

Fourteen

KEVIN: *Stand back, snake! / This flute can make a sound so shrill / You'd think it was a dentist's drill.*
SERPENT: *What'th a dentitht?*
-The Glass Flute, Scene vii

I peeked out. In what was left of the light, it was impossible to see who it was, because, like us, the intruder chose to work in the dark. They made straight for Jason's vest. There was a wet rustle of fabric, as if the visitor were searching the pockets, and then the tiny, annoyed "Tsk" sound that indicated disappointment. Get a male friend and then a female friend to make that noise. You'll find that there's no gender difference. It's about the only sound in the human linguistic spectrum that's entirely asexual. The person left as quickly and quietly as s/he had come.

We didn't move until we heard a car leave.

"Did you hear a car arrive?" I whispered to Tobin through a gap in our curtains. We were still masked from the room, but I realized, once I thought about it, that our hiding place would have made us plainly visible from the exterior. Seeing us from outside would have been like sneaking backstage to see two people peeking out into the audience from the wings.

"I might have heard a car subconsciously," Tobin said. "My heart rate increased, and then I heard a door open."

"Who do you think it was?" I said and stepped out into the room.

"Could have been Juliet," Tobin said.

"No way. She'd have turned on the light and walked in as if she owned the place," I said.

"She does."

"I know. So it can't have been her. Did you get a look at them?"

"Nope. I was making like a hatrack," he said.

"You're never going to get your junior detective's badge at this rate," I said.

"Don't want one. I've got the decoder ring already," Tobin said. "And it's telling me we should get the hell out of here."

"Agreed." We slipped out of the room and tiptoed down to the shop. Don't ask me why we tiptoed, but we did. The residue of the cat-burglar thing, maybe.

"So, what were they looking for?" Tobin asked, gathering some papers together and stuffing them into a worn satchel.

"The notebook, guaranteed," I said, patting the pocket where it was safely stashed, creating a wet spot next to my hip. "I don't know why, but when I get it dried out and the pages aren't sticking together, maybe it'll tell us."

Tobin killed the lights and carried Jason's cardboard *Flute* paperwork box to George's truck for me. I was loaded down with the prompt script (Jason's now mine) and the various bags and baggage I seemed to have accumulated during the day. I'd have to get a briefcase, or a cool satchel like Tobin's. Somewhere at home I had a thing I used to carry in my stage management days. I think it was in the closet, stuffed with orphan socks. I'd have to dig it out.

"See you at nine tomorrow," he said, driving away in his buttercup yellow Neon, into which he had folded himself with extraordinary ease, as if he were one of those collapsible bridge tables. Big guy. Really small car.

I fired up the beast and headed home, yearning for Lug-Nut, peace and some dinner. It had been an insanely busy day, and my life, apparently, had changed. I was now a stage manager, with responsibilities coming out the wahzoo, a paltry one-week rehearsal schedule, a two-month touring schedule and a lot of forms to fill in. My broken nose throbbed, and I also had what I believed was a murder on my hands, which I absolutely had to solve, even if there was no corpse in sight. It was obvious the Laingford OPP wasn't up to it.

The peace I was looking for at home didn't materialize. I'd dropped in to Rico's for a quick cappuccino on my way home, rehashed the day's business and gossiped a bit about the cast. Neither of us had been inclined to talk much about Jason. I think we were afraid that if we did, his being dead would turn out to be true. I had cut my visit short, because the subject had been hanging in the air above our heads like a bad smell.

As I passed the shack where the Neighbours from Hell lived, I couldn't help but notice the big bonfire, the beat-up pickup trucks lining the dirt road and the hectic figures staggering around in the orange glow. My window was open, and I could hear the music and the barking dogs above the rumble of the Ford's engine. The Neighbours were partying, Big Time.

I pulled into the driveway and found Luggy and George sitting on the porch. George was cradling his head in his hands and Luggy's hackles were up. Luggy was tied to the porch railing too, which was unheard of.

"Hey, George. Trouble?"

"I don't know what to do," he said, tight-lipped. "The noise.

It's horrible." Next door, heavy-metal rock music was blaring, the dogs were barking and the night was shattered by it.

"Has this been going on long?"

"Since dusk. They have been shooting guns. The dogs are howling. I think they shot one of them."

"You're kidding."

"I am not. There was barking, barking, for hours and men shouting at them to shut up. Then some shots and yelping." George was profoundly upset. He was almost in tears.

"Let's go inside," I said.

The Neighbours from Hell were a good acre of woods away, but sound carries beautifully in the bush when everything's dry and there are no leaves on the branches to absorb the sound. The trees can perform acoustic miracles. The din, which came in waves like a bad headache, ricocheted off the tree-trunks, surrounded the house and poured through the window screens. The windows were open, because, in spite of the noise, it was an incredibly beautiful spring night.

George and I had shared dinner, done the dishes, and were now trying to relax beside the woodstove in the kitchen. The dogs next door were still at it, although the music had stopped.

We shared the highlights of our respective days. I told him at length about finding Jason's vest and all that went after. I tried very hard to be balanced and objective—to give the "Jason had a hissy fit and walked out" theory as much weight as the "Jason fell in the Kuskawa River and sank to the bottom" gambit, but I'm not sure I pulled it off. I had a sense of *déjà vu* as I pleaded my case, hearing my own words eight-odd months ago, when I was trying to convince George Hoito that my best friend Francy hadn't murdered her husband. I'd been right then, too, but if this were anything like last time, there'd be a second murder before George agreed with me.

"The young man will show up," he said. "He'll need to be sure his disappearance is causing some concern."

"Oh, I think he'll show up. I just think he'll be too drowned to care," I said.

He countered my story with the news that my aunt Susan had told him she was selling her business. I don't know which upset me more, the mystery of Jason or this revelation and the fact that Susan hadn't told me first.

"How can she go out of business? People rely on her and she's thriving. Besides, she's run that store since I was a baby."

"She has two reasons," George said. "The new feed store on the highway is undercutting her prices and carrying the American stock she refuses to sell. That means people aren't relying on her as much as they used to. And the other is something she wants to tell you herself."

"Oh, God. She's not sick, is she?"

"No, no. Nothing like that."

"So?? What is it? What's this reason number two?"

"You'll have to wait until you can see her."

"Wait? For the weekend? I'm in rehearsal every day until Sunday."

Our voices had been getting progressively louder, not because we were having a difficult time seeing eye to eye, but because the barking was, I think, subconsciously making us angry.

"Sometimes," George said, "I play a game with myself. I listen very carefully and try to guess how many dogs there are. Once, I counted seven. Tonight, I hear a hundred."

The spring peepers would usually have started their evening song by now, but they're a choir that likes to be centre stage, and they were waiting for the warm-up act to finish their set. Even Poe was bothered, which wasn't like him at all. He stayed on his bookshelf above the woodstove, huddled into an angry black ball of feathers. He shivered the way he does when it's really cold and muttered occasionally to himself.

The dogs barked on, and George poured an unusually hefty slug of Glen-unpronounceable into our coffee mugs. He drank most of his in a mouth-scalding gulp.

"Maybe if we get drunk, we won't hear them any more," he muttered.

"Have you tried calling the police?" I asked.

"They told me it was a bylaw problem," he said.

"So you called the Town?"

"They said we were zoned rural," he growled and poured another slug into his empty coffee cup.

I had a rehearsal the next morning, so I didn't join him.

"I live here for 26 years in peace. I pay my tax. Why will nobody give me an answer?" George said.

"I guess we could go over there…" I said.

George grabbed my hand and stared into my face. "You will not—I will not go over there. People like that, you stay away from. Don't even let them see your face. They are dangerous."

I was inclined to agree. Anyway, it was a bit too late in the game to pay a visit with a blueberry pie and a Howdy Neighbour dinner invitation, and going over there in anger would be stupid. The dogs barked on, sometimes frantically, sometimes ferociously, but incessantly, with only the occasional pause to fill doggy lungs with air.

"I don't suppose they have a phone, do they?" I was sort of joking. Bad timing.

George slammed down his mug and stood up. "They do not even have a proper toilet or an outhouse," he shouted. "They have no electricity. They have nothing!" He was generally a controlled man, and he had shouted at me only twice before—once when I was about to sever my toes with an axe, and once when had I almost thrown up in his barn. Finns are slow to boil, but when they do, duck. I admit I flinched.

He stomped off towards the bathroom, and I prepared to go. I had to do some work on my prompt book and dry out Jason's notebook, and Lug-nut needed to be further away from the barking, or he'd start pissing everywhere.

I went out to George's mud room to look for a rope or something for Luggy. With the noise the Hell-hounds were making, he'd be over there like a shot as soon as I opened the door. Lug-nut was big, but I'd tried George's trick and counted at least three barkers, and they all sounded like Cerberus.

The mud room was screened in and open to the night. As I started thumping around, looking under the pile of coats, boots and tools, the barking dogs re-doubled their efforts. Maybe they could hear me, or smell Luggy or something, but they were suddenly a heck of a lot louder.

The door to the house opened behind me and George brushed past, at great speed, ignoring me. I grabbed Luggy's collar and watched as George ran out onto the porch, down the steps and into the driveway, carrying his shotgun. The gun's an antique in perfect working order, made when they didn't care how much noise the thing made, as long as it fired lethal stuff out the business end. It had two clumsy grey barrels, an oak stock and a kick that could knock you down.

The dogs were going postal. George stood, his legs planted wide, and lifted the big old gun to his shoulder, aiming straight up at the sky. Then he fired. The noise was prodigious. I lifted my hands to my ears.

For a split second, everything was still. Every dog on the planet stopped barking and I stopped breathing. Then, with a roar that I swear must've been heard at the Cedar Falls Dinette in the village, George let fly.

"SATANAN PERKELE! HILJAA!!"

Then he stumbled off into the dark, still carrying the shotgun, towards the dwelling next door. Lug-nut, no longer held, flamed off after him like a hot arrow.

Fifteen

CAT: *The words that mothers say are often true / and spoken when their child is feeling blue / There's other people far worse off than you.*
-The Glass Flute, Scene vi

George had told me not to go over there, that the people next door were dangerous. Normally, a remark like that would have had me doing the opposite in about five seconds. I hate being told what I can and can't do, but in this case I agreed with my old friend. However, George was likkered up (as we say around here) and armed, and though it was unlikely he'd shoot anybody, it made him more dangerous than the unknown entity of the Neighbours from Hell. Also, my dog was involved. As I plunged into the bush after them, I could hear Lug-nut's bark mixing with the cacophony of the neighbour's dogs. Visions of enormous vet bills swam before my eyes.

"George, get the hell back here, you idiot!" I yelled. It was sort of like trying to recall an untrained dog. You can call out a name over and over, in an increasingly desperate and angry way, and the person or dog being called is about as likely to come as they are to grow another head. George was beyond reasoning, and my only hope was to catch up to him before he burst out of the bush into the midst of the partying neighbours.

In rural Kuskawa, just like in any rural neighbourhood, there's a highway you never see from the road, a criss-crossed grid of forest paths between houses, established by dogs and children, discovered and made use of by adults and the occasional deer. The width and clarity of an inter-household path, if you cared to study it, would tell you the degree of intimacy between neighbours. Abandoned cairns, forts and toys would indicate that the children living in adjacent houses were friends. A canine companion would be able to tell you if other dogs he knew had passed that way by sniffing at markers and leaving his own. The path between my cabin and George's house was well-worn, strewn with chewed Luggy-sticks and bootprints. There used to be a path between my place and that of my old friend, Francy Travers, who lived near the Cedar Falls dump, but she died last year, and the overgrown trail would be able to tell you that, if you asked it. There was no path at all between George's house and the Neighbours from Hell.

The light from the bonfire next door glimmered through the trees. The party people had turned off their music some time ago, around the time that George and I were finishing dinner, but the dogs were still barking, now using the fully-engaged warning voices that herald the approach of strangers. Obviously, they were tethered, or they'd have been on top of us by now. I couldn't hear any human voices, though.

I caught up to George while we were still masked by trees. He was standing behind a large oak, propped against the trunk, his shotgun at the ready like a Rambo-movie sniper. Lug-nut was right at his heels, silent and quivering. When George heard me, his head whipped around and he pointed his gun at me, lowering it as soon as he saw who it was. I'd had a gun pointed at me only once before, on purpose that time, but this was equally as frightening. In the darkness, George's eyes seemed to glow.

"What are you planning to do, George?" I whispered. "Pick the neighbours off one by one?" I was so mad at him I could feel myself shaking.

"They must be inside," he said. "They are so used to the sound of barking dogs that they do not hear them any more. I wonder how their children can sleep. We could go right up to the windows, and it wouldn't make any difference."

I looped the rope I'd brought through Lug-nut's collar.

"We could go home, and it would make even less of a difference, which would be a good thing," I said.

The Dogs from Hell were looking right at us. There were six of them visible in the light of the bonfire. Each was staked out on a short tether, about three feet long, far enough apart so they couldn't touch each other. There were no feed bowls or water bowls in sight, and their ribs stuck out. Three of them were mixed German Shepherd types, with intelligent faces and enormous eyes. If they'd been in better shape, they'd have been beautiful. Two of the dogs were scrawny hounds, contributing to the general din with soulful houndy-howls. The sixth was a small, mixed breed puppy which couldn't have been more than two months old. The chain to which it was tied probably weighed more than it did. Its yips were ear-splitting. According to George's earlier count-by-ear, there were supposed to be seven of them. Had number seven been shot, as George suspected? It was too dark to see if there was a furry body stashed nearby. The whole scenario was horrible. What was worse, in a way, was that the dogs were plainly doing their job, warning their masters that there were intruders, and the masters were oblivious.

"Just look at them," George said, "tied like animals."

"They are animals," I said. "But I know what you mean.

This isn't right." Both of us, I think, once we saw the conditions under which the Dogs from Hell were living, lost a lot of our anger about the noise and instead, channelled it to where it belonged, toward the owners.

"I want to see how they live," George said, creeping towards the windows.

"Why?" I called after him. "Hush, Luggy! That's enough, dammit!" I could hardly blame my dog for barking, considering that his fellow canines were making such a racket, but just because the next-door kids are foul-mouthed brats, it doesn't mean you like when yours is, too. Luggy's eyes bulged as I yanked on the rope attached to his collar. Is that how animal abuse starts? Probably. He didn't quiet down at all, so I tied him to the tree we were standing by, told him to stay, and fell into sneak-step behind George.

The light coming faintly from the windows was too orange to be electric. There was a trickle of smoke oozing from a rickety chimney, and the woodpile was exactly that, a heap of raw logs and branches from the bush, unstacked and scattered everywhere. If they were burning green wood, they'd be prime candidates for a chimney fire, and the roof didn't look like it could handle more than a spark without going up like a funeral pyre.

As we moved closer to the house, the dogs all at once gave up. Maybe they were just exhausted. They'd been barking non-stop for the entire day. They hunkered down on their chains, heads between their paws, looking at us and whining. Luggy shut up, too, and they all just lay there. I had the sudden urge to set them all free and let them play tag.

Just at the edge of the yard, the dark silhouette of an outhouse could be seen.

"George," I said in a low voice, "you know what? They live

just like I do. No electricity. No plumbing. Wood heat. It's just the same."

"It is not the same," George said. "You live in peace and order."

"Not always," I muttered.

We had crept up to the windows—peeping Toms, both of us, and I didn't feel very good about myself while I was doing it, but pure nosey-parker instinct ruled the night. Mixed with my vague feeling of wrong-doing was an intense fear and excitement. What if the neighbours had been watching us all this time and were waiting, hiding, with shotguns of their own?

Through the small, filthy window, we could see a bit of the interior. There was an oil lamp on a kitchen table, throwing shadows around the room. A man sat at the table, his head on his arms, a hand clasped around a bottle of spirits. He appeared to be asleep. Another man was passed out, half-propped against the wall. Beyond him, in another room, a battered sofa contained a few more figures, all apparently asleep.

Both rooms were crowded floor to ceiling with litter, green garbage bags spilling their contents. There were piles of newspapers and take-out food containers. The kitchen counter was buried under a mountain of dirty crockery, and some of it was stacked on the floor. One whole corner was devoted to beer empties. Redeeming them at the beer store would have been like a lottery win. There wasn't a clear surface in the whole place.

Looking into the heart of this chaos, I saw myself. I knew it wasn't all that difficult to let things get like this. Let the dishes go another day, forget to take the recycling box out, save the empties for a rainy day and call it your bank. Get used to the squalor, because as it mounts, the enormity of it becomes too much to contemplate. Denial sets in, followed by indifference. Before you know it, you've forgotten what a nice clean kitchen counter looks like, and if the counter was miserably ugly and stained to begin with, what's the point? Factor in the hopelessness of unemployment, addiction and hunger, and you've got all the makings of a slum. That's what this was, and rather than being disgusted, as I'd have expected myself to be, I felt an enormous, overwhelming pity.

George let out a defeated sigh, perhaps feeling as I did. When your anger has turned to pity, without the cause of action, you wind up being patronizing and judgmental. For the self-aware, it's a very unpleasant feeling.

Without a word, we turned to go. The dogs whined again, but did not bark. I turned back once, just before we moved into the forest. In the tiny window, set in the eaves of the shack, I caught a glimpse of a small face, peering out, and a tiny hand, waving goodbye.

Sixteen

DRAGON: *Your quest is noble, kid, but doomed to fail / I'll whack you with one flick of this here tail.*
-The Glass Flute, Scene x

I am inside the house of the Neighbours from Hell, my home, and I am very pregnant. Outside, Lug-nut is chained to a short tether and barking ferociously. I know that this is because he is hungry, but there is nothing left to feed him. Becker, my husband, comes in, throws his hat onto the table and demands food. I tell him that there isn't any and remind him that he spent all the money on his new breathalyser machine, which he wears on a heavy key ring at his belt.

"I bought it so I could keep an eye on you," he says and makes me blow into it. His eyes widen.

"You're going to have puppies," he says, and then punches me in the nose.

I woke to find Lug-nut standing over me, holding my cell-phone gently between his teeth and batting it against my face. It was ringing, and he finds the noise impossible to ignore. When the phone rings, he has been known to break normal rules, like the ones that say "don't get on the bed" and "don't touch'a da merchandise."

"Thanks, Luggy," I said and took it from him, probing tenderly at my poor nose, which didn't take kindly to being smacked with a piece of plastic, however lightweight.

"H'lo?"

"Sorry, Ms. Deacon. Did I wake you?"

"Becker. You just decked me," I said, still half-asleep.

"Excuse me?"

"Oh, nothing. A dream, that's all. Yes, you did. Wake me, that is. Not deck me."

"You dreamed I decked you?"

"It's okay. You made me take a breathalyser first."

"All in the line of duty," he said cheerfully, showing remarkable wit for seven in the morning, which is what it was. "Look, I'm sorry to be calling you so early, but I wanted to talk to you before you went to work. Seeing as you've got a phone, now." The last time Becker and I had enjoyed dealing with each other, I was telephone-free and nobody was calling me at the crack of dawn.

"It's a work perk," I said. "How did you get my number?"

"From the contact sheet you gave me yesterday. I'm sorry to have to tell you this, but we think we've found your stage-crew guy, but the body's pretty messed up. I thought we should get someone who's not family, but who knows him, to identify the body before we call his parents," he said.

My gut wrenched. Messed up? Yuck. Why me?

"Why me?" I said.

"Because you saw him the night before last, you know what he was wearing, and you have experience with bodies," he said, a trifle smugly. "And you don't have an emotional connection to him," he added.

"Thanks a lot. Does this mean I'm not a suspect?" I said. The nice thing about cellular phones is that you can move around while you're having a conversation. I shuffled off to the kitchen, lit the burner under my camp stove, let Luggy out for a pee and put some water on for coffee.

"I didn't say that. But I would appreciate you dropping in at the hospital morgue before you head in to work."

"I have to be at the theatre at nine for a production meeting," I said.

"This should only take a few minutes," he said. I told him I'd meet him at the hospital at eight-thirty. If they had found Jason, especially if he was "messed up", it would mean a real investigation, not just a missing persons report. If that were the case, I wanted to stay on Becker's good side so I could make sure he didn't make any stupid mistakes, as he had the last time.

The number of unidentified bodies that show up in Kuskawa is very small. While I'd never visited the morgue at Sikwan District Hospital, I was willing to bet it would be claustrophobic and low-tech, which meant that there would be none of that "viewing the deceased by video tape" stuff, which I hear the bigger centres offer by way of making the experience less unpleasant. Keeping this in mind, I skipped breakfast.

The weather was shaping up in true Northern Ontario fashion. While the mornings were still see-your-breath chilly, the moment the sun came up, the maple-syrup-coloured light bathed everything in a gentle warmth, which made the hayfield steam gently in a fresh-baked kind of way.

The black-fly had moved in, too, the scourge of the landscape. Seen through a fine mesh of bug-netting, May and June mornings in Kuskawa are spectacular. Seen with the naked, unscreened eye, the view quickly becomes obscured by a thick cloud of biting insects. Later on in the season, the mosquitoes would hatch, adding their hungry whine to the general background noise. Both insects are blood-feeders, and spring conversations commonly stray to the question of which of the two is worse.

Visitors to the area tend to react more to black-fly than to mosquito bites, although both can raise red, itchy welts, but the black-fly actually razors through your skin, while the mosquito merely slips its proboscis through until it finds lunch.

Black-flies crawl into your hair and nibble your scalp, crawl up your trouser-legs to get at your shins and into your sleeves for a snack on your wrists. They're silent and can be deadly if you're lost in the bush without the proper protection. Black-flies rarely bite indoors. If they get in, they'll gravitate to your windows and skitter up and down, looking for a way out. That's when you exact your revenge, with palm or folded magazine, creating a scene of carnage on the window pane. The blood smeared there will be yours, half-digested. I know this is gruesome stuff, but it's part of the Kuskawa reality. They never tell you this in the tourist brochures, but I think it's only fair to warn you.

The illusion of a lovely spring morning was quickly dispelled when I stepped out onto the porch to test the air before I went down to tend to the goats. Swarmed, immediately. I went back in to get my bug hat and overalls, thinking, as I suited up, that the costume of the intrepid Kuskawa native was not much different from the sweaty black get-ups used in *The Glass Flute*. I made a note to mention it, the next time Meredith or one of the others complained about the costumes. "It's traditional up here," I'd say.

After doing the chores and letting the goats out for an early spring frolic in the pasture, I dropped in on George. He was suffering from a massive hangover and wasn't exactly scintillating company. The Dogs from Hell were, not surprisingly, barking.

"Today I will call the Animal Shelter again and insist they do something," George said. "By the time you get back from the theatre, it will be quiet."

"You might want to think about calling the Children's Aid, too," I said. "The conditions over there are pretty horrible for a kid." The memory of that little face in the window was haunting me.

I knew that one of the hardest things a neighbour can do, no matter what the circumstances are, is to call in the authorities when they suspect that a child is being abused. Nobody likes to rat on somebody else, and the average person still maintains that what goes on in the home is a private matter. And so it should be, to some extent, but when there's a child at risk, a neighbour who suspects nastiness is forced to do battle with her or his own concept of What Is Right.

In the past couple of years, some particularly ugly cases of child abuse in the city, coupled with a shockingly ineffectual and underfunded child welfare system, have made the public sit up and take notice. But there's a difference between reading about child abuse scandals in the paper and dealing with one right next door.

This train of grumpy thought carried me all the way into Sikwan, and by the time I pulled into the hospital parking lot to help identify Jason's body, I was ready to bite someone's head off.

It was an appropriate state of mind, actually, because that appeared to be the method of dispatch used in the case of the poor soul who lay in several pieces on the gurney in the morgue.

Seventeen

WOODSMAN: *Cutting trees is not the game it seems to you, my child / Just try it for a minute and you'll learn the woods are wild.*
-The Glass Flute, Scene vi

Becker was waiting for me in the lobby. He looked a little impatient, which wasn't fair, as the time was exactly eight-thirty, and I'd rushed my whole morning for his sake. I'd called Rico and told him I had an unexpected morning errand, and to be ready early. I didn't elaborate. I was nervous enough as it was, without having to satisfy Rico's Insatiable Curtiosity all the way to Sikwan.

I dropped him off at the theatre, where he was planning to spend the rest of the week hanging around the office with Sam and Kim, who were helping to organize the benefit. It surprised me that he'd want to, considering everything, but maybe Shane's pretty apology had cancelled Rico's earlier reservations.

Becker hadn't shaved, and his hair had that just-out-of-bed look. I had an impure thought and marvelled for a moment that the human libido picks the most inopportune times to rear its peculiar head. Golly. In a hospital lobby, just before viewing a cadaver. How romantic.

"Morning, Becker. Where's your partner?"

"Busy"

"You're sure it's Jason?"

"No, we're not. That's why you're here. If you can give us a positive ID, we'll get the ball rolling." He led the way past the receptionist's bullet-proof kiosk to the elevators.

"So, if it is Jason, you'll want to come back to the theatre and interview everybody properly this time," I said, trying to keep the accusation out of my voice. Becker pursed his lips and punched the elevator down button. Off to hell, the two of us. "Actors have short memories for everything but their work," I added. "We may have missed the opportunity to pick up the nuances."

"We?" Becker said. "There is no 'we' here, Polly. If this turns out to be a homicide investigation, I'll expect you to behave like an average citizen and mind your own business." The elevator reached rock-bottom and pinged ominously as the doors opened. It was cold down there.

Somehow, movies and television have managed to glamorize the clinical side of dead people. The men and women who perform autopsies, manipulate dead flesh and oversee the realm of the corpse have achieved a level of celebrity formerly reserved for athletes. When an actor portrays a forensic scientist, she or he is usually presented as brilliant, oddly sexy, humane and possessed of a sardonic humour. They may be carving up cadavers, but by heck, they also have a thriving social life and the stink of death never makes it to the big screen.

In the morgue of the Sikwan District Memorial Hospital, the stink of death was masked, not very well, by one of those automatic air-freshener things plugged into an outlet on the wall. The result was unspeakable, a mixture of chemicals, corruption and lilac.

"Nice atmosphere," I said, following Becker down a dim hallway. There is no need for cheerful lighting, I guess, when most of the residents aren't looking at anything. "That lilac air-freshener smells exactly like the one they used in the outhouses at the summer camp I went to when I was a kid." It did, too. And it was no more effective in the morgue than it had been in the privy.

The morgue attendant was unlike the movie version. She was middle aged and plump, more Nurse Ratched than Quincy Jones. Her eyes were masked by a pair of coke-bottle glasses, and she watched me very closely, as if I were an interesting case.

The body was lying on a gurney in the middle of what appeared to be a storage room, where it had obviously been wheeled for the viewing. In another room, I supposed, there would be a steel meat locker thing (as seen on TV) with nice drawers and bodies filed neatly with toe-tags attached. I wondered why they used this space and not the meat-locker-room for this kind of thing. The gurney was wedged between a bouquet of mops and some supply shelves filled with linen. Not exactly the place where the bereaved would feel comforted. Cutbacks, I supposed.

This body, revealed when Nurse Ratched pulled back the sheet covering it, had suffered, as they say, some trauma. It was also a heck of a lot longer dead than Jason would have been, if it had been him. The face was sort of caved in, and there was something dreadfully wrong with the flesh. I won't even talk about the eyes. Well, I will. Think about grapes. Boiled ones. They could at least have closed them, I thought. The body was thoroughly water-logged, soaking the sheet which covered it and making a puddle on the floor. There was no sound but my own rather laboured breathing and the drip-drip of the wet lump of ex-humanity in front of me. The smell was excruciating. Becker pulled the sheet down further, revealing the interesting fact that the head was only partially attached to the body. It hadn't been severed very neatly—there were pale, raggedy bits and fleshy-boney bits poking out here and there. I was extremely glad I had not eaten breakfast.

The torso, what I could see of it, appeared to be clad in a snowsuit.

"Just about thawed out now, Officer," Nurse Ratched said.

"You mean this body was frozen?" I said.

"Yup. Stiff as a board when they brought him in. The Kuskawa River water's still awful cold this time of year."

I turned to Becker, realization dawning. "Becker," I said, softly, "you know that there's no way this could have been Jason. Jason disappeared yesterday, not two months ago."

Becker smiled slightly. "We pulled him out of the river last night. Got a call about midnight. He washed up on shore near the Port Mortimer marina. I didn't get a chance to see much of him until now, though."

"One glance would have told you it wasn't Jason," I said.

"Maybe, but you seem so interested in doing my job for me, I thought I'd better get you down here just to give you a chance to chip in," he said. "You don't have any idea who this is, do you?"

I was numb. Becker had used a convenient body to try and teach me some sort of sick lesson. Or maybe he thought this was funny, I don't know. I was determined not to show him how disgusted I was.

"Morrison doesn't know about this, does he?" I said.

"Oh, he knows about the body all right. He's going through the paperwork right now. We think it's probably one of about a dozen snowmobilers who went through the ice this winter. Got mangled around by the ice break-up, probably."

"But Morrison doesn't know you called me," I said.

"Listen, Polly, he feels exactly the way I do about your Nancy Drew act." Nurse Ratched covered the face of the corpse and stood, staring at me. He had put her up to this, I was sure. It was probably their little secret. Heck, they probably did this all the time. He'd call her up and say "Hey, Babe, I've got someone I want to gross out. Would you take a body out of the freezer for me?"

"I doubt this is even legal," I said to her. She shrugged and wheeled the gently thawing sledder away. I turned to Becker and looked him squarely in the eye. "I know you think that Jason's alive and sulking somewhere, and that's fine," I said. "It's obvious that you're not interested in pursuing any kind of inquiry, and of course that's up to you. But there's nothing you can do to stop me from asking questions of my own, and if Jason does turn up dead, I'll make it my personal mission to tell your superiors what an asshole you are. As if they didn't know already." I turned my back on him and fled. I was upset enough to start crying, which is what I tend to do in times of extreme emotion, and I wasn't going to give him the satisfaction of seeing it.

By the time I got to the theatre, I had brought myself reasonably under control. Becker's plan may have been to warn me off poking around on his turf, but it just made me more determined than ever. Turf, schmurf. What happened to Jason McMaster, stage manager, was very odd, and I wanted to find out more. Seeing a drowned, ice-battered body wasn't going to stop me, no matter what Becker thought.

As I lifted the heavy bag containing my stage-management stuff off the bench seat of George's truck, I remembered that I hadn't even looked at Jason's notebook. I'd left it drying beside the woodstove at home. As soon as the rehearsal day was over, I'd zip home and devote my evening to it. I was sure it contained something that would help explain why Jason had vanished off the face of the earth.

Tobin and Juliet were waiting for me in the boardroom next to Juliet's office. It wasn't used very often, even though Juliet did have a board, but she was in complete control of the Steamboat operation, and the board only met once or twice a year to review the books and drink scotch. The president of the board, Harvey Ogilvie, was a Sikwan barrister who dabbled in amateur theatre and deferred to Juliet in every respect. Word was that they were sleeping together, which was highly likely.

"You're late," Juliet said. It was ten after nine.

"I know. I'm sorry, Juliet. The police called me down to the hospital to identify a body," I said.

"They found him??" She stood up so fast, she knocked her seat over. Tobin looked at her with interest.

"Nope. It wasn't him." I didn't elaborate, but I must have looked a little green, because both of them became solicitous.

"Oh my dear, how dreadful for you. Are you all right?" Juliet said. "Was it very horrible?" Her eyes gleamed, and she picked up her chair, pulled it in closer to me and sat down again. I just nodded, and Tobin poured me a coffee.

"I don't really want to talk about it," I said, giving Tobin the kind of look that meant I'll talk about it later. "Let's get down to business, shall we?"

"Right," Juliet said, her voice taking on an official, artistic director tone. "We're glad you're taking over the job, Polly. We've looked at your résumé, and you're obviously very experienced at touring. But do you know anything about pyrotechnics?" I knew that there were several flash-pots in the show, small pyro devices that went off at exciting moments when Kevin fights the bad guys, but I hadn't had a chance to find out about them.

"Jason had a lot of pyro experience," Tobin said. "He was ASM for a LiveShow production of *Guy Fawkes: The Musical*, and he pre-set all the smaller flashpots. It's one of the reasons we hired him."

"Do I have to get a licence or anything?" I said.

"Not for the small stuff, but if anyone asks, you're qualified," Juliet said and winked. "Tobin will show you what's involved. It's not very difficult. You just have to be very careful to follow the same procedure every time. And don't let the actors near your equipment."

Tobin and I arranged to have a pyro-lesson after rehearsal, and I felt an excited twiggle in the pit of my stomach. Blowing things up sounded like fun.

We dealt with several other technical matters, including the van-load, which would be rehearsed towards the end of the week as if it were part of the show. Jason's prompt-book (which included a script covered with blocking notes, the time sheets, prop lists and schedules) had a preliminary sketch of what goes where. Jason's hyper-efficiency had led him to label each and every item in the pack with a name, so that each piece of equipment was the responsibility of a particular actor.

Before Shane came aboard, the actor who was supposed to play Kevin had been a guy called Steven Higgs. Juliet told me that Higgs was very short, barely five feet, and a master puppeteer who had worked on the *Fraggle Rock* TV series. Jason had taken Higgs' size into account, and assigned only the small stuff to him. Since Shane was a strapping six-footer, the list would have to be reworked. I noticed that Jason had given the balance of the small stuff to Amber. The heavy pieces, which included the lighting boxes and the black drapery (which weighs a ton) bore Meredith's and Brad's names. I knew Meredith would take pride in being able to lift one of the 80-pound lighting crates by herself, but I didn't think Brad would be able to. The first pack would, as usual, be an actor-management nightmare. It was the stage-manger's job to stay in the van and arrange the pack. This job is uncomfortable and hard on the back, as I knew very well. It occurred to me that by the end of the tour I would probably be a few pounds lighter and a good deal stronger.

Before the meeting ended, I brought up the matter of the driving, telling Juliet about Meredith's request the day before.

"She's pushing for everybody to take a turn," I said. "I'm not prepared to let that happen."

Juliet's eyes widened for a fraction of a second. "Meredith did mention this to me," she said. "I don't see anything wrong with the idea. I told her that I would discuss it with you. The driving bonus isn't that much money, after all."

"It has nothing to do with the money," I said. "It has to do with control. If you let the actors drive, you open the whole tour up to a kind of anarchy that can get out of hand." I knew this from experience. When the deputy is the back-up driver and the navigator, the SM and the deputy develop a kind of intuitive understanding that makes the travelling smooth. Routine on the road is extremely important. Without it, the bickering becomes unbearable. I told her so, adding a short, hair-raising anecdote about an actress who insisted on driving the scenic route along a coastal highway in California during the U.S. tour of *Can't Read, Won't Read*. "I'm driving and I get to pick the route," she'd said. I was young and inexperienced then. We were two hours late for our gig, we burned out our brakes and very nearly cannoned off the cliffs into the Pacific. I've never forgotten it.

"If you want the driving to be shared, I'm off the show," I said.

Eighteen

KEVIN: *It's lonely on the road, Cat. Why don't you come with me?*

CAT: *You're human, kid, and driven. Creatures like to wait and see.*

-The Glass Flute, Scene v

With Juliet's word that I would have my way on the driving issue, my mood began to improve. It had already been a stressful morning, and the rehearsal hadn't even started yet.

The rehearsal space was deserted. I didn't bother turning on the fluorescent overheads yet (they buzz like a swarm of angry bees), and the morning light filtering through the small, high windows in the top floor room was soothing. The main curtains on the playing box were closed in pre-set position, ready for the top of the show. We would begin blocking that morning.

I spent a few moments going over the notes from the production meeting, which were written in a spiral-bound notebook similar to the one Jason had used. The stage manager's job is largely a matter of co-ordinating a million little details, and if they don't get written down, they tend not to get done. I had scribbled a note to myself to look at the mouth mechanism of the Kevin puppet, which Shane had said was a bit loose, so I went backstage to get the puppet from its pre-set position behind the stage right curtain.

Kevin wasn't where I had left him the night before. Nothing ticks a stage manager off more than someone mucking about with her or his preset. It's like someone going through your purse—it feels like an invasion. If something is moved from preset before a show, it can be disastrous, which is why we tend to be sort of anal about it. Clicking my tongue in annoyance, I stepped past the side curtain and into the box, expecting to find the puppet on the playing shelf where I suspected that Shane had left him after some last-minute practice, after the rest of the cast had gone home. It showed enthusiasm, at any rate, I thought benevolently. Still, I would have to have a word with him about the sanctity of the preset.

It was pitch-black in the box. Rather than open the curtains, I flipped the switch on the ultra-violet lights, and all the preset props and puppets sprang into glowing reality. As I stepped forward, something soft brushed my face. I looked up and nearly choked on my tongue, because Kevin was hanging from an overhead pipe centre stage, limp and dead-looking, with an audio cable tightened around his little terrycloth neck.

Oddly, my first thought was not that Shane had played a prank, but that Becker had somehow managed to get into the theatre and had strung up the puppet as a warning to me— another of his sick lessons. The last time I had interfered in police work, I'd found my best friend Francy hanged in her own kitchen. It was ridiculous to think that Becker was responsible, of course, but that was my first thought. My second thought was to get to the bathroom as quickly as possible, because I was about to throw up. The dead puppet had done what the half-frozen snowmobiler had not.

"Anybody here?" It was Shane's voice. Oh, golly. I swallowed carefully, three times, and called out in what was supposed to be a strong voice, but sounded more like a kid with a stomach-ache.

"I'm in the box, Shane. Would you come here a second?" If he had done the dirty deed, I knew I'd be able to tell as soon as I saw his face.

"Everything okay?" I heard him walk across the room.

"Fine, fine. I just need your help."

There was a rustling of material and Shane joined me in the box. The UV lights made his white T-shirt and his teeth glow. UV makes human flesh go a sort of dull greeny-blue colour, and he looked like a Martian. He was looking at me expectantly, and I pointed upwards. He followed my gesture and when he saw Kevin, he let out a moan I don't think I'll ever forget. It was full of sorrow and shock, and quite genuine. He may have been a good actor, but there are some things you can't fake. His face went white—I know this for a fact, because it started to glow like his shirt. A second later he was very, very angry.

"You think this is funny, do you?" he hissed at me, his face inches away from mine. "Who told you, Polly? Who?"

"Told me what?" I said, stepping back.

"You know damn well what, or you wouldn't have set me up like this. Telling me to come in early for some extra coaching, and then luring me back here to show me...this."

"I didn't tell you to come in early," I said.

"You didn't leave that message at the motel?"

"No, of course not. I have enough to do without giving any of you guys extra coaching. Besides, you don't need it. But I'd have thought you had enough respect for the puppets not to pull a stunt like this."

"You think I did it? Kill my own character? You must be crazy."

"Then who did?"

"I don't have a clue, Polly. Look, there was a message, I

assumed it was from you, at my room last night telling me to come in early. I was kind of worried, because I thought I did okay yesterday, and your note sounded like I was a puppet-retard or something, and needed remedial help."

"Retard" is not my favourite word, but I let it go. "Well, whoever sent you the note was the one who strung up Kevin, I guess. I have a nasty feeling we have a nutbar in the cast. You promise it wasn't you, Shane?"

Shane just looked at me.

"Okay, okay. It wasn't you, and it wasn't me. We'd better take him down before the others get here. Grab that step-ladder from backstage, would you?"

The audio cable which had been used to hang Kevin was, again, from Ruth's keyboard. One end had been made into a very professional-looking noose, and the knot used to tie the cable to the overhead pipe was equally as neat. The cable was ruined, which meant there would be no music again until I went to visit Fish. I made a mental note to ask Ruth to strike her equipment every night from now on, and we'd lock it in the storage closet.

"Shane?" I said, after he had replaced the backstage ladder and I had preset Kevin in his proper spot

"What?"

"What was it you thought somebody had told me that would have made me pull this ugly trick?"

"Ancient history, Polly. I'd rather not talk about it, if you don't mind." Actually, I did mind. If Shane was holding some sort of clue as to who our prankster was, I wanted to know about it. Then I remembered Meredith's crack the day before, about Shane turning tricks in Toronto. I'd forgotten about it in the excitement of Becker and Morrison's pseudo-investigation.

Whatever the "ancient history" was that Shane alluded to,

it was obviously painful. I couldn't make him talk about it, but I resolved to do a little digging into our star's background.

Shane and I agreed not to tell the cast about the morning's incident. The schedule had been screwed up enough the day before, and there was a lot of work to be done. We opened the show in less than a week, and in the biz, the show takes precedence over just about everything else in the world. Even puppet murder. After having spent time on Day One getting used to the puppets and how they worked, the next challenge for the cast was to learn the intricate blocking patterns of *The Glass Flute*.

"Blocking" is one of those terms that has been used by theatre people for ages, but hasn't got a clear derivation. It might have come from the woodworking practice of sketching or "blocking out" the general shape of something before cutting it. It also might refer to the areas of the stage, which are divided into squares, or blocks and labelled "down stage right", "up centre" and so on. Blocking simply means where you're supposed to go and when you're supposed to go there.

It's up to the actor to write down all her or his blocking into their script, so a scene is performed the same way, every time. It's up to the stage manager to write down everybody's blocking in the master, or prompt-script, because actors and directors always forget to take notes. It's an art that is deadly dull to everybody except stage mangers, so I won't go on about it.

Because the show is choreographed like a ballet and the lines are all sung or spoken in verse (doggerel, actually, but then Juliet isn't Will Shakespeare), having one's part down cold is more than usually important.

The scripts were mailed to the cast the month before the first rehearsal, along with the contracts and the invitations to Juliet's costume ball. It was expected that they'd be more or less line perfect ("off-book") at the start of the rehearsal period.

This was not usual for most theatre companies, but we had an insanely short rehearsal period, so any head-start we could get was welcome.

The only person with an excuse for not having a reasonable handle on his lines was Shane. Because of his last minute casting, he hadn't even seen the script until his arrival. Luckily for him (and for us) he was a remarkable quick-study. When we started the laborious process of blocking, he was off-book for the first three scenes.

Meredith was off book completely, no surprise, as she'd done the show before, and Amber was well on her way.

"I don't want to hold anyone back," Amber said to me during our mid-morning smoke break. "Shane and I worked on lines until about two a.m. last night. It's amazing how fast he can pick them up, eh? He was like that at theatre school, too—a quick-study."

"Was Jason in the picture when you guys were at Kingsway together?" I asked.

"Well, sort of—near the end," she said. "Shane and I had been seeing each other pretty steadily for a couple of months, but then he got the lead role in the year-end production opposite this other girl. I auditioned for the part, but I didn't get it, which really hurt my feelings. So he was rehearsing with her during the day, and hanging out with her at night. I knew it was over."

"They were running lines, I take it," I said. I wasn't trying to be facetious. It's just that theatre people bond very tightly, very quickly, when they're all in a show together. Frequently, they end up sharing a bed. It's a work-perk, like my cell phone.

"Yeah. Running lines to begin with, then running something else," Amber said. "Jason was SM-ing the show, and I started hanging out with him instead. We've been together ever since."

133

No wonder then, that Jason had flipped out when he heard Shane was on the show. An old flame. Not even really so old. According to their résumés, Shane, Amber and Jason had been at the Kingsway Theatre School together in 1997, the year Shane had graduated.

Amber had been a second-year acting student, which is probably why she hadn't been cast in the lead role of the year-end show. That part would have been reserved for one of Shane's contemporaries. Jason was a third-year techie in 1997. In their mid-twenties, all of them, so the hormones must have been just a-raging.

I was dying to ask Amber if her pregnancy had something to do with her old flame, but I was too polite (or chicken, depending on which way you look at it). Because she had told me the news in confidence, I wasn't about to go blabbing it to the artistic director, but I wondered how it would affect the tour. I don't know a heck of a lot about babies, Miz Scarlett. Still, I couldn't help but be curious. Would Amber be puking in the school washroom during early-morning set-ups for shows? Should she be exempted from carrying heavy stuff? I suddenly remembered that Jason had booked her to carry fluffy cargo like the puppet bags and the tool boxes. Had he suspected that his girlfriend was with child? Is that why he had proposed?

Amber read my mind, which saved me asking.

"I didn't tell him about the baby," she said. "I think I told you that already. Anyway, I'm getting rid of it, I decided. I have an appointment next week, and I've already talked to Ms. Keating about it, so it's okay. She said I could have a puppy instead."

"Excuse me?"

"To take on tour. You get to take your dog, so I get one too. To help get over the grief. I've got one picked out already," she said. Lord help us.

Nineteen

PRINCESS: *At home, I sit and sew or rest or play / The king says working makes your hair go grey.*

KEVIN: *All day I tend the fire and care for Mom / My hair's not grey—I think the King's a bum.*

-The Glass Flute, Scene viii

Bradley, it seemed, couldn't remember a line if his life depended on it. This became apparent quite early on, and by the end of the day, it was worrying everybody. If Brad had been a spy, entrusted with state secrets and passwords, we would be horribly dead by now.

"I'm sorry, guys. I just can't seem to retain anything today," he said. We had finished a rough block of the show and were working Scene Four, between the Princess and the Woodsman. Meredith and Shane were running lines (in the literal, not the carnal sense) for Scene Five, with the Cat and Kevin puppets, at the other end of the studio.

Juliet was showing some impatience, which was understandable. Brad was a reasonable puppeteer, but if he couldn't remember his lines, the show would be in trouble. There was very little room for error in *The Glass Flute*.

"Bradley, darling, you haven't been smoking too much of that wacky-tobaccy have you?" Juliet said. "I understand it's hell on the memory. If you have, cut it out until the show's up, would you?" Brad's reaction indicated that she may not have been far off the mark. He reddened and said something inaudible to Amber, who let out a little yelp of laughter.

"What was that, Brad? Didn't quite catch," Juliet said.

"Nothing, Juliet," Brad said. "You may be right, though. I'll cut back on the herbal remedies forthwith." We struggled on with the scene.

PRINCESS: *It's hard to be a princess when you're lost and cold and scared / I'd ask that stranger over there to help me if I dared.*

WOODSMAN: (Chopping at a tree with an oversized axe) (Singing to himself) *Oh, I'm a lumberjack, and I'm okay...*

PRINCESS: *Excuse me, sir, for barging in, when you've got work to do.*

WOODSMAN: (Looking up) *A voice! I heard a voice—and look, I see a princess, too.*

"When the Princess starts speaking, freeze the axe in mid-air," Juliet said. "I think it would be funny if it just stayed like that, frozen in mid-swing."

"We'd need someone to hold it," I said.

"What are the others doing at that point?"

"They're waiting to come on for Scene Five. As long as he goes back to the axe and takes control of it again just before the end of the scene, either Meredith or Shane would have time to deke backstage and grab their puppets for the next bit."

"Let's try it. Shane, dear? Can you be in this scene, please?"

Shane left Meredith and headed for the box. We ran the opening lines again, and as Amber spoke the princess's line, Brad's Woodsman puppet checked his upward swing of the axe and Shane stepped smoothly in behind Brad to hold it in place. During a performance, because the actors were dressed in black, none of the mechanics would be visible to the audience. The axe would be suspended in mid-air on its own. Meredith moved in to watch as the scene continued.

PRINCESS: *I'm hoping you can help me find the path that leads to home / I'm lost you see, and hungry and I hate to be alone.*
WOODSMAN: *I've never seen a princess in the woods without a guide / You're not exactly dressed for it. What made you come outside?*
PRINCESS: *The King wants me to marry and I don't like who he chose / I ran away to hide last night and practically froze.*

While the two puppets were having their exchange, Shane, as the axe, involved himself in the conversation, by making the axe listen. This is not an easy thing to do. Animating an object that has eyes and limbs is one thing, animating an axe is another. Somehow, the prop sprouted a face, and as the Princess and the Woodsman talked, the axe turned from one puppet to the other, cocked its head and nodded sympathetically. Out in the audience, Juliet, Meredith and I chortled with delight.

"What's so damn funny?" Brad said, breaking character.

"The axe, Brad," Juliet said. "It's got a life of its own." Brad didn't say anything, just glowered at Shane.

"Let's incorporate that all the way through the Woodsman scenes," Juliet continued. "If the axe has a personality, it could keep trying to get away from the Woodsman. We could do some nice slapstick bits."

"I don't want all my scenes upstaged by an axe," Brad said.

"Maybe we could give his lines to the axe as well," Meredith said. "Shane doesn't seem to have a memory problem." This was just plain bitchy, considering how early in the process we were, but it looked like Juliet was actually considering it.

"What kind of a voice would an axe have?" she said.

"Sharp. Choppy," Meredith said.

"No. He'd be blunt," said Amber.

"A little dull, but with an edge," Shane said.

"Excuse me," Brad said in a wounded voice, putting the Woodsman puppet down on the playboard. "While you all go ahead and axe my part, I'll just slip into the wardrobe room and slash my wrists."

"Brad, come back. We were only kidding," I called, but he had left. The bathroom door slammed.

"Is he, like, crying in there?" Amber said.

"No, he's just taking a hissy fit," Meredith said. "He'll get over it, once he knows he's not really losing lines."

"Well, it's something to keep in mind," Juliet said, very quietly.

"Smoke break," I said.

Juliet had given me my cell-phone when I started my puppet-making contract, because she said that if you work for Steamboat Theatre, you're not allowed to be unreachable. The need to be in touch with her employees was obsessive, as I found out later in the afternoon when Juliet called me into the board room. On the long table, its hood up and humming faintly, was a laptop computer.

"I want you to have this for the duration," Juliet said. "I'll expect you to e-mail me the show reports every night when you're on the road, plus performance notes and so on. It's a direct line to God, dear." By "God", I assumed she meant Juliet Keating.

"Can't I just phone you every night?" I said. The thought was unpleasant, like being allowed outside for a run in the woods and then finding that someone had attached a two-foot leash to your collar. Still, phoning was preferable to computer-ing. As far as computer-literacy was concerned, I was seriously challenged.

"No, I'm not always available by phone. Besides, e-mail will give you more leeway as to when you file your reports. You can't call me after ten p.m., but you can send an e-mail any time, day or night."

"Juliet, I haven't got the foggiest idea how to drive one of those things. They scare me." I'd used Kim Lee's big computer to re-do the cast list, but she had done everything for me except type in the names. I'd had the impression that putting a computer-illiterate person at the helm of her machine was as dangerous as letting a three-year-old operate a chainsaw. Now here was Juliet, handing me one for my personal use and pretending that the damn things didn't bite.

"Oh, don't be a baby. Anyone can use a computer," Juliet said. "They're very simple. Sam will give you a lesson." That would be Sam Ruttles, the theatre accountant, who worked in a tiny closet-space at the very back of the building. I hadn't seen him since he presided over the bar on Sunday night. I hoped he would be more generous with his instruction than he was with the company scotch.

Sam was summoned, and he and I went on a journey through cyberspace that gave me vertigo. All that stuff in such a small box. I took a lot of notes and Sam, surprisingly, was a gentle and patient instructor. He had me "surfing the Net" like a teenager in less than half an hour.

"This could get addictive," I said, as our lesson ended. "How does Juliet expect me to do any work, handing me one of these? I could lock myself in a motel room and never come out again."

"You'll find that the novelty will wear off after a while," Sam said. "Just avoid the chat-lines, or you'll end up having an online affair with some charmer from Newark, you'll arrange to meet and end up boffing a complete stranger in an airport bar."

"The voice of experience?" I said.

"Yup. My last marriage ended up that way," he said.

"Oh, Sam, that's too bad. Is she still with him?"

"Not her—it was me. I meet a lot of women that way."

"Oh." The twinkle in his eye told me that he was perfectly serious. Sam is right weird. I closed the lid of the laptop and added it to my growing collection of business buffle. Cellphone, laptop, briefcase, van keys. "Just gimme a pager and a power suit," I muttered.

The remedial computer class had taken up most of my lunch hour, and I still had to get out to Fish Gundy's to pick up replacement cables for Ruth's keyboard. Ruth had not been called for the morning rehearsal, but we were due to work on the music in the afternoon.

As I drove the scenic route through the Kuskawa Falls Park to downtown, waving absently at the kiddies who greeted the theatre van like an old friend, I reflected how paid employment can change your lifestyle completely.

It was only twelve-thirty, and I would normally have been working quietly at my cabin, carving the head for a marionette, maybe, or sketching. I would have risen at seven to feed and milk the goats, but it's entirely possible that I might have gone back to bed for an hour or so afterwards. I'd have a leisurely lunch, maybe, spend a while practicing my guitar, then I'd have gone for a long walk in the woods with Luggy and dropped in on Rico for espresso in the afternoon.

As it was, I'd already driven more in one day, interacted with more people and performed more tasks than I'd normally drive, see or do in a month. There was also the matter of the dead sledder and the puppet-body I'd found that morning. No time to think about them. No time for reflection. Just go, go, go. I wasn't exactly stressed, but my brain felt full, as if it were a bowl brimming with water. One more drop in there, and it would spill over and I'd lose something. That's why I had my spiral-bound notebook. Without the notebook, I'd be wandering around Sikwan, dazed and disoriented. I imagined that Jason's notebook, getting progressively less squishy as it dried by the stove at home, would have been similarly important to him.

Fish was gobbling Thai noodles and giving his son a violin lesson when I entered the emporium. Jake Gundy, a very small and beautiful eight-year-old, played the fiddle like an angel. They were working on a complicated Bach thing, the notes cascading over and under themselves at an impossible speed, the bow a blur. I stood quietly, bewitched, until the last note, then applauded softly.

"Sounding good, Jake," I said.

"Thanks, Ms. Deacon," Jake said, politely. He was a miniature version of his miniature father, with his mother's stunning Asiatic cheekbones and eyes. He was the sort of little boy you feel compelled to pick up and cuddle, particularly as his manners were impeccable, but one has to control impulses like these, for the sake of dignity, the child's and one's own. I compensated by beaming at him. He beamed back, then began putting his violin away.

"Jake's getting ready for the Kiwanis music festival," Fish said. "He's coming along well with his piece, but the pizzicato section's giving him trouble."

"My fingers are still too short," Jake said. "Glenn Gould used to do finger exercises and soak his hands in warm water before he played the piano, but Dad won't let me do that."

"Gould was a genius, but he was nuts," Fish said. "If you

start obsessing about your hands, you'll lose your edge."

"Sure, Dad. I gotta get back to school. I'll wait outside for my ride, okay?"

"Okay, kid. Love you."

"Love you, too," Jake said, hefted the violin case under his arm and raced to the door.

"Seems like he was in diapers yesterday," I said. "What happened?"

"I know," Fish said. "Jake and Fiona will be in high school in six years, and we'll be the grown-ups we used to write joke songs about." He finished his noodles with a slurp and stood up.

"Nose-job looks good," he said. "Swelling's gone down, I see."

"It's feeling better. Thanks, Fish." I didn't know whether he'd really bought my line about the nose-job or whether he was just being kind. Didn't matter. If someone says I look good, I don't really care whether it's true or not. It's the thought that counts.

"Did you ever find that stage manger you lost?" he said.

"Not yet. We think he drowned, actually. At least some of us do, but the police don't seem to be too interested in looking for him."

"I did see a bunch of divers and police boats in the bay this morning," Fish said. "Maybe it just took them a while to get started."

"No, that was something else. A snowmobiler washed up at Port Mortimer last night. They're probably dredging for his machine."

"There was a lot of that going around this winter," Fish said. "I heard there's about ten guys floating around under there, like a kind of winter tourist soup."

"They'd better get them out before the summer people come," I said. "Those synthetic snowmobile suits can play havoc with the water quality." Okay, so we were being callous. You get that way if you live in Kuskawa, unless you're a sledder yourself.

Every winter, the peace of the Kuskawa landscape is shattered by the howling of snowmachines. They belch fried fossil fuels into the woodland air, frighten the animals and travel at speeds that break the sound barrier. Every snowmobile club does its best to train its members to sled responsibly, but that's an oxymoron, like military intelligence and jumbo shrimp. They'll achieve responsible snowmobiling when they build machines that run on hydrogen or electricity, are soundless, and would lose in a race with Donovan Bailey. In the meantime, the winter watchword for many of us is "No ice too thin," or, as one local put it, "The lake is safe for ice fishing when the snowmobilers stop falling through."

Fish fired up the wok he keeps in the back of the store and whipped me up some noodles while I picked through his box of audio cables. I only had a few minutes left before I had to get back to rehearsal, and I hadn't eaten breakfast on account of my early morning date with a corpse.

"There's been a run on audio cables lately," Fish said, handing me a steaming bowl. He'd thrown some shrimp in there for good measure, and I wolfed it down. "This seems to be the last one of this kind in stock. I'll have to order some more. Popular item."

"New fashion statement, maybe," I said with my mouth full. (You can do that with really good friends.) "People using them as necklaces, eh?"

"Well, they have a certain utilitarian charm, I guess," Fish said. He tied one on. With an audio cable around his small neck, he looked just like the Kevin puppet.

Twenty

SERPENT: *You thay you're off to find the fruit of life, my little man? / It'th dynamite you're playing with; control it if you can.*
-The Glass Flute, Scene vii

By the end of the rehearsal day, things were shaping up nicely. Brad had spent his entire lunch hour in the bathroom, working on lines, and he was off-book in three scenes. The threat of having one's part shrunk, so to speak, is an amazing motivator. Someone once said "There are no small roles, only small actors." Nonsense. There are small roles and big roles, and actors want big ones. Size matters, okay?

It was the end of Day Two, and we'd blocked the show, worked some scenes and rehearsed about a third of the music. I spent some time with Ruth after the actors were released, going over the sheet music. The songs had been written in 1980 by Juliet's flame of the time, Solomon Lollipop, a kids' entertainer who went on to become a million-selling tour-machine. He's a big, bearded, huggy-bear type with a light tenor voice and gallons of charisma. You may have taken your kids to see him at some point. He hits every small town in Canada once a year, packs arenas and gyms and gets all the kids and their parents to sing along to "Buddle-Buddle-Stomp-the-Puddle". Parents loathe him: kids love him. It always works out that way.

The melodies themselves were gorgeous, but the lyrics needed updating from time to time. We had made some minor changes as we rehearsed, so we went over the alterations to make sure we both had the same ones.

Juliet had requested a new number, "Axe Me No Questions", for Brad to sing. We were going ahead with the idea of making the Axe a character, and while the prop would have no actual lines, it was allowed to make sort of whiny, inarticulate noises from time to time.

This put added pressure on Shane, but he was enthusiastic and had won Brad over by sheer force of personality. The two actors had spent the last half hour of the day working up a schtick for the Woodsman's first entrance—the kind of slapstick comedy that Juliet had envisioned when the idea popped out during morning rehearsal. The schtick was screamingly funny, and Juliet had asked Ruth to write the song as a kind of reward for Brad, who had finally accepted that he was going to be upstaged by a foam rubber axe.

I had helped Ruth write a number of songs over the years, including some really neat ones for Shepherd's Pie's fourth album, *Maple Tree Market*, due out soon in a record store near you. We decided to get together that evening to work on the new number. I also took the opportunity of being alone to tell her about the earlier puppet-hanging and to suggest that we put the keyboard, amp and speakers away in the wardrobe room closet (which had a lock) every night.

"That's a pain in the butt," Ruth said. "Couldn't we just strike the cables and leave everything else?"

"I'm just worried about your stuff," I said. "I don't know who pulled the stunt, but it's the second time in two days that someone's used your cables for weirdness, and I don't think the person has a lot of respect for property. We're better off storing the valuables, I think."

"What about the puppets and props?" Ruth said. "We can't strike everything every night."

"Actually, we can, or we should fairly soon," I said. "The cast is going to have to get used to setting everything up in the shortest time possible. I was going to do a strike and set-up on Thursday, anyway. We'll add another strike and load at the end of the day tomorrow and haul everything downstairs to do the pack for the first time. It'll be brutal—it always is. But then all the stuff will be safely inside the van, which I'll be driving back to Cedar Falls every night. We preview Saturday, after all, and then we're on the road next week, God help us."

"And in the meantime?"

"In the meantime, we lock up your equipment, and the puppets are on their own. I just hope some of them know karate."

"The Kevin puppet didn't."

"No, poor little guy. I wonder if the person who did it was targeting the actor playing the role."

"Now, why would anyone want to hurt Shane?" Ruth said, her voice dripping with sarcasm. "He's beautiful, talented, a certified chick-magnet and a violent drunk. Everybody loves him."

"You weren't in here doing puppet-murder earlier, were you?" I said.

"Nope. Not me. I was in bed until eleven. Part of my contract, darling. Music rehearsals in the afternoon only."

"Except for yesterday," I said.

"That wasn't planned. Juliet informed me of that in the wee hours of the party on Sunday night. I told her I'd only do a morning sing-through if she gave me fifty bucks. She did, too. Cash."

"Well, you are the famous folk singer," I said.

"That's me. Oh, by the way, don't worry about making Rico wait around. I told him I'd give him a ride home." I'd totally forgotten about him, actually. Shows what a caring friend I am.

"Thanks, Ruth. Tell him I'll pick him up at the regular time tomorrow." It was really time for Rico to get another car, I thought. His vintage Caddy had died that winter, after a long battle with chronic radiator-trouble. I'd been doing a lot of chauffeuring ever since. Not that I minded, but Rico was a bit tight with his cash, and I would have appreciated the odd twenty for gas. These unworthy thoughts embarrassed me, so I switched the subject.

"Hey, you know what? Juliet gave me a computer."

"She's corrupting you, Polly. First the cellphone, now this. You'll be moving to Toronto and trading in goat futures next. Listen, with this computer—avoid the chat rooms, okay? Now, I've gotta go. See you tonight."

As she left, I wondered if Ruth, too, had met some sexy woman from Newark on the Net. Not likely. She and Rose had been together for twenty years, and a cyber-flirtation wasn't her style. Still, my interest was thoroughly piqued by that point. I made a mental note to check out the chat rooms at the first opportunity, then headed downstairs to keep my appointment with Tobin, master of blowing things up.

There are three pyrotechnic devices, or flashpots in *The Glass Flute*. They're guaranteed to thrill the Nikes off the preteen audiences and scare the holy heck out of their teachers and caregivers. In the show, the fireworks are synonymous with evil. The first pot goes off with the entrance of the serpent.

"The first one is easy to set up," Tobin said. "It's placed in the branches of the tree at the top of Scene Seven, just before the serpent flops out of the branches and lands on top of Kevin."

I'd seen the video and I knew what the effect would be—a sharp pop and a small flash of fire, plus a lot of sparkly smoke.

Tobin unsnapped the lid of the Pyro supply box, which held the explosives. The box was marked with all sorts of skulls and crossbones and danger signs, which I thought wasn't the best idea, considering we were going to be unloading everything into school gyms across Ontario. Any kid getting a gander at that would be insane not to take a look.

"There's a padlock," Tobin said, seeing my expression.

"Oh, good," I said. "I get the only key, right?" Tobin nodded and took out a small plastic bottle full of grey powder, one of several in the box. The bottle was labelled #1, in bright pink lettering.

"This is the stuff that makes the bang," he said. "It's volatile, and you want to be sure to use only the tiniest bit." He opened a small plastic cannister and extracted something that looked like a match, except that it was made of thin red wire, with a grey blob on the end. The end of the match was split into two copper leads.

"These are electric matches," he said. "They're expensive, and hard to come by. We get them from a place in the States, and I've only got enough for the first week of the show. The ones we ordered haven't come in yet. However, we're going to waste some of them now so you'll understand how they work." He produced a nine-volt battery and pressed one of the leads onto the positive ring-thing on the battery-top.

"Fired by itself, the match is harmless," Tobin said, and pressed the other copper lead onto the negative ring. There was a tiny snap and a spark.

"That's your triggering mechanism," he said.

He showed me how the battery fitted into a little metal

box, about the size of a small pack of smokes, with a red "go" button soldered on top. Originally, the box had held one of those flavoured coffee powders. A wire ran from the box, and at the end of it were two copper leads corresponding to the leads on the match. You with me so far? Good. Don't try this at home, kids.

"This is makeshift," he said. "It works, but it can't take rough handling. I'll be sending you out with a soldering kit in case it gets wrecked."

"Gee. Electronics and Pyrotechnics 101, as well as computer lessons," I said. "My brain hurts."

"That's why Juliet's paying you the big Kuskawa bucks," Tobin said, without much humour. He put the battery box down and took a moment to tell me about a friend of his who had SM-ed the *Flute* some years ago and had lost a couple of fingers in a stupid pyro accident, because he got careless. I paid more attention after that.

"If you follow the same procedure every time and observe the usual precautions, you'll be fine," he said. He took another match out of the tube and laid it on the table we were working at. Then he slipped a long piece of soft-looking paper from an envelope.

"This is the coolest stuff in the world," he said, allowing enthusiasm to creep into his voice. He ripped a small piece off, whipped out his lighter and set fire to the scrap, which ignited, flashed and disappeared with a woof. "Flash paper," he said. "The magician's secret." It looked like thick Kleenex and had a sheen to it.

Tobin tore off another scrap, about two inches square, placed it on the table and poured about a quarter teaspoonful of the pyro powder into the centre of it. Then he placed the head of the match on top, carefully wrapped it up and tied it with a piece of sewing thread. The result was something that looked like a big Q-tip. He wired the leads of the match to the leads of the trigger-box wire, then he handed the box to me.

"Pyro demonstration number one," he said, grinning.

"Shouldn't we do this outside?" I said, feeling distinctly nervous.

"Heck, no," Tobin said. "This stuff is designed to be fired off in theatres, places where there's lots of curtains, paper and flammables. Where there's smoke, you won't find fire."

"How far away do you have to be?" I said.

"Just don't put your face directly in front of it," Tobin said. "Even then, it would only singe your eyebrows. My friend got hurt because the pyro power spilled and then someone tripped the trigger, which he'd wired up first to save time. Bad move. This stuff's safe, as long as you're in control."

"Okay, then. Here goes," I said and pressed the button.

It was beautiful. There was a loud pop, a shower of sparkly stuff, a big puff of smoke and it was gone in a moment. The spent match cooled in seconds, and Tobin untwisted it, then made me set one up.

My first flashpot was a bit big, too much powder and flash paper, the next one was too small (to make up for it), and, like Goldilocks, I got it just right on the third try.

We made up Q-tips of the same powder to construct the second and third flashpots, which were set off in specially-made bowls—pots, really, from whence came the name. The bowls were metal, wired with thick cable and triggered by a Pyro-pack, a remote switchbox that could be set ten feet away from the flashpot.

Neither of the other two was dangerously big. After all, they would be set off in the curtained playbox, fairly close to the actors and the puppets, but they used more powder, a combination of several different types from the plastic bottles.

Setting them off was a hoot, and I could have spent hours making bigger and bigger bombs. Tobin told me that the compulsion to do so was what led to accidents.

"Always stick to the recipe," he said. "Don't give in to the temptation to experiment. It's part of the preset and has to be just so."

At some point during the tour, I was supposed to pass on my secret flashpot expertise to another cast member, just in case something came up during the set-up that required my absence, like the van being stolen or something. I figured I'd probably pick Meredith, whom I expected knew how to do it already, or had a pretty good idea, considering that she'd done the show before. Letting Meredith play with explosives didn't seem terribly sensible, but heck, she was the Equity deputy.

We put the pyro supplies carefully back in their death-box, and Tobin handed me a small padlock and key.

"I hereby confer on you the mantle of pyro-master and the key to Armageddon," he intoned. "Use it at your peril." I locked the box solemnly and took it upstairs, where I put it in the lockable closet with Ruth's equipment. The phantom trickster was not going to get the chance to muck about with this stuff.

As I was packing my briefcase, laptop and paperwork box into George's truck, the Laingford OPP cruiser pulled up beside me and Morrison stuck his head out the window.

"Polly," he said, "I think you'd better follow me to the station."

"If this is another 'identify the body' trick, I'd rather eat ground glass," I said.

"It's no trick, kid. Your friend George is in the lock-up, climbing the walls, swearing in a foreign language and calling for you. We were thinking you might be able to talk some sense into him."

Twenty-One

MOTHER: *You're all I have to light my world, my son, so please take care / to lose you in my final hours would be too much to bear.*
-The Glass Flute, Scene i

Morrison gave me a police escort all the way up the highway to the Laingford cop-shop. It was kind of fun, following a cruiser that was breaking the speed limit, flashing its lights and sticking to the fast lane as people pulled over and slowed down. George's truck struggled valiantly to keep up.

When we got to the police station, Morrison took a moment before we went in to tell me what had happened.

"We got a call a couple of hours ago from a guy who said he lives next door to Mr. Hoito's place," he said. "Guy was pretty incoherent, crying and slurring his words, so we figured he was drunk, but he was plenty upset."

"Where was he calling from? George told me they didn't have a phone."

"He was calling from a neighbour's about a kilometre away. He said he ran for help after Mr. Hoito kidnapped his grandkids."

"What? That's ridiculous."

"Well, we thought it was pretty odd, considering what we know of George Hoito, but we had to check it out, Polly."

"And what did you find?"

"Well, the two kids were definitely at Hoito's place. They were locked in an upstairs bedroom, and they were scared but unharmed. Hoito was fine until we asked him to make a statement, and then he went sort of haywire and started spouting Polish, or whatever it is he speaks."

"Finnish."

"Finnish, then. He was so mad he was practically frothing at the mouth, and we couldn't get a word of English out of him."

"What about the guy who called?"

"We picked him up at the neighbour's on the way to Hoito's farm. He was drunk all right and loaded for bear. Said he left the kids playing in the yard and went inside to make dinner and when he went to get them, they'd disappeared. He used one of his dogs to track 'em, he said, right to Hoito's farmhouse."

"Why did he think they were kidnapped?" I said. "Couldn't they have just, you know, wandered over for a visit?"

"Mr. Gamble—that's the guy's name—said that Hoito threatened him with a shotgun."

"Oh. And George? Was he drunk too?"

"Didn't appear to be. Why do you ask? He got a drinking problem?"

"No," I said. "What about the parents? There's a pregnant woman and her spouse who live in that shack too. Where were they?"

"No sign of them. Gamble says they were gone when he woke up this morning, and he hasn't got a clue where they went. Says they've done it before, though. They leave the kids behind and take off for two or three days, and then turn up again with no warning."

"Where are the kids now?"

"Back with Grandpa, of course."

"Geez, Morrison. Did you see that place? Isn't there an alternative?"

"We called in a social worker to do an evaluation. They're being monitored." I could only wonder what kind of criteria, after an evaluation, would deem the slum next door to George an appropriate place for two small kids.

"Couldn't you rack 'em up as abandoned?" I said.

"Not with a blood relative handy," Morrison said. I could see he didn't like it either. "Let's go have a chat with Hoito," he said, and we stepped inside.

"Hello, Ms. Deacon," Becker said. He was sitting at his desk filling in a bunch of forms. He was inordinately cheerful, which ticked me off. "Come to bail out your buddy?"

"Hey, Becker," I said. "Found any more sled-sicles lately?" I wasn't about to let him think for one minute that his little caper of the morning had affected me one bit.

"No more so far. We're going fishing again tomorrow," he said. "The perp's through that door, first cell to your left. Hasn't said a word in English since he got here, except your name."

"Why's he so chipper?" I muttered to Morrison as we passed by his desk and headed for the cells.

"Well, actually, he's loaded for bear too," Morrison said. "The happy face is his way of pretending nothing's wrong."

"So what's wrong?"

Morrison gave me a mournful look. "We've been assigned to marine duty," he said. "Starting next week. Until we find the eleven other snowmobilers in Kuskawa Bay, we're gonna be shipmates."

"Isn't that a great gig, though?" I asked. "Deck shoes, sunscreen and short-sleeved shirts? Stopping speeding babes on Seadoos and giving them stern warnings?"

Morrison glowered. "Not in the middle of May it isn't," he said. "The ice is barely out of the lake, the wind is cold, and police boats are tubs."

"Oh. Sorry about your luck, Earlie." We reached the cells and there was George, sitting on the side of a cot with his hands clasped between his knees, his head down. Seeing him like that made my heart hurt. There's a sweet little bald patch on the top of his head, which I rarely get to see, as he's over six feet tall. He wears his yellowish-white hair long, pulled back in a pony tail, and he usually cuts a commanding figure. Now he just looked forlorn and crumpled. What the hell had happened in the past few hours? Why was he refusing to speak?

He looked up as we approached.

"Polly," he said, "I am sorry about this."

"Me, too, George. What's going on?"

"I lost my temper," George said. His accent was very thick—far more so than normal, and I was suddenly very worried about him. Had he experienced some sort of weird mental episode? Had he regressed, or something? Was he all there?

"George," Morrison said, using a gentle voice I'd never heard from him before, "if you're not comfortable telling us what happened, I thought you might be able to tell Polly. How about it?"

"I was waiting for you," George said directly to me, ignoring Morrison. "You know what it has been like. They do not."

"What's he talking about?" Morrison said. I felt like an interpreter in a bad cop-film.

"Can we go somewhere less austere?" I asked. "An interview room, maybe? Tim Horton's?"

"We can't release him till we get a statement," Morrison said.

"Has he been charged with anything?"

"Gamble wasn't willing to press charges, but we still have the evidence of the kids being over there, and there was a shotgun propped against the wall. We confiscated it. It's licensed, so that's okay, but you can't go threatening people with a firearm, George."

George glared at Morrison and perked up a bit. "You can charge me with death threats if you choose," he said. "I would have killed him gladly, for what he did to those little boys."

"Let's go somewhere else and talk about this," Morrison said. "If you've got a legitimate complaint, we'll follow it up."

"Meanwhile, those kids are back with that guy," I said. "Did you ever think of that, George?"

"Oh, I have been thinking about it," George said, as Morrison unlocked his cell and led us both to an interview room I had been in once before, after a psycho had tried to kill me. It brought back all sorts of happy memories.

"You two stay here," Morrison said. "I'm getting coffee and Becker."

"Two creams and some compassion, please, Earlie," I called as he left the room.

"Okay, George," I said. "Spill." He shook his head.

"No. I will only tell this once," he said.

"What's got into you?" I said. "I know the dogs were driving you crazy, but did they really do the trick? You're scaring me, the way you're acting."

"I'm acting the way you told me to act," George said. "You told me to think about calling the Children's Aid. I did think about it. All day I thought about it, as the dogs were barking and the man was shouting and the children were crying. I thought about it, and then I thought I should be sure before I made the phone call."

Becker and Morrison came in. Morrison was carrying a pot

of coffee, cups and the fixings. George stopped talking, as we all performed the oddly formal act of coffee-arranging.

"You thought you'd be sure before making the phone call," Becker said to George, indicating that he had probably been sitting in the next room, observing us through the obvious one-way mirror-thing in the wall.

"So I went over there, very quietly," George said, taking a sip and grimacing.

"We're recording this," Morrison said.

"Good," George said. "Then I will only have to describe it once. Polly will tell you that there are dogs chained behind the dwelling. The chains are very short, and the dogs are not fed very often and they have no water. They bark all day and all night."

"If you have a complaint about animals, you can call the Humane Society," Becker said.

"This is not about the dogs," George said. "It is about the children. Today, the dogs barked as they always do, and the man was shouting at the children and the children were crying. All day long, barking, shouting, crying. I could not think. I became very angry. Then a dog screamed, and a child screamed, and the dogs went into a frenzy. I heard two shots and I heard the man say, very clearly, 'that will teach you.' Everything was quiet. I thought something horrible had happened, and I went through the woods, hating the pictures that I saw in my head. I came onto the edge of the clearing, and saw the bloody bodies of two dogs, piled one on top of the other, near to where I was standing." George's voice began to shake.

"Closer to the shack, there were two children with dog collars around their necks, chained close to the ground. They were on their hands and knees and they were making whimpering noises. In the doorway of the shack, the man stood.

He said, 'One more sound out of you and you know what'll happen.' Then he went into the house and shut the door."

"Jesus," Morrison said, quietly. "Go on."

"I waited. I did not know what to do," George said. He was weeping now. "I could have gone back to my nice home and called the police, but that would leave the children chained like dogs to the ground with a madman to watch over them. I waited a very long time and then I went forward. The children watched me, but made no sound. I looked in the window and the man was asleep, like last time."

"Last time?" Becker said.

"We checked the place out last night," I said. "They were having a loud party, and they were all flaked out on the floor."

"I rescued them and took them home with me," George said. "We did not speak very much. I gave them some milk and biscuits and prepared myself to call the police, when the man appeared with one of his remaining dogs. That is when I lost my temper. I fired at him and he ran away. I thought he would be going back to his slum to get his own gun, so I put the boys in my bedroom and told them to stay there."

"Why didn't you call us then?" Morrison said.

"I was frightened," George said, simply. "When you came and I saw him in the back of your police car, I knew that I would have to have Polly to stand by my story."

"And the kids are back with Grandpa," I said. "Good move, George."

"We'd better get out there," Becker said. "Morrison, you call the CAS, and I'll get the cruiser. I just hope the kids are all right."

"What about evidence?" I said. "It'll just be George's word against this Gamble's, won't it?"

"Unless this guy's got the stamina of a moose, he would

have been too drunk to do anything with the bodies of the dogs," Becker said.

"I have the dog collars," George said. "I unchained the boys, but there was no time to remove the collars."

"And maybe the kids will talk," Morrison said.

"It sounds like the kids, if they're okay, are going to need more than an invitation to talk," I said.

"You can thank your friend for some of that," Becker said and walked out. Morrison was right behind him. He left the door open.

"I guess you're free to go," I said to George.

He said nothing, just followed me out.

Twenty-Two

KEVIN: *It may be safe to stand aside and let the tough ones take the ride / but if you watch and don't join in, how can you ever hope to win?*
-The Glass Flute, Scene v

Just because a guy has been accused of putting dog collars on his grandchildren and chaining them to the ground, it doesn't mean that he goes directly to jail without passing Go. Yes, the kids were "taken into care," as they say, that night, after the CAS worker got a look at the living conditions in Home Sweet Hell. They found the kids sleeping in cardboard boxes upstairs in the attic room, and Grandpa had of course denied everything. In spite of what Morrison had told me, no CAS worker had had a chance to visit the home since the "kidnapping" incident. The duty worker was swamped that day, Morrison told me later.

After George had made his statement, the police had picked up the social worker and taken her with them, out to the shack. The dwelling did not, apparently, score very high on the grading system provided in the new government book on Things You Can't Do To Your Kids. The children, Tyler and Wade, were removed and placed somewhere safe, where presumably a qualified person would try to get a statement from them about the dog collar incident and anything else that might be relevant.

Grandpa, on the other hand, was not apprehended. The cops told us that we should get in touch with them the moment we heard the parents had returned. So now we had a solitary, very annoyed, evil neighbour living close by, probably carrying a pretty hefty grudge. I just hoped that the charges looming over his head would be enough to keep him from sneaking up on George and trying to exact some sort of revenge.

"I am not worried," George said, but I don't think he was telling the truth. He had aged drastically in the last couple of days and moved like an old man.

Grandpa next door was down to one dog. The Humane Society had been called in after they found the bodies of three dogs on a midden heap next to the outhouse. They had all been shot. For some reason, they had only taken three of the remaining four away. It seemed like a pretty miserable sentence for the one that was left, but the Humane Society works in mysterious ways. Anyway, that cut down on the noise considerably.

"I shall sleep well tonight, anyway," George said. "Do you want to stay here? The bed in the little room has clean sheets." I had gone up to the cabin earlier to get Luggy. I'd left him chained that morning, which I absolutely hate to do, but the dog situation next door made it the only option other than leaving him indoors. I planned on taking him to rehearsal with me from then on. George's casual offer of a bed for the night was unusual. The only other time he had offered was in the fall, when a murderer had been on the loose in Cedar Falls, and he had been concerned for my safety. This time, I suspected, he was a tad concerned about his own well-being. I said I would stay, but I was due at Ruth's place to help write Brad's new song. George's face took on an abandoned goat-kid look.

"Of course, she might like to come over here," I said. "She

hasn't visited for a while."

"I would like that," George said.

"I'll call her."

On the phone with Ruth, I sketched out the situation as briefly as I could, and she said she was on her way. The best thing for George right then, we agreed, would be a bit of distraction. I could only imagine the nasty images that were floating around in his head. Some goofy music was just the thing. Ruth said she'd bring her portable keyboard.

The rest of the evening passed pleasantly. George didn't contribute much to the song-writing process, but he sat contentedly in his chair, listening, with Poe perched on his shoulder and Luggy at his feet with his head on George's knee. Often, when a human is in distress, animals know to move in and do the comforting thing. From time to time, Luggy licked George's hand and Poe nibbled his ear. He fell asleep there.

"What do you think makes people pull that kind of shit on a kid?" Ruth said, quietly, after George had dozed off. We were working on the chorus of "Axe Me No Questions."

"I think maybe the person who treats a child badly was treated that way themselves," I said. "It's the only way they know to make a child 'behave'."

"Slap it around and tie it up?"

"Well, this guy controls his dogs by doing that. Maybe for some people, dogs and children are similar creatures. And if they've had rough handling as a child themselves, they sometimes see it retrospectively as an effective method. You know, 'My old man used to beat me to keep me in line, and it didn't do me no harm,' type of thing. It's like the whole spanking issue."

"Spare the rod and spoil the child," Ruth said in a fire-and-brimstone voice.

"That's it, although Pastor Garnet once told me that the word 'rod' in that quote was referring to a shepherd's staff, used to guide the sheep in the right direction only, not beat them. A shepherd would never, ever clobber a lamb, he said. It would make it fear him."

"Another Bible misquote, co-opted by the dinks," Ruth said.

"Yup."

"So, this song. What have we got so far?"

Ruth played a tinkling, ballad-like introduction on her keyboard, then launched into it.

A woodsman's worth is measured
by the sharpness of his axe,
Without it, he's a slacker,
just a hacker to the max,
but when your tools are handy
for the job there is to do,
You're ready to work steady cutting wood
the whole day through.

I joined in the chorus.

My axe and I are friends who work together,
Through rain and snow and any kind of weather,
I keep his blade all shiny,
coz it sometimes gets all piney,
and I sharpen him because I know it's wise.
Axe me no questions,
don't need no suggestions,
Axe me no questions
and I'll tell you no lies.

We still had a couple of verses to go, but the tune was catchy, and Ruth had added a wood-block percussion to the chorus that was perfect.

She left a little before ten. As George was snoring, I patted his shoulder softly to nudge him awake.

"Kaarina?" he mumbled in a frightened, child-like voice. That was the name of his long-departed wife. Mention of her was extremely rare. I would have given anything in that moment to have been able to whisper something reassuring in his ear in the Finnish language to ease his waking.

"It's me, Polly," I said. "You might as well go to bed, George. I'll do the barn." He thanked me gruffly and stumbled off to his room.

It didn't take long to do the last chores of the day. The goats get milked and fed at seven in the evening, and though we were late getting back from the cop-shop, George had gone down immediately to deal with them. All I had to do was freshen their hay and water and dole out the evening treat, which was carrot bits and broccoli stems left over from our dinner preparations.

Luggy came with me and we both stopped for a wonderful moment on the path, gazing upwards. It was a crystal-clear night, the moon was nearly full and the peepers were beginning to compose tentative love songs. An owl hooted and passed overhead, searching for unwary mice. It was quiet enough to hear the air whistle through its wings, and the absence of barking was blissful.

I had tried to feel some empathy for the people next door. I had done my best, but I was kidding myself. The bad karma that I'd personally pumped out into the atmosphere about these folks was probably gathering like a storm cloud, ready to whack me in the behind sometime in my future. To be truthful, I was absolutely delighted about the shattering of whatever it was they called their household. I was glad of the peace and quiet.

The goats moaned their thanks for the treats and nosed them politely, but it was kind of late and they weren't all that interested. I took a moment to pick up and cuddle the new kids, who were warm and sleepy and amenable to hugs, which they tend to struggle out of when they're more alert.

After I got back to the house, I was wide awake. I poured a finger of George's Glen-unpronounceable scotch and, borrowing his phone-jack, the way I'd been taught, plugged the laptop into the Internet.

"Look out, Web, I'm coming aboard," I muttered and started looking for a chatline.

After about an hour, I understood how marriages could be destroyed by web-addiction. It was like walking into a huge masquerade party full of excited, uninhibited people. It wasn't that the conversations online were interesting—most of them were deadly dull, but the potential for finding somebody fun to talk to was limitless. A typical chat room conversation goes like this:

```
HOTDOG: so where you from layla?
STUD MUFFIN:hey witch wanna whisper
LAYLA: Dayton, Ohio. You?
WEBWITCH: sure talk to me dirty
big boy
POISON PEN HAS ENTERED THE
CONVERSATION
HOTDOG: Hi Poison Pen
STUD MUFFIN:Hey PP
LAYLA: Hi poisons
POISON PEN: hi folks
```

(Webwitch and Stud Muffin have gone into private session, which can be engineered by clicking on a whisper icon on the screen. Nobody can see what they're talking about. Nobody would want to, of course.)

```
HOTDOG: I'm from Australia.
POISON PEN: Anybody seen HARRY?
LAYLA HAS LEFT THE CONVERSATION
HOTDOG: bitch.
```

Not all of them are this bad, but most of them are. In spite of the subject or interest listed for each room, the form stays the same. You may be in a "book" chat room or a "pet lovers'" chat room, but a version of Stud Muffin, Webwitch and Hotdog will be in all of them, greeting each other inanely and brokering to talk dirty. Perhaps one of the reasons people spend so much time in chat rooms is that they are desperate to find a conversation that isn't like all the others. It rarely happens.

After a couple of hours, I'd had enough. I'd used the predictable nickname Goatgirl and I'd exchanged greetings with Beer Baron from Florida, Beauty Queen from somewhere in Germany, and a masher from Vancouver calling him(her?)self Spyhole, with whom I whispered for a line or two, receiving some of the most improper suggestions I've ever heard in my life.

GOATGIRL (As they say) HAS LEFT THE CONVERSATION.

I had never been a TV person, and I'm not the type to spend long hours at a typewriter or word processor. What's weird about the concept of sitting for a long time in front of a screen is that the real world completely disappears. As I left chat-room-land, I felt my mind shake itself like a wet dog and re-orient to the room I was in, physically. Lug-nut was lying at my feet, looking at me in a perplexed kind of way. Certainly, when I work on a puppet, I'm absorbed in what I'm doing, but I like to think I remain aware of sounds and vibrations (squirrels in the rafters, the state of the fire in the woodstove and so on). I realized that, while I was online, the Neighbour from Hell could have come in and set a fire in the kitchen and I wouldn't have noticed a thing. (Well, Luggy would probably have commented, but you know what I mean.) Cyberspace takes you far, far away. I don't know if that's a good thing or not, but it might go some way towards explaining why people get hopelessly hooked on it. As a means of escape, it beats any drug I've ever tried.

Before logging off, I practised checking my e-mail, just as Sam had taught me. To my surprise, there were two messages. The first was from Juliet.

```
To: pdeacon@kuskawa.com
From: steamboat@kuskawa.com
Subject: Internet use

Dear Polly;
Congratulations on your inaugural visit
to the world of e-mail. By now, you will
have tried out the chatlines and perhaps
surfed the Internet. I only hope that you
were using a Bell-line telephone connection
and not your cell-phone. Be warned: I pay
for every minute of airtime that you spend
on the cell. If you access the Net via
your cell-phone, it's more than a dollar
a minute and it had better be for business
purposes, or it comes out of your paycheque.
I suggest you keep a log of your Internet
use.
Juliet.
```

Considering that she gave me the infernal technology to begin with, I didn't think her tone was quite fair. However, I was glad of the warning. My stomach felt quite queasy at the thought that, if I hadn't been at George's, I would have used the cell-connection without thinking, and I'd owe Juliet close to two hundred bucks for the privilege of being propositioned by Spyhole in Vancouver.

The next message was from Becker, of all people.

```
To: pdeacon@kuskawa.com
From: oppbeck@kuskawa.com
Subject: welcome to the real world

Dear Ms. Deacon;
My colleague tells me you're online, so I
got your address from your boss. Welcome
to the real world. It's about time you
took advantage of modern technology
instead of running away from it the way
you do.
If anything comes up about Jason
McMaster and you can't get me by phone,
you can leave a message for me at the
above e-mail address. The investigation
into his disappearance continues.
Sincerely,
Detective Constable Mark Becker,
Laingford OPP
```

For three years I had been totally unreachable—no phone, no datebook, no commitments, no cash. Then, when employment struck like a ripe melon in the side of the head, I got wired so fast it felt like they'd implanted a microchip in my brain. Too much vulnerability, too quickly.

After Becker's stupid dead body trick that morning, I had been planning to ignore him completely for the foreseeable future. I had given him courtesy at the Laingford cop-shop over the George/Hell Neighbour affair, but nothing more. Now, for some reason, he was sending me e-mail, and my gut reaction was, annoyingly, to be very pleased.

I have heard that e-mail communication has prompted a renaissance in letter writing. What I discovered during my affair with a laptop was that e-mailing is not letter-writing at all. It's e-mailing. Letters require a legible hand, more than thirty seconds of thought, and the act of licking a stamp. E-mail is only one step away from blithering on the chat-lines. There is an inherent pressure, when the machine is humming and the online time's a ticking, to answer quickly. I discovered that what you type in an e-mail message can be sent without sober second thought. All it takes is the momentary downward pressure of one finger.

I drafted a couple of replies to Becker's e-mail, therefore, on a piece of paper before I typed and sent one.

```
To: oppbeck@kuskawa.com
From: pdeacon@kuskawa.com
Subject: You're welcome to the real
world

Dear Detective Constable Becker;
Thanks for your note. This computer was
thrust upon me for work-reasons, and
while it would give me no greater
pleasure than to establish an e-mail
correspondence with you, I can't afford
to pay for it. Perhaps, as my employer
was kind enough to give you my e-mail
```

address, she might also be approachable about the matter of remuneration for the time online.

I have made some progress in my investigation into the disappearance of Jason McMaster, but it's all flaky, Luddite stuff that you wouldn't think was important. Let me know when you find his body.

Cordially,

Polly Deacon.

Twenty-Three

CAT: *There's safety in numbers—it can't be denied / with your friends right beside you, you don't have to hide / But someone must lead us and someone must follow / a quest by committee's just too hard to swallow.*
-The Glass Flute, Scene vii

Amber Thackeray, I concluded at the beginning of the third day of rehearsal, was stark raving mad. She had arrived late, with an assortment of satchels and tote bags strung about her person. In her arms, cradled in a baby blanket, was a small puppy. Amber's face was alight with love, and she crooned to the creature enthusiastically as she introduced it around.

"This is Portia," she said. "You know, like in *The Merchant of Venice?* I played her in my second year at theatre school. She's only six weeks old, and she already knows her name."

Portia the puppy, an expensive yellow lab, by the looks of her, gazed balefully out at the world from her nest of blankets, yawned and then burped.

"Oooh. I think she needs to go," Amber said and began wriggling to remove the straps of her various purses. Shane sprang forward and helped her divest, then he followed her outside. We were all in the lobby, doing the coffee-thing and waiting for Amber. She wasn't more than five minutes late, but most professional actors learn to be obsessive about time, if they're to survive.

As I watched the dog-people in the cast (I was one of them) gather around the puppy and make oodgie-woodgie noises at it, I reflected that the success of our preparation time for *The Glass Flute* depended on Amber keeping it together. If the dog made her late, or distracted her, the show would suffer. Right then, the dog was distracting everyone.

Of course, I was smart enough to keep my mouth shut. After all, Lug-nut had been introduced to the cast not ten minutes earlier. Luggy isn't a cute puppy, though. Even with dim pink lighting, a good makeup person and a bit of distance, he'd still look like a big old junkyard dog. A myopic mongrel with yellow eyes and clumsy feet, he is, however, old enough to know his place and keep it. I inherited him, and his life pre-Polly hadn't been nice. He had been used as a hunting dog, kept hungry and isolated, and my home represented a significant upgrade in his lifestyle. This made him reasonably obedient and remarkably good-natured.

He went to each cast member in turn, sniffed politely at extended hands, then padded off to his usual spot on the floor by the lobby sofa. He'd hung out with me here often while I was building the puppets and Tobin, Juliet and I were the only ones in the building. I'd been meaning to bring him along again, because he's pleasant to have around, and he's quiet. Now that the dog/evil neighbour situation made Luggy-life at home untenable, I had let him come with me a couple of days earlier than planned. When Amber walked in with the puppy, he lifted his head, sniffed the air and then rolled his eyes at me in a weirdly human way. Obviously, we felt the same way about the infant versions of our respective species.

Rico, who was emphatically not a dog person (he and Lug-nut tolerated each other, nothing more) wandered off into a back office to commune with Sam.

Meredith was not altogether delighted with the presence of two canine colleagues. She didn't insist on their removal, which was generous of her, as that would have precipitated an ultimatum from me, and probably from Amber as well. Had she been genuinely afraid of dogs, it would have been awkward, seeing as the Equity Green Book doesn't have a section on canine involvement in theatrical productions. I expect that she would have been well within her rights to threaten workplace discrimination if it had come to a showdown. I had already made Juliet put Luggy's presence into my contract, and our fearless leader had obviously okayed Amber's puppy, for reasons that were unclear. Meredith was the kind of person who is perfectly capable of taking a grievance to a higher court, and she knew we knew that. During Amber's "Meet my puppy" scene, Meredith sat glowering on the sofa, nursing a coffee and probably plotting ways to use the dogs as a bargaining tool. I suddenly saw our van-driving dispute in a new light and trembled inwardly.

I needn't have worried about the puppy interfering with rehearsal. Juliet, like a good matriarch, had made Arrangements.

When we entered the rehearsal room, Amber squealed in delight. In a corner of the studio, Juliet had constructed a puppy playpen, with the help of Tobin and Sam. I hadn't been up there yet, but I should have guessed, because Tobin kept making dog-jokes in the shop when we were having a smoke. I thought he was talking about Luggy.

The playpen was constructed out of wooden latticework, left over from the set of *The Gardening Show*, an educational snoozer commissioned by a generous government in the early eighties. The latticework still had its fabric flowers and fake grass attached, which would turn into some interesting canine bowel movements later in the game.

Inside the playpen was a wicker basket with a pillow in it (both from the props room) and a tray that had once carried fake food for *The Eat Rite Revue*, with water and feed bowls (props from the same show) at the ready. The *pièce de résistance* was a brightly-coloured, moulded plastic toddler's playhouse, with a slide and everything.

"Oh, it's sooo cute!" Amber cried and took possession.

"I think I'm going to be sick," Meredith muttered.

Juliet appointed herself nanny, and while the pup's occasional whimpers were heard throughout the course of the morning (attended to when Juliet deemed it necessary), the rehearsal was undisturbed. Lug-nut took on the role of prison-guard, settling down on the outside perimeter of the pen and patrolling the boundaries regularly to make sure everything was secure.

I had moved the strike and set-up schedule forward a day, in case the jokester was planning another assault on the puppets. The sooner I had the cast rehearsed in the fine art of taking the set apart and putting it back together again, the sooner we could put everything under lock and key in the van.

According to the Theatre for Young Audiences Agreement, the set-up and take-down time for a set isn't supposed to take more than forty minutes from start to finish. The time-limit is there to encourage theatre companies to keep the size and scope of the sets down to a minimum and protect the actors and stage managers from burnout. Technical directors and set designers take it on as a personal challenge. Over the years, they have perfected the art of building massive, complicated sets that fit together like Meccano or Lego, come apart into a million different pieces so they can fit into the van, and can be unloaded and set up in forty minutes, provided the cast does everything at a brisk trot, has eaten a hearty breakfast and doesn't make any mistakes.

According to Meredith (who, in case anyone had forgotten, reminded us that she had done the show before), the set-up/take-down time on the last tour was about thirty minutes. Perhaps the entire cast of the last show was made up of triathletes. I didn't ask.

The black velour curtains that were used to create the play-box mini-theatre were heavy, but reasonably simple to deal with. They either fit like sleeves over the steel pipes of the frame, or were velcroed on. For transportation, they had to be folded and rolled like pastry, plush side in, and placed in a series of big hockey bags, which were marked according to which side of the playbox they belonged to (stage right, stage left, proscenium curtain, etc.) The puppets were packed away in wheeled touring cases, according to the "what's where" chocolate box diagram on each lid.

The frame itself was held together with key-clamps, ingenious connectors invented by a Canadian engineer with a vendetta against theatre people. The key-clamps allowed technical directors to construct extensive scaffolding which was strong, safe and came apart easily—a designer's dream and an actor's nightmare.

I put Amber and Shane on curtain duty and Brad and Meredith (did I mention she'd done the show before?) on frame construction. Meredith had come to rehearsal with her own Allen key, a pricey Lee Valley tool with an ergonomically designed hand-grip. I gave Brad a plain one from the tool box.

Recognizing that Meredith already knew how to strike and set up the frame as efficiently as humanly possible, I left her alone to talk Brad through the process. She gave instructions in a kindergarten-teacher tone, and I just prayed that Brad would keep his cool.

We left the set in pieces on the floor when we broke for lunch. Amber and Shane headed off to town with the dog to parade it up and down Main Street, after Juliet had explained to Amber that puppies need to be socialized as soon as possible.

"Let people pet her and introduce her to all the other dogs you meet," she said.

"Since when did Juliet become a dog-wrangler?" I muttered to Tobin, on my way down to the shop. I was carrying the big pink daisy that has a cameo appearance in Scene Nine. One of its petals was hanging by a thread, and its mouth was torn a bit in one corner.

"She's got a bunch of dog-books on her desk," Tobin said. "I guess she's reading up on it."

"Vicarious puppy-parenting, you think?"

"Seems so. I would have pegged Juliet as a cat-person, though, not a Barbara Woodhouse type."

"Wonders will never cease."

I left the daisy downstairs on the shop table, its mouth propped open so the air could quick-dry the contact cement repair I'd made. I looked around for Rico, in case he wanted to do lunch, but Kim said he'd gone out already.

Brad was waiting by the front door. "Can you give Meredith and me a lift into town, Polly?" he said. "We want to go to that vegetarian place." Meredith emerged from Juliet's office, looking smug, and joined him.

"Sure," I said. "You need a ride back, too? I've got a lot of errands to run." Sharing my lunch hour with Meredith and Brad was not in the script.

"No, we'll walk," Meredith said. "We're on a plan."

"A plan?"

Brad grinned a little sheepishly. "Meredith's helping me lose weight," he said. "We're jogging together in the mornings before rehearsal, and power-walking at lunchtime. Meredith used to teach aerobics, eh?" I'll just bet she did, I thought. I could just imagine her up there at the front of one of those classes, screaming commands into a Madonna-style headset microphone, wearing one of those high-cut leotards that are reserved for those with buns of steel. She'd be a tyrant. Still, she obviously had Brad eating out of the palm of her hand (even if all he was getting were celery sticks and tofu), and he could stand to shed a few pounds.

Bonds do form quickly in rehearsal, I knew this, but the speed with which we had established factions was slightly disturbing. Amber and Shane were glued together, the missing Jason having been apparently wiped from Amber's memory. I figured that they'd likely remain that way throughout the tour and speak as one, but at least they'd be on my side. Meredith and Brad, on the other hand, could present a dangerous united front if any issues came up that needed arbitration.

In the van, Meredith raised one.

"I think we should draw up a list of every day we're on tour, with a seating plan," she said. She was sitting in the front passenger seat, and Brad was on the bench seat in the back.

"Why?" I said.

"Because it's more comfortable up here," she said. "I know you like the deputy to navigate, but I think it's only fair that everyone gets a chance to sit in the comfortable seat, seeing as you're not willing to let anyone else drive."

"I agree," Brad said. "Riding shotgun is way more fun." He sounded like he was fifteen years old.

I allowed myself a small, weary sigh.

"Sure, Meredith, if you think it's important. I don't think

I'll have time to get around to it, though. Will you take care of it?"

"I'd be glad to," she said. "In fact, I've already done it. Juliet loves the idea." So that's what Meredith was doing in the artistic director's office moments before. I should have guessed. It annoyed me that Meredith had proposed an idea to Juliet before running it past me, but it was a minor thing, and at least I hadn't been petty about it. If I'd offered any argument, I suspected it would have given the actress a great deal of pleasure to tell me that Juliet had okayed it already. Perhaps, I thought, I should have a quiet word with Juliet and suggest that Meredith have a rider attached to her contract, making her the assistant stage manager. Juliet could give her a few extra bucks, and I could give her all the scut work she could handle. That might cool her jets.

I dropped them off at the Green Beanery and headed up to the post office to pick up the package of dancewear I'd ordered from the costume shop in Laingford.

On the way up the street I saw Amber, Shane and the puppy, attracting the kind of attention you'd expect from passersby. Three beautiful, fair heads, three expensive, gorgeous creatures with perfect teeth and contented smiles. A young woman with a camera had posed them on one of Sikwan's downtown benches and was taking their picture. I recognized her as a reporter for one of the local newspapers and figured it wouldn't be long before the golden children were front page news. Hmmph. Luggy and I had never been in the paper, although there had been a grainy shot of George and me coming out of the Sikwan courtroom during the trial of Francy's murderer.

After lunch we put the set together again and continued to work through the script, perfecting puppetry technique and fine-tuning the blocking. Ruth was scheduled to join us for the afternoon so we could start fitting the music in. She was on hand to play the music live for the first week, but when we were on tour, we would be performing with audio tapes. The tapes would gradually replace Ruth towards the end of the week. There was no point in messing around with tapes before we started doing runs of the show, because of all the stops and starts involved in early rehearsals. We only had a week, though, so the sooner we could stumble through it, the better. Having Ruth on keyboard in rehearsal, knowing we'd only have tapes in performance, was like being an astronaut at a pre-lift-off banquet. You know the future holds nothing but food-in-a-tube for the duration.

When we got to Scene Nine, just before Ruth was due, I realized I'd left the flower puppet drying in the shop and went down to get it. I passed her on the stairs.

"Be warned," I said. "Amber's got a puppy up there, and at some point we'll have to give it a lesson in staying away from cables."

"Oh, God," Ruth said. "Another cable trashed? That was my last one."

"No, the puppy didn't touch your stuff. She's being seriously chaperoned, but she won't be for always, you can bet on it. They're waiting for you. I'll be up in a sec."

Down in the shop, I discovered that someone had made a few adjustments to my repair job. The big foam flower was on the work table where I'd left it, but it was horribly disfigured. The pink petals which had surrounded the face had been torn off, rolled up into a sausage-shape and stuffed cruelly into the puppet's mouth. There was an audio cable wrapped around its neck.

Twenty-Four

DRAGON: *How dare you touch my treasure pile? How dare you touch my stuff? / It took me years to steal this, but I'll never have enough.*
-The Glass Flute, Scene ix

I have to admit that I was more than a little miffed. I don't often lose my temper, and if I'm angry I cry more often than I yell. However, this deliberate vandalism of my work felt like a kick in the kidneys. I was, after all, the puppet designer on this show, and I'd built the pink daisy myself.

A foam rubber sleeve, painted green, was the stem, which grew up out of a plastic flower pot-base, rather along the lines of an Audrey-the-plant puppet in *Little Shop of Horrors*. The flower pot has a hole in the bottom, and the puppeteer (Shane, in this case) wears the puppet like a bulky, full-length glove. The arm becomes a living stem, and the hand goes into the flower-head, to work the simplest of hand-puppet mouths. It's a fun character to manipulate, because the neck/stem is pliable, which makes the head more expressive. The mouth is small and lined with soft terrycloth, so the hand operating it can do neat things, like bunching the material up to make the lips purse. It was one of my favourites. I'd soft-sculpted a wide, sweet face that exuded flowery innocence. The day before, Shane had worked the daisy like a master, giving it exactly the personality it needed to come alive.

The little mouth was stretched and distorted now, choked by the thick pink sausage of foam rubber. The audio cable around its neck was neatly knotted. Another puppet murder, horribly sexual this time.

I guess I overreacted a bit. I pounded up the stairs, two at a time, to ask Kim to call the police. Then I continued on up to the rehearsal room.

Ruth was just coming down to find me.

"My audio cable's disappeared again," she said.

"It's downstairs," I said, "wrapped around the neck of the daisy." Kim appeared at the bottom of the staircase.

"Polly, the police want to know the nature of the injuries," she said. I had gabbled to her that there had been an accident in the shop. (I told you I overreacted.)

"You called the police?" Ruth said. "Are you crazy, kid?" The cast had come spilling out of the studio to see what was happening.

"Someone's murdered the daisy puppet," I said to them. "And someone hung the Kevin puppet yesterday, and they've used audio cables every time and Jason's vanished and don't you guys think this is serious?"

Meredith turned to Juliet, who was beside her on the landing.

"Now do you see what I mean?" she said, loudly enough to make sure I heard it.

"Polly, dear, what do you mean someone's murdered a puppet?" Juliet said. "What were you smoking at lunch?"

"Come down and see," I said, beginning to feel like a fool. "But don't touch anything. Becker will want to see this." Fat chance. I went to the phone, where an OPP dispatcher was waiting patiently on the end of the line.

"The other lady said there was a shop accident," she said. "Do you need an ambulance?"

I tried to explain.

"You're saying that someone has vandalized a puppet? That's too bad, ma'am, but I don't think you should be calling us," she said.

"Is Becker there?"

"Excuse me?"

"Detective Constable Mark Becker. Is he there, please?"

"Um, not at the moment, ma'am. Would you like his voice mail?"

I said yes, and there was a click.

An androgynous, "just stay calm" recorded voice came on the line. "Welcome to the Laingford OPP voice mail system," it said. "If you know the extension of the person you are calling, please enter it now." I waited for other options, having no idea what Becker's damn extension might be. The receptionist could at least have connected me directly, I thought. The cast members, along with Ruth, Juliet and Kim were heading for the shop stairs.

"Press One for our staff directory, or spell the first three letters of the name of the person you wish to speak to." I stabbed at the buttons, struggling with my mild numerical dyslexia to spell what I thought was "BEC."

"Don't touch anything down there, okay, you guys?" I called to the group on the shop stairs. The voice-mail system clicked once, then delivered a brain-liquefying, high-decibel fax screech into my ear. I slammed the phone down and followed the crowd.

"If one of you did this as a joke, it's not the least bit funny," I said. They were gathered in a circle around the violated puppet on the work table.

"What makes you think one of us did it?" Meredith said.

"Nobody here is that sick," Amber said. I was more interested in Shane's reaction. The day before, when he had seen the Kevin puppet hanging in the box, he had moaned and turned sheet-white. This time I didn't catch his initial reaction, but his lips were set in a thin white line, and he looked ill.

"That puppet was fine at twelve-thirty," I said. "Whoever set this up did it sometime between then and now."

"We've all been in the studio, Polly," Juliet said.

"Not everybody, not all the time. People were out at lunch. We all came back at different times. People left to go to the washroom. We weren't working with everybody at once. Kim, did you see anyone go down to the shop?"

"I've been working on the benefit project with Sam and Rico in the back," Kim said, looking uncomfortable. Generally, she never left her desk. Maybe she was feeling guilty about being away from standing guard over the front door.

"Well, I left for a lunch thing at 11:30, so I'm out of the loop," Rico said. I looked at him, surprised. It wasn't as if I was accusing my friends, was it?

"It was probably some kid who snuck in from the park," Brad said. "Spring fever and a dirty mind, you know? This is gross, Polly, but it's not exactly murder. Any more than Jason taking off was murder. Can we get back to rehearsal? I want to try my new song."

"We're not doing any music until I see if this audio cable still works," Ruth said, moving forward.

"Wait! Don't touch it!" I said. Obviously, everybody thought I was crazy. Maybe I had been smoking too much dope, or maybe I'd just had too much on my mind and was seeing crime in pranks and murder in a simple case of lover's sulk. Whatever the case, my credibility as a competent stage manager and all-round sane person was being undermined, big-time.

"Oh, for crying out loud," Ruth said.

"Polly, that cop's not going to come and take fingerprints off a goddamn puppet," Meredith said.

"Okay, so he's not. But I think this is beyond just a bunch of dicking around. Where's Tobin?" I knew he kept a Polaroid camera around for shots of van packs and the occasional record of a nice bit of pyro circuitry.

"He went to Toronto about an hour ago to pick up the UV bulbs," Kim said.

"I'd like to get back," Juliet said. "We can talk about this later, Polly." I had been standing there, feeling like an escaped nutcase, scanning the shop for the camera. There it was, on the supply shelf next to a tin of contact cement. I grabbed it and took a quick shot of the mayhem before Ruth removed the audio cable from the daisy's stem and everybody trooped silently back to rehearsal. Ruth gave me a speak to you later look, and so did Juliet. I expected a carpet-call before the day was out.

Shane lagged behind and spoke to me quietly at the bottom of the stairs.

"You free after rehearsal, Polly? We've got to talk."

"Sure, Shane. About this prank-stuff, you mean?" He nodded.

"Falls Motel Pub," he said. "Around five-thirty?"

"Okay."

To say I was intrigued would be putting it mildly.

The cable, in spite of having been used as a garrotte, worked fine. Ruth was shutting me out, which hurt, but the rest of the rehearsal was her baby anyway, so I stayed out of it, taking notes.

Brad loved his new song and Shane, as the Axe, came up with a peculiar little wordless voice, sort of nasal and full of humour, to accompany Brad's singing. We would have to keep a lid on Shane's enthusiasm, though, because the Axe tended to interject with an expressive whine whenever the Woodsman had a line. It was funny sometimes, but not every time, and Brad's patience was not a commodity plentiful enough to squander.

"Sorry about being short with you down there," Ruth said softly to me as she handed over the photocopies of Brad's new song. "Rose called to say her brother is probably going to die soon, so she's staying on for another two weeks. I'm feeling bitchy and abandoned."

"That's okay," I said. "We'll talk about it after, if you want." She squeezed my hand and the music rehearsal continued.

At the end of the day, Amber volunteered to put the puppets away into their road-cases.

"We might as well get in the practice," she said. I had been wondering how to bring the subject up myself, for fear of further puppet-mayhem, and I appreciated what I recognized as a sympathetic gesture.

"I was going to suggest that," Juliet said.

It was Brad who noticed that the "what's where" chocolate-box diagrams had been tampered with. The diagrams on the lids of both the red case and the blue case had little drawings of each puppet or prop, and how they fit into the box. The drawings for the Kevin puppet and the daisy puppet had ugly red X-es drawn through them, in what looked like crimson lipstick.

"The puppy did it," Meredith said.

Twenty-Five

CAT: *That flute packs more potential than you think, my little friend / Keep it safe and never lend it, or you'll meet a sorry end.*
-The Glass Flute, Scene v

The cast was on break and nobody came downstairs to have a smoke with me, so I had time to brood by myself, sitting at the worktable where the violated daisy still lay, corpse-like. I decided to start a kind of log-book of incidents after that. I turned to the back of my stage manager's notebook and wrote "Weirdness" at the top of it, then lit a cigarette and prepared to write down every odd thing that had happened so far, but before I could get to my list, I had to give the daisy back some of its dignity.

I removed the rolled-up foam petals from the puppet's mouth and unravelled them. Like a pink twinkie, the outer wrapping surrounded a special filling—a tiny scrap of paper, many times folded. When it was opened up and smoothed out, it turned out to be a piece of a photograph, torn from a magazine or something, with a glossy finish. The people in the photo were smiling. It looked to be part of a group shot, because there were legs and torsos filling in the background. The fragment showed a man's face, with weathered, dark features and a kind of rakish charm, flanked by two other faces that were vaguely familiar, both young men. Other faces and bodies in the shot had been torn away, leaving only those three. The young men were younger versions of Jason and Shane, I thought. Somebody, and I was sure that it was a member of the cast, was trying to tell me something.

I started my Weird Incidents list.

1. Shane is taken in by Rico's outfit. When he discovers this, he goes berserk and tries to kill him.

2. Jason's vest is found floating in the shop pool. No Jason. (Okay—I was willing to entertain the possibility that Jason had scrammed when Shane arrived. I didn't buy it, but I was willing to borrow it.)

3. The vest is moored to the deck with an audio cable from Ruth's gear. It's tied in a neat knot.

4. Meredith implies that Shane has once been a hooker. (The nasty remark just before Becker arrived in the studio.)

5. Amber reveals that she's pregnant.

6. Somebody sneaks into Juliet's office at night to search the pockets of Jason's vest.

7. Somebody hangs up the Kevin puppet with another of Ruth's audio cables, and Shane says a message was left for him to come in early.

8. Somebody violates the Daisy puppet and leaves a cryptic photograph behind, to be found by the person who would ultimately have to fix it.

There were seven incidents so far. Amber's pregnancy could hardly be called an incident, an accident maybe. While I hadn't a clue as to who was responsible, I was reasonably sure that there would be more weirdness. Three of the incidents were decidedly sinister. I was still expecting Jason to show up dead, although nobody else seemed to agree with me. The two puppet murders were just plain spooky, and I was convinced that they were connected to Jason's disappearance in some way.

I did a quick glue-job to stick the petals back on the puppet head and stashed the photo in the envelope flap at the back of my notebook, along with the polaroid of the scene of the daisy crime. No matter what anybody said, I was going to go and show this stuff to Becker and Morrison. At least then they'd know that something peculiar was going on, even if they weren't interested in pursuing it. Then, when Jason turned up dead, there would be a file of sorts for them to go on. I wouldn't even take the credit, dammit, just as long as they used it.

After the break, we began the arduous work of hauling all the equipment downstairs and learning how to pack the van. Jason had left his "who lugs what" list in his promptbook, and we followed it, more or less, just because it was there. He'd assigned light stuff to Amber and to the original actor, Steven Higgs, whom Shane had replaced. He'd given Brad heavy stuff, but then he hadn't met him and didn't know (Brad told me while we were striking the set) that he had back trouble. So I just switched Brad's and Shane/Steven's list. Some of the puppets (the dragon and the serpent) were too bulky to fit into the road cases and had their own personal hockey bags for transportation. Amber got those. Brad and Amber got the steel pipes that made up the frame, which were heavy, but bungee-corded together in groups of three, they were easy to carry with one person on each end. Shane and Meredith hauled the lighting boxes, the drapery bags and the road cases. I hauled the sound equipment that we would be using on the road, a tapedeck, amp and speakers. There was no point in loading Ruth's keyboard, because she wouldn't be joining us on the road, but we did need to include the sound gear in the pack, because it took up a fair amount of van space.

By the time we got all the stuff downstairs, everybody was sweaty and red-faced.

I'd backed the van up to the loading door at the side of the theatre and we began the pack, following the pattern Tobin had taped to the back door. The frame pipes went in first, on the floor, followed by the big road cases and the lighting boxes. It was satisfying, in a way, like building something out of Lego. Every available cranny in the pack was used. Sometimes, we had to take stuff out and fit it in a different way, and when we had finished, there was still one puppet bag left, forgotten beside the loading door.

"If that happens on the road, we're dead," Meredith said. "Whose responsibility is that one?"

"Mine," Amber said, in a small voice. "Sorry. I thought I accounted for everything. We could put it on the seat in the back."

"No room, with all of us crammed in there," Meredith said.

"Chill out, Meredith," I said and tossed the forgotten puppet bag on the back seat. "We'll remember it next time."

I slammed the rear doors of the van, packed to the roof with equipment, and sighed with relief.

"Well done, guys," I said. A tiny little beep sounded behind me and I turned to see Meredith, a grim expression on her face, holding a stopwatch.

"From when we started carrying everything downstairs to now, it took us seventy two minutes and forty seconds," she said.

"Not bad for the first bash at it," I said.

"Unless we can shave a half-hour off that, we'll be getting into some serious overtime issues," she said. "The Green Book allows for forty minutes, tops. If the load takes over an hour, it'll cut into our lunch break and travel time. It's big bucks, and I can't be responsible for waiving the OT fees."

"Overtime! Terrific," Shane said, sarcastically. "That'll mean more cashola on the paycheck. Let's do the whole thing in slow motion from now on."

"We could cut your big song at the end," Brad said to him. "That would shave off a boring fifteen minutes."

"Juliet's not going to like this," Meredith said.

"Meredith, this was the first strike, load and pack we've done. It will get faster, it always does. Now would you put your stopwatch away and relax, please?" I said. It was the official end of the third rehearsal day, and Meredith had very cleverly let a huge emotional fart over what was supposed to be an atmosphere of mutual congratulation and positive karma. I wanted to strangle her.

"I think we should both keep time sheets when we're on the road," she said. "Just to make sure they're accurate."

"If there's overtime due, then it'll be submitted and paid for," I said. "You can keep an extra log of our hours if you want, but your time would be better spent working on your puppetry techniques." I know that was snarky, but I couldn't help myself. Shane snorted and Amber giggled nervously.

Meredith's face contorted, but she didn't say anything. She stormed back into the building, headed, I imagined, straight for Juliet's office.

"Let's call it a day," I said. "Ten a.m. tomorrow, please."

Shane stayed behind for a moment to confirm that we were meeting for a drink at the motel pub and then melted away. I stood leaning against the Steamboat Theatre van, feeling irritation, frustration and stage-manager's angst turning my neck muscles into Kuskawa granite. My shoulders were up around my ears, my back was killing me from stooping and lifting in the confined space of the van, I had a headache and I realized I'd forgotten to eat lunch. Three days into rehearsal and I felt like I'd aged ten years. This, I reflected, is why I gave up the theatre biz and moved north. Coping with the complicated egos and adolescent needs of actors is no picnic. At this rate I would be getting through an ounce of homegrown a week.

Lug-nut, who had helped with the load by carrying my briefcase down to the van, dropped it gently at my feet and sat leaning into my leg. If he had been Rico, he would have said "Polly, take me home, please."

"I know, Luggy. Thanks for babysitting the pup," I said, and stroked his head. He gazed at me with his tongue hanging out, drooling on my shoe. Of course all he'd understood of that was "Bluh-blah, LUGGY. Blah blu-blah-blah-SITTING bluh-blah." Seeing as he was sitting already, there wasn't much there for him, but then he was used to me blithering on at him. Dog owners end up doing that after a while, at least this one does. Amber was doing it already with her puppy, Portia, speaking in a high-pitched baby-voice that I predicted would drive everybody on tour absolutely insane inside a week. She and Shane were leaving together by the front door as I was entering the lobby. From the back, you'd think they were new parents, the way she held the dog, wrapped in a blanket, and the way Shane opened the door for her and carried the numerous bags of puppy paraphernalia out to the car. In another week or two, Portia would be too big to carry. I wondered if Amber actually knew what kind of breed she'd bought, and if she would ever let the poor creature walk about on its own four paws.

I went to the back office to check in with Juliet. Rico had left two hours earlier with Ruth, after the music rehearsal. I'd told him that I was supposed to meet one of the cast after work on a private matter, and he said he'd ask Ruth for a ride. Seeing as Ruth lived at the opposite end of Cedar Falls (Rico's antique shop was on the way for me), I hoped he was duly appreciative. Probably not, though. He's a sweetie, but he's a bit Rico-centric.

Juliet was nowhere to be found, which I thought odd, as she had indicated rather heavily that she wanted a chat with me about my reaction to the daisy murder. Still, I wasn't about to hang around for a dressing-down. I fired up the van and headed out.

The Falls Motel is a mid-range establishment on the other side of the river from the Steamboat Theatre space. It is close enough to the falls to get a view of the cascade, but it's hardly "at the foot of the mighty Sikwan Falls", which is what its flyers claim. However, it's clean and cheerful, with spacious rooms, kitchenettes (how I detest that word) and balconies overlooking the water. I was not surprised that Amber and Jason chose to stay there, but I would have expected Shane to get a room at the prestigious Sikwan Empire, a gorgeous, five-star resort hotel a couple of kilometres downriver. Shane, after all, was loaded, or at least that was the impression he gave. His clothes were very expensive, he drove an Intrepid, and besides, Juliet had told me so.

I arrived at the Falls Motel Pub a little before five-thirty, and because I was meeting Shane Pacey (who may have been in mid-flirt with Amber, but was still mind-numbingly gorgeous) I scooted into the ladies' room to freshen up. I hadn't had the pleasure of seeing myself reflected in a mirror since early that morning, when I'd once again plastered on the makeup to hide the bruising around my eyes. My nose was still swollen, and no makeup could hope to hide the fact, but I'd slapped it on anyway.

The face which greeted me in the bathroom mirror was shiny and quite unlovely. I had spent the last few hours hauling theatre equipment, and the resulting perspiration had caused what little mascara I wore to slide down my face, making me look like the sad clown in a black-velvet painting. I wondered how long I'd been looking like that, and why none of my dear co-workers had alerted me. My hair was sticking up in front, where I'd repeatedly pushed it away from my face during the van pack, there was a smudge of grime on my forehead, and the foundation I'd blended (just like they tell you in the magazines) into my skin had worn off in patches, but gathered in the creases around my nose and on my chin. The tip of my turnip nose was glowing. If I washed my face, and just left the makeup covering my black eyes, I'd look even more grotesque. Saying a mental "to hell with it," I ran hot water in the wash-basin, grabbed a handful of paper towels, pounded the bejeezus out of the "press once" soap dispenser and washed it all away. I also splashed some water on my bangs to erase the rooster-crest. The result was not as bad as you'd think. I like to go bare-faced most of the time anyway, and my eyes were now more yellowy than purple. I wouldn't win any beauty contests, but at least it was me.

The face-washing had delivered a sharp smack to my ego as far as "being pretty for Shane" went, which was just as well. I go off on these sad little tangents from time to time, reverting back to the hormonal "Pick me! Pick me!" thought patterns of a fifteen-year-old. Maybe we all do, I don't know. Anyway, the face that stared back at me after I'd finished was familiar and comfortable. I decided to toss the Max Factor as soon as I got home.

Shane was waiting for me at a table on the patio of the pub.

The early evening sun was golden and warm, and he was basking in it, his eyes shut, his legs outstretched. All you needed to do was take a picture, stick a trendy brand-name in the corner of it, and you'd sell a million of anything. He had changed from his rehearsal clothes into a pair of olive-green pants and a khaki T-shirt with cut off sleeves. He was drinking beer from the bottle and when he lifted it to his lips, hardly opening his eyes to do so, it was one of the most sensual things I've ever seen. His arm muscles rippled, for heaven's sake. I think I must have stopped walking towards him, just to gawk, because a waitress said "excuse me" behind me, and then squeezed by with a loaded tray, making a tiny "tsk" sound with her mouth.

Shane noticed me and lifted a hand in greeting.

"What're you drinking?" he said as I sat down. The waitress was at his side instantly. I could feel her checking me out, the "what's he doing with her when he could have me?" kind of thing. Very bad karma.

"I'll have one of those, please," I said to her, pointing at Shane's Kuskawa Cream Ale. "I'm glad to see you supporting local business, Shane."

"It's good stuff. I'm taking a case home with me when this gig's over." He lifted his bottle in a toast to his surroundings. "This place is great. I'd forgotten how much I love the north."

"You mentioned that you grew up here," I said.

"Yeah. That's what I wanted to talk to you about. These things that keep happening. Jason disappearing and that ugly shit with the puppets. Polly, I think someone's out to get me."

At last, I thought. Someone who is taking this business seriously.

"Why do you think that?" I said. The waitress came back with my beer in what must have been Falls Pub record time.

"Thanks, Alison," Shane said and gave her a ten. "That's fine," he said. Beer was only three bucks, but maybe he was paying for both. Anyway, it figured that he knew her name. Waitresses at the Falls Pub don't wear nametags. They barely wear clothes, come to that. Shane waited for her to go away before he answered my question.

"There's some things you should know about me," he said, softly. "I don't know where to start, though. Amber's meeting us here in about fifteen minutes, and I don't want her to hear this, but I think you should. She probably knows this stuff anyway, from Jason."

"What stuff, Shane?"

"Well, I think you're right about Jason being dead," he said. "And I think whoever did it is trying to pin it on me."

Twenty-Six

PRINCESS: *In the palace there's a rule that says you're not allowed to speak / Unless the grown-ups say so; not a whisper, not a squeak.*
-The Glass Flute, Scene viii

"Kuskawa is full of secrets," Shane said. "Anyone who grows up here could tell you that. It may be Toronto's cottage-country playground and heaven's waiting room for a million retirees, but there's a lot of shit below the surface."

I knew that as well as he did. Kuskawa, for all its monster cottages, thriving tourism business and pristine wilderness, had its seamy underbelly, just like everywhere else. You just don't get to read about it in the newspapers, because community weeklies tend to promote church socials and local heroes and avoid the court reports. Occasionally, there is a messy death, such as a traffic fatality, prompting one or two stern editorials and a call for a road-study at the council level. Or it might be a nasty case of domestic unpleasantness, with no names mentioned, because everybody knew everybody else, but you have to live here a long time before you get the real dirt.

"I grew up here, too, Shane," I said. "I know."

"You weren't here in the late eighties, were you?" he said. I shook my head. I'd been working in touring kids' theatre in those days, for a company out east.

"This thing happened at Laingford High," Shane said. "A teacher died, and it was pretty gruesome. A lot of kids were affected, and they covered it up, sort of. If you ask about it now, they'll call it 'The Incident' and that's all they'll say."

"Were you affected?" I said.

Shane's face twisted. "Yeah, you could say that," he said. "This guy, Mr. A., he was the drama teacher. He died just before we opened a rock-musical production of *Hamlet*. He was directing and I was Hamlet."

"Don't tell me," I said. "Jason was stage-managing."

"Well, no, he was only a Grade Eleven student then. I think he was running follow-spot."

"So what happened?"

"Mr. A. was found in his office, strangled with an audio cable. We were pretty good friends, and I kind of flipped out, a lot of us did."

"That's awful, Shane. Did they find out who did it?"

"That's the thing. Nobody was really sure what happened, and the police investigation never turned up anything."

"You're kidding."

"I couldn't handle school after that, so I left and went to Toronto. I was in Grade Thirteen then, anyway. Nobody ever talks about it any more."

"So you think that Jason's disappearance and the puppet-stuff with the audio cables is linked to 'The Incident,' as you call it?"

"It has to be. You see, there were some people who thought I might be involved with his death in some way. The police asked me a lot of questions, and everybody knew that I was spending a lot of time at the cop shop. That's partly why I left town."

"And now, ten years later, someone's trying to throw

suspicion your way again, is that it?"

"Well, think about it. If somebody killed Mr. A. ten years ago and got away with it, the case is still open, and the killer could strike again. The only obvious person with a motive for killing Jason would be me, because of the Amber-thing. The puppet stuff is meant to point to me. Whoever it is wants to stir up enough old memories to get the police interested in me again. It's the perfect set-up. Ten years after Mr. A. gets killed, Jason McMaster buys it and I'm the fall guy."

"But who would know that you're back in Kuskawa, working for Steamboat?"

"Lots of people do," he said. "I'm kind of hard to miss." He said it so unselfconsciously that it didn't sound like a brag. It was just the truth.

"This is totally off the wall, Shane. Why are you telling me?"

"I don't want to talk to the cops, Polly. That's exactly what this somebody wants. I know you've been involved in this kind of stuff before, so I thought you could help. You know, find out who the somebody is."

"And if I do figure out who it is, what then?"

"Maybe you could tell the cops—I don't know. I hate the thought of people thinking I was mixed up in Mr. A.'s death, but people have long memories up here. They may not talk about it, but they never forget. Whoever killed Mr. A. wants me to take the blame."

"You should really go to the cops with this," I said.

"I can't. I don't want to go through all that again. It's what I'm trying to avoid by talking to you, don't you see?" Shane was being downright emotional, and it was hard to resist. His eyes were moist, and he had taken hold of my hand in a most familiar way, which I rather liked.

"Well hi there, you two. Can I join you, or is this private?" Amber appeared next to our table, carrying her puppy. She spoke the words in a friendly way, but there was steel beneath the cotton candy, and her eyes were slightly narrowed. Shane snatched his hand away and sent me a "don't say a word" look.

"I was just leaving," I said. "How's the puppy, Amber?"

"Oh, Portia's just perfect," she said, brightening at once. "Of course, she's not house-trained yet, and she just made doo-doo on the carpet in my room, but I think I'm getting to know when she needs to go. Look! She knows her name." The puppy had, indeed, opened its sleepy eyes and had commenced chewing on Amber's hand. "Juliet says I have to let her get used to the feeling of having her mouth touched, so I can brush her teeth when she gets older," Amber said. "Ow! Easy, Portia." It was going to be a long haul. It still rocked me that Juliet had okayed the puppy-on-tour thing. Allowing Lug-nut to come along was different. He was a grown-up and reasonably trained. Portia was going to create havoc, I was certain.

I bid my fellow Steamboat shipmates a fond farewell, thanking Shane for the drink (which I'd only half-consumed) and went out to the van, where Luggy was waiting patiently on the passenger seat. I'd left George's truck at the theatre and would be bringing him in the next morning to collect it. From that moment on, I would have my own set of wheels and a company gas card. It gave me a feeling of freedom, even though the van, fully loaded, weighed a couple of thousand pounds.

On the way home, I mulled over what Shane had told me. He certainly seemed sincere, but then he was an actor, and a good one. It was gratifying to think that someone other than me and possibly Tobin thought that Jason was dead. I didn't want Jason to be dead, you understand, but I was sure he was. Shane had been convincing when it came to "somebody" having a motive to do the puppet stuff, and if the somebody had truly hastened Jason's death in order to renew the suspicion that Shane was responsible for a decade-old "Incident", then we were dealing with a nutcase. I just hoped it wasn't anyone in the cast. On the other hand, it would have to have been someone connected with Steamboat somehow, in order for them to know about schedules, and to know the space well enough to sneak around murdering puppets.

I went through the personnel list in my head as I drove in the slow lane along Highway 14, hugging the shoulder as the spring lumber trucks passed me, doing 140 clicks in a 90 zone. When I first moved to Cedar Falls, I'd regularly scribbled down the licence plate numbers of the trucks and phoned them in to the cops. It must have driven the local constabulary crazy, but it made me feel better.

Could Juliet have bumped off Jason and violated my puppets? It seemed unlikely, unless she lost her mind when he spurned her advances the night of the party. I couldn't see her damaging company property, though. Anyway, Juliet and Shane were old friends. She probably knew about the Incident and couldn't care less.

Amber was out of the question, and I couldn't see Bradley knocking off Jason for any reason whatsoever. Meredith was a good bet, though. She obviously knew something about Shane's past and made no secret of not liking him. She was trying to sabotage my stage-management authority and she seemed to like power. However, she had no connection to Kuskawa as far as I knew, and there was no reason why she'd know about the Incident. That left Ruth (no way), Kim and Sam, Tobin and I guess Rico, seeing as he'd been at the theatre every day since the party.

I was stumped. I resolved to check out the Incident with

Morrison, or even Becker, if he'd listen. I also planned to keep an eye on Meredith. Why had she accused Shane of "turning tricks"? What did that have to do with anything?

There was a police car parked outside George's farmhouse, next to Aunt Susan's lime green station wagon and George's Toyota. My heart hammering, I jumped out of the van and ran, expecting the worst. The Neighbour from Hell had attacked, I was certain, and George was hurt, even dead. I felt instant rage, the kind that tells you that a person you love fiercely has been harmed by someone who must be killed. I think I even snarled.

On the porch, there was rather a lot of blood, and when I saw it, I did the brave, sensible thing and blacked out.

Twenty-Seven

WOODSMAN: *If you're a princess, don't you have a duty to obey? / Do what you're told, and bide your time—you'll find your prince one day.*
-The Glass Flute, Scene iv

I am not generally a squeamish person. During the birth of goat kids, which involves a fair measure of less-than-attractive hot liquid matter, I'm in there up to my elbows, making comforting goat-noises. When I broke my nose at the party, I was reasonably stoic about the blood part. Just held a wodge of paper towels up to my proboscis and tried not to think of how much it hurt. Every month (guys can skip this part if they want) women have no choice but to deal with several gallons of the stuff, and while I know some menstruating people who are acutely embarrassed about the whole process and hide the evidence from sight as if it's shameful, I don't know of anyone who actually faints. In a way, it's rather useful to have your body remind you on a regular basis that there's healthy red stuff gooshing around inside you, just below the surface. It keeps you careful. I think this is why men tend to cut themselves more often than women do. Empirical evidence, I know. I don't think anyone's done a study yet. Guys keep cutting their fingers off with power saws and jackknives because they forget that they can bleed. Women remember.

This inner strength, however, dissolves when I see gouts of blood that are neither my own, nor birth-related. The blood on the porch of George's farmhouse was, I assumed, human, and smeared about as if the source had somehow been used as a mop. George's porch is painted white, and the effect was dramatic; hence my swoon.

I only blacked out for a couple of seconds, sort of crumpling up on the porch steps. I came to almost immediately, with Lug-nut's reassuring dog-breath in my face and a pair of police boots directly in front of my eyes.

"Hey, Polly. You okay?" Becker said and touched my head. "Did you damage anything?"

I groaned and struggled to sit up. Becker helped me by putting his arm around my shoulders, and I leaned into him, smelling clean police-uniform and his distinctive aftershave. (Obsession for Men. He told me once that his ex-wife buys it for him every year as a divorce-iversary present.)

"George," I said. "Is George dead?"

"Dead? Of course not. Just really angry. Morrison's sitting on him inside." An image flashed into my mind of Morrison's large rear end filling the sofa and my old friend's head poking out angrily from underneath. I chuckled.

"Thank God. What happened, Becker? It looks like the slaughter of the lambs, here. I thought…"

"I can imagine what you thought. Not as tough as you look, eh? No, I'm sorry. Keep still. This mess is pretty disgusting, but it's goat blood, not human."

"So what happened? Why is Susan here?"

"Ms. Kennedy says she was here when it happened. Good thing she was, too, or your Mr. Hoito could be in big trouble."

"WHAT HAPPENED?" Becker still had his arm around me.

I didn't move away because it was a little bit chilly, and I didn't have a sweater on.

"The way he tells it, the dog from next door attacked one of his goats."

"On the porch? The goats never come up here."

"Mr. Hoito says—"

"I saw it, too," Susan said, emerging, with Morrison and George behind her. "We heard your van arrive, then a thumping sound. Did you fall on the steps, Polly? Are you drunk? Goodness. What happened to your nose?"

I realized I hadn't seen my aunt since the Sunday night party. Typical that she'd say all that in front of two cops.

"I'll tell you later, and no, I'm not drunk. Just felt a little woozy, Susan. The view from here isn't all that pleasant."

Susan looked around at the porch, her lips set in a thin line. "I've seen worse," she said. I didn't ask her where.

"So what happened?" I said.

"We were playing Scrabble before dinner," she said. "I heard a noise on the porch and looked out the window. A man and a dog were at the front door, but it was obvious he wasn't a casual visitor. He had a big feed bag with him, and whatever was inside was struggling. Then he opened the bag and said something to his dog and out popped one of the goat kids and the dog just ripped it apart. It was utterly horrible. It was over in moments, and the man and the dog ran away."

I felt sick.

"The Neighbour from Hell?" I said, rhetorically.

George let fly with a string of Finnish invective that I couldn't hope to translate, which was probably just as well.

"George wanted to follow and shoot them both," she said, "but I wouldn't let him. We called the police, and I must say, they came very promptly." She nodded in approval at Becker and Morrison. "I just hope that they'll treat this with the severity it deserves."

Becker had removed his arm from my shoulders as the others came out, and now he stood up.

"With your statement, Ms. Kennedy, we should be able to do something. I called Animal Control, and the dog will probably be destroyed. They're on their way, now."

"It's not the dog's fault," Susan said. "It's the owner of the dog who should be destroyed." George muttered in agreement.

"The best we can do is lay a cruelty to animals charge and a vicious dog charge against him," Becker said. "Plus damage to private property, I guess. Have you checked that the goat was one of yours, Mr. Hoito?"

"Of course I have checked," George said. "Do you not think that I went down to the barn as soon as Susan would let go of me? That madman and his dog might have destroyed the whole herd. Yes, it was one of mine. Who else keeps goats around here? The kid was called Keanu—a buck I was rearing to be the next sire. He was valuable."

Becker looked at me. "Is that the little guy you introduced me to last fall?" he said. I was surprised that he remembered. We had gone on a date, Becker and I, half a year earlier, and I'd taken him down to the barn because he'd never seen a goat before. The evening ended badly, but the early part of it was straight out of a Harlequin romance. Keanu, a fluffy newborn goat kid with impossibly long legs and ears and the body of a kitten, had jumped into my arms and Becker had shaken its hoof after the formal introductions were made.

"That's the one," I said softly. "Keanu was shaping up to be a terrific buck. He was smaller than you'd expect, but he had a lot of personality—curious, you know? Always liked to come and check out what you were up to. Buddy next door wouldn't have had any trouble catching him, although putting him into a feed sack was probably a struggle."

The remains of the goat kid, Keanu, had been wrapped in a green garbage bag and placed at the bottom of the porch steps. I hadn't noticed it until Morrison picked it up and put it in the trunk of the cruiser. Amazing, really, how little bulk there was. Alive, a six-month-old goat kid is a whirlwind of energy, all legs and bleats and inquisitive nose. Dead, it's about the size of a small suitcase. I didn't ask to see it. Judging from the mess on the porch, there wouldn't be much to recognize or to pat goodbye.

The cops got ready to leave, saying they were going next door to pay the Neighbour from Hell a visit. The Animal Control vehicle hadn't shown up, but they said they wouldn't wait for it.

"They will shoot the dog right away?" George asked. It sounded as if he would have liked to watch.

"No, Mr. Hoito. There are formalities that have to be observed," Becker said. "You and Ms. Kennedy will have to make formal statements. We'll do that tomorrow at the station."

"What about the guy?" I said. "You're not going to arrest him? As soon as you're gone, he could come over here again."

"There's not much we can do about that, Polly," Becker said.

"Can't we file a restraining order or something?"

"You can apply to do that, certainly, but these things take time."

"So you're saying that this guy, who just murdered one of George's goats on the front porch, never mind what he did to his grandkids, gets off scot-free and we have to sit here quaking in our boots for the foreseeable future? Isn't this incident, as you'll probably call it, sort of like a death threat?"

"What Mr. Gamble did or did not do regarding his grandchildren has no bearing on this incident," Becker said. "They're unrelated."

"How can you possibly believe that?" I said.

"If it came down to a court of law, any previous tendency toward criminal behaviour in one case is not admissible evidence in relation to another," he said.

"But it's obvious that he did this goat thing to get back at George for squealing on him, isn't it?"

"That's conjecture only. You can't put someone in jail for uttering a death threat to a goat," he said.

"He didn't utter a death threat to a goat," I said. "He killed one."

"Public mischief," Becker said.

"Mischief??" George roared. "You call this mischief? Does this man have to murder us in our beds before it becomes a serious matter?" He didn't wait to hear the answer but stormed back into the house, heading, I feared, for the scotch.

"Oh, it's a serious matter already," Becker called to George's back. "It's just that we can't arrest him and take him away. He has rights, you know."

"And we don't? Don't you think he's a danger to us?" Susan said.

"I didn't say that," Becker said. "I think you should lock your doors tonight."

"Oh, excellent. Lock our doors. Thanks, Becker," I said.

The Animal Control vehicle, a battered green pickup with a Ministry of Natural Resources logo on the side, came down the driveway, and Becker went out to meet it. Morrison jingled his keys and turned to Susan.

"I finish my shift at midnight. I'm coming back," he said.

"Thanks, Earlie," Susan said. "I think I'll stay, too."

"What about Eddie?" I asked, thinking of Susan's sixteen-year-old ward, Eddie Schreier.

"Eddie can look after himself for one night," Susan said. "He's not a baby, Polly. I'll call him. Besides, it's not fair to get him involved in this. He's had enough grief in his life already." Eddie's mother was in a psychiatric facility in North Bay, and his father had moved to the States. He had been living with Susan since the previous fall and was doing well, though Susan said he still had nightmares about the events surrounding what was known as the Cedar Falls murders.

"Well, if you two are going to stay with George, I'm going home," I said. "I've got some work to do, and I'm beat."

"Is that wise?" Susan said, making it plain that, in her opinion, it wasn't.

"I don't think old man Gamble even knows there's a cabin up there," I said, referring to my place, which was hidden in the woods on the hill at the back of George's property. "He has no reason to connect me with this mess. If you're worried about my safety, don't. Luggy'll be with me."

Morrison, who had been through this kind of thing with me the previous fall, when there had been a killer on the loose and I had been directly involved, knew better than to comment. He just gave me one of those "Earl the Destroyer" warning looks left over from his pro-wrestling days. I grinned at him.

"See you later," he said to Susan and headed for the cruiser. He had a word or two with Becker, who glanced over in my direction and shook his head. Then he called out: "Check your e-mail," and they left, followed by the Animal Control guy.

"I don't envy them their jobs," Susan said.

"That's a switch," I said. "You used to think cops were the scum of the earth." She glared at me.

"Everyone has the right to change her mind," she said. "Since getting to know Earlie, I have come to appreciate the kind of thing they're up against. You would do well to have a bit more respect for them yourself, Polly."

"Excuse me?"

"That Becker still seems quite fond of you." She was dead serious. I was flabbergasted.

"I recall you telling me not so long ago that I was insane to get involved with him. You practically disowned me," I said.

"Speaking of disowning," Susan said, "you won't have to worry about inheriting the feed store and being chained to grain, as you used to call it, for the rest of your life. I put it up for sale today."

"Oh, so you want me to chain myself to a policeman instead," I said.

"If we're going to have an argument, we might as well channel the energy into something useful at the same time. Let's get some nice buckets of cold water and sluice down the deck while we talk. I don't imagine George will be up to the job, and it's the least we can do."

"Just what the doctor ordered after a hard day of rehearsal," I said, but followed her, because she was my aunt and had been my guardian growing up, and I was programmed to do what she said—except when it came to my personal affairs.

Twenty-Eight

MOTHER: *You've grown into a big boy now, I've taught you right from wrong / So when you walk alone, my son, I'm with you all along.*
-The Glass Flute, Scene i

"I'm tired," Susan said. We were washing the goat blood from the floorboards of George's porch, working in the appropriately crimson light of the setting sun.

"Rest, then," I said. We had been working in silence for some time.

"I mean I'm tired of fighting the good fight," Susan said. "Tired of struggling to keep the store afloat when that damned Agri-Am down the highway keeps undercutting me." The Agri-Am had opened the previous summer. It was like an agricultural Wal-Mart, full of low-end American and Chinese goods at rock-bottom prices and U.S.-imported grain that was cheaper than the local stuff. They had a fleet of little delivery trucks with star-spangled cows painted on the sides and a frequent-buyer plan that gave away rubber boots and milking pails with every feed order.

When the Agri-Am first opened, Susan had gone to the local town council, demanding to know why an American-owned "big-box" feed store had been allowed to set up shop without a public debate. Council had told her that the market ruled, and a little healthy competition would be good for her. The mayor was an ex-boyfriend of hers, and they had been feuding for years. At first, Susan's regular customers had remained loyal, but slowly and surely, the insanely low prices, huge parking lot and teenaged cashiers in fake cowboy outfits had won out.

"I'd keep fighting if I were younger," Susan said, "but I'm going to be sixty-nine next month, Polly. I just haven't got the oomph any more."

I didn't know what to say. I had grown up in Susan's feed store, learning to sling bags of grain and birdseed, getting my first practical math lessons on her old brass cash-register and stealing pairs of zip-up overalls to wear to school, thereby creating fashion trends amongst the nerdy set. Susan had always insisted on carrying nothing but Canadian goods. She'd order American stuff if you asked for it, but it was banned from her shelves. There was a big sign in her window—"100 PER CENT CANADIAN PRODUCTS ONLY SOLD HERE." I'd done a project in Grade Eight on Canadian/U.S. trade issues, and she'd helped me gather the information with the enthusiasm of a zealot. When the North American Free Trade Agreement was signed in the late 80s, we'd had a wake in the store—a bunch of us drinking Baby Duck and stomping around wearing rubber boots made in Mississauga.

"Do you think anyone will be interested in carrying on the business?" I asked.

"I don't know, dear," she said, looking sadly at me. She had always hoped I would. When I told her I was planning to pursue a career in the arts, she had been supportive, but melancholy. "Terry Morton says she's interested, but I don't know how she can possibly afford it. Her father certainly won't help her. He wants her to become a funeral director." Theresa Morton had been working for Susan for years. She was the daughter of Hunter Morton, who ran the big funeral home in town. Funny how our elders still waste a huge amount of energy choosing our career paths for us, then wringing their hands in despair when we go astray. Terry told me once that for her first date with a boy, Hunter had insisted on chauffeuring the young couple to and from the Laingford Odeon in the hearse. Now there's an incentive to follow in Papa's footsteps.

"If you sell the store, what on earth are you going to do with your time? And what about Eddie?" I asked. I suspected that I knew the answer already, but I had to hear it from Susan.

"Well, George has asked us to move in here," Susan said. I didn't say anything. My aunt and I get on reasonably well together, but the thought of her living right next door and taking over George's life (and mine, I might add) was not terribly appealing. Still, Susan and George had been pillow-buddies for about a year now and were obviously very fond of one another. It was none of my business what George chose to do with his life, but I couldn't help feeling a wave of jealousy. He was my friend more than he was her friend, I felt, even though they were sleeping together. It was Susan who had engineered my moving into George's homestead cabin in the first place; she had known him before I did. But still, having your mother-figure move in on your adult turf was disquieting. I wanted to say all this, but I didn't. I didn't really have to. Susan's nobody's fool.

"There's enough room in George's life for all of us," she said. "It's not as if we're going to get married, Polly."

"It's not that," I said. Actually, I whined it, sounding like a seven-year-old who's putting up a fight about going to the dentist. How could I possibly say "I love you, go away" in a nice way?

"It would take some of the responsibility for the goats off your shoulders," she said.

"I like helping with the goats," I said. "It's not like it's a chore." In addition, my contribution to the workings of George's farm was payment in lieu of rent. It allowed me a modicum of self-respect, in spite of the fact that my income (pre-Steamboat, anyway) was about $6,000 a year. It was complicated. It was my life.

"Well, we can work the details out as we go along," she said. "I've told him I would be delighted to move in, and anyway, if I sell the store, I won't have anywhere else to go."

"You could buy a condo in Florida," I said. I was only kidding.

Susan's left eyebrow shot up and nestled in her hairline. It's a trick she has. I can do it too, a bit, but she has it down to an art. "You really don't want me here, do you?" she said. "You'd banish me to the blue-haired ghetto first."

I backtracked, explained I was being facetious, and spent the next little while filling her in on all the details of my life at Steamboat Theatre, to put her off the scent.

"It sounds like George will need some help around here when you're on tour, anyway," Susan said, quite reasonably. Oddly enough, I hadn't thought that far ahead. Once Juliet had dragooned me into doing Jason's job, I'd been too preoccupied with the logistics of doing it to think about how it might affect my life on the farm. Of course I wouldn't be able to do the chores, if I was waking up in a seedy motel in Kenora, scheduled to do a show at the Kenora Public School and Young Logger's Academy. I could only agree with my aunt, which I did, not very gracefully.

"I don't expect the store to sell right away, anyway," Susan said. "It's not as if it's a waterfront property or a frozen-yoghurt franchise. It's a failing agri-business. If it were a car, I'd be selling it for scrap."

It was only later, after we'd tossed the pink water over the side of the porch and I'd said my goodnights, that I realized I'd never, ever heard Susan sound so defeated. Some help I'd been. "I don't want you here—go to Florida," I'd more or less said. How sensitive. I felt my face burning with shame as Luggy and I tromped up the hill to the cabin.

I warmed up a tin of baked beans (comfort food) and prepared to fire up the laptop, so I could check my e-mail. (Gosh, how glib that sounds. How quickly the Luddite turns cyber-puppy.) It was chilly in the cabin, and I lit a small fire, discovering in the process that Jason's drowned notebook had slipped down between the woodstove and the wall. I fished it out and brought it to the table, where the oil lamp was casting a cheerful glow. It had dried out to the extent that I could separate the pages without tearing them, and like any waterlogged book, it was now three times its original thickness.

The first few pages were full of the predictable and panic-striken notes of the young stage manager who has blithely taken on a gig without realizing the extent of the work involved. The first page was titled: "Production Meeting", dated the beginning of the week before, when Jason had arrived at Steamboat. There were scribbles about pyro stuff, lighting stuff and what appeared to be preliminary notes about the van pack. He was an experienced enough stage manager to know the "If it ain't on the page, it ain't on the stage" rule, and every little thing was written down.

It got interesting a bit further in.

"Background," Jason had written at the top of the page. Then each member of the cast and production staff was listed, with curious little notes beside each one.

"Juliet Keating: Fucking Harvey Ogilvie, chairman of board," it said. "Guy is married."

"Tobin Boone: Deals dope." Now this I didn't know. My friend was holding out on me.

"Sam Ruttles: Money guy. Petty cash? Check records." It looked like Jason had been collecting stuff about every one of us, even if there was nothing to collect. I felt the hair prickle at the back of my neck. When had he had time to go snooping around getting this kind of information? I read on.

"Ruth Glass: Dyke singer. AIDS?" This was pushing it, and I was beginning to get pissed off. If anyone else had seen this, I could understand why they might have been tempted to push the little creep into the Kuskawa River.

"Polly Deacon: Dope smoker. Likes cops. Used to date Drew Franklin." Now where did he get that esoteric piece of gossip? Drew was the reason I'd moved to Kuskawa in the first place. Our breakup hadn't been pretty, but it was more than three years old, and the only thing unresolved about it was a phone bill that Drew claimed I owed him for. How on Earth had Jason made that connection, and why the heck did he think it was important enough to include in his little hate sheet?

He had a shoplifting charge on Meredith (I'll admit this little tidbit gave me some pleasure), a failed marriage and three small children on Bradley (no surprise and hardly scandalous) and the accusation of gayness on the guy who was supposed to play Kevin, Steven Higgs. Higgs' name had been crossed out, though, and what Jason had done to the page, presumably when he'd been told that Shane Pacey was replacing him, was the notebook equivalent of road rage.

"Shane Pacey: Fucking bastard!!!" was scrawled with a heavy hand and underlined several times, and the hand which had written it had pressed hard enough on the paper to tear it.

Staring at the notebook, which was blank after this page, I wondered what to do about it. Here was a fairly interesting list of motives, perhaps not enough to point in one particular direction, but enough to suggest to Becker and Morrison that Jason was obviously a rather nasty little chap who liked to get his jollies by collecting dirt on his co-workers. More than ever, I was convinced that Jason was adding to the snowmobiler soup at the bottom of the Kuskawa River.

I dialled the server from the cellphone (see? I can talk the talk) and logged on.

Twenty-Nine

DRAGON: *There's little I like better than the glitter of a gem /
But I'm also fond of maidens—can you offer one of them?*
-The Glass Flute, Scene x

[You have mail]
"Hey, Luggy," I said. "I've got mail."

There were thirteen messages in all. Normally, I didn't get much mail. In the previous year, the only stuff that had come through old-fashioned channels and arrived in envelopes had been a couple of nasty "pay up or you're toast" notes from Petrocan (addressed to George, whose name was on the card, but given to me because I was the one who used it) and a bi-annual, chatty letter from an old friend on the east coast. I'd had a Christmas card from Rico in December (a lovely picture of a nearly naked bodybuilder wearing a Santa hat—I'd hung it in the outhouse) and an anonymous note from the States telling me that if I didn't repent me of my sins, I'd burn in Hell, which I suspected came from Eddie Schreier's estranged father, Samson, who had reason to dislike me. That was it. I have never been a subscriber to magazines (the people who produce them sell your address directly to their advertisers, who sell it to marketing firms, et cetera) and I refuse to fill out "Win a Free Widget" contest ballots.

Because of this, I haven't had a piece of junk mail in years.

Eleven of the messages on my e-mail were from people I didn't know, offering me schemes for making money in my own home, exhortations to do all my shopping on the Internet and opportunities to set up my own website. I can just imagine a Polly Deacon website. Polly dot com. A picture of me and Luggy on the rickety porch of the cabin, with the inscription "nothing to report."

I deleted them all except for two. One was from steamboat@kuskawa.com, which I assumed was Juliet's, and probably contained a written reprimand for my reaction to the daisy-puppet murder. I decided to smoke a joint before I read that one. The other was from Becker.

```
To: pdeacon@kuskawa.com
From: oppbeck@kuskawa.com
Subject: Flaky, Luddite stuff

Dear Polly;
If you have found out anything about the
Jason McMaster case, I'd expect you to
tell us. It's not for you to decide what
is important to the case and what is
"flaky, Luddite stuff", as you call it.
Like I said in my last message, the
investigation is ongoing. Just because
you don't see us at the theatre, doesn't
mean we're not working on it.
Mark Becker
```

I wrote back right away, not even bothering to draft my message first. After all, I was calling on Juliet's nickel.

```
To: oppbeck@kuskawa.com
From: pdeacon@kuskawa.com
Re: Flaky, Luddite stuff

Dear Becker;
I thought you had concluded that "the
Jason McMaster case" was simply a matter
of a young guy who was miffed because
his girlfriend's former flame was back.
If the investigation is truly ongoing,
there are things you should know. Jason
was collecting dirt on everybody at the
theatre (I can prove this) and somebody
has pulled a couple of sick stunts at
the theatre that seem to allude to a
death that happened in Laingford about
ten years ago. If you're interested, I
can tell you about them. Have you fished
up any more bodies yet?
Polly.
```

I pressed "send" and the message disappeared, presumably transformed into an electronic gibber, skittering through the phone lines into the belly of whatever infernal machine processed it. It still blows me away that this actually works. If I'd been born in Alexander Graham Bell's time, I would have denounced him as a loony.

Then I logged off, rolled a small joint and smoked it, cobbled together a cheese sandwich and started cleaning up my worktable, perfectly well aware that I was procrastinating about reading Juliet's message. Perhaps if I waited a few minutes, the laptop computer, like the proverbial homework dog, would eat it and I'd have an excuse for having missed it.

It didn't.

```
To: pdeacon@kuskawa.com
From: steamboat@kuskawa.com
Subject: preview

Polly;
I know this is short notice, but we've
arranged to do a preview of the show at
Laingford High School on Friday
afternoon. Please inform the cast
tomorrow morning, and tell them not to
worry about it. Most of the audience
doesn't speak English. As you know,
Laingford is sponsoring a group of Kosovar
refugees, who arrived in Kuskawa last
week, and the show is a way of making them
feel welcome. There will be about 50
people, adults and children, plus town
officials and some people from the
Salvation Army. I'll talk to you about it
tomorrow night. Please put the cast
through a couple of runs of the show
tomorrow. I'll be in Toronto until about
6 p.m.
Juliet
```

I just sat there, staring at the screen, my mouth open. The cast was going to go ballistic. To schedule a preview of a complex show like the *Flute* after only four days of rehearsal was totally insane. Our preview wasn't supposed to happen until Monday, and we hadn't done a complete run yet. There was no way Ruth would have the show tapes ready by Friday, and nobody was entirely off-book. Not only that, but we hadn't integrated the flashpots into the show yet, either. This was a recipe for disaster.

I'd heard about the Kosovar refugees coming to Kuskawa. There had been a big splash about it in the local newspapers, a welcoming ceremony and a general atmosphere of "aren't we wonderful to be doing this?"

The group of fifty Kosovars who were welcomed into the heart of northern Ontario cottage country had languished in a camp in Macedonia for more than a month, after being expelled from their own country by the Serbian army. They'd been flown to Canada by military jet and housed on an army base in Petawawa for another month or so, before being "adopted" by the Laingford Town Council. The provincial government had generously donated a property it owned in the region. It was, ironically, an abandoned summer camp on the shores of Lake Kimowan, complete with cottages, several dilapidated outbuildings, a main dining hall and a beach. In a frenzy of well-meaning preparation, Laingford council had repaired the cottages, painted over the "Camp Gitchee-Goomie" sign and organized a district-wide drive for food, clothing and household goods. The community had responded with the boundless enthusiasm of an elementary school classroom getting ready to receive a new pet.

When they arrived, the Kosovars had been photographed mercilessly by the local media, their faces scrutinized for signs of gratitude. The presentation of *The Glass Flute*, I suspected, was being offered in order to coax a smile or two from Kuskawa's newest citizens. In most of the pictures I'd seen, they'd been pretty grim, and Laingford council must have been disappointed. I wasn't sure how they'd react to our puppet show. If they didn't speak much English, the story would be hard to follow, and while the pyrotechnics would certainly produce a reaction, I wasn't sure the bomb-traumatized Kosovar kiddies would be crowing with delight. I said as much in my reply to Juliet's e-mail, but I doubted that it would make much difference. Juliet's big on community involvement.

"Is she crazy?" Meredith said, after my announcement of the news the next morning. Her voice rattled the casement window and Amber's puppy, Portia, who had been asleep in her playpen, woke up and immediately started yipping.

"Shut that dog up!" Meredith said. "Christ, this is the most unprofessional outfit I've ever had the misfortune to be associated with. A measly one-week rehearsal period, then the chicken-shit stage manager walks out on us, then we get hit with a preview for a bunch of immigrants way before we're ready and the director waltzes off to Toronto, leaving a hippie puppeteer in charge. I'm calling Equity." She headed for the door.

"Scared you'll look like an incompetent idiot up there?" Shane said. Meredith stopped and squared off against him. Showdown. Everybody scrambled for cover.

"I think it's kind of exciting," Amber said from the door.

"Meredith, chill out," Bradley said from the safe side of the stage manager's table.

"I won't look half so stupid as you'll look, Pacey," Meredith said.

"I guess Ruth'll be playing live, eh?" Amber said, trying for a segue with a frantic smile, looking at me, willing me to do something.

Smarting from the "hippie puppeteer" crack, I was inclined to wade in and pour kerosene on the burn by using a highly improper Anglo-Saxon epithet referring to the nether regions of the human female.

"Yup, Ruth will," I said.

"You're just afraid you'll dry in the middle of the opening

scene and crack up like you did at Gananoque," Shane said. "Wanna be blacklisted again?"

"I didn't know you were at Gananoque," Bradley said to Meredith.

"So, if Ruth plays live, then if we screw up, she can get us back on track and, like stall, right?" Amber said to me.

"I did not crack up, Pacey. I had mono," Meredith said.

"Bullshit. You went crazy and wrecked the show. Nobody but kid's theatres has hired you since," Shane said.

"Listen, Meredith. The audience doesn't even speak English," I said. "If you lose a line, nobody'll notice."

"I never lose lines," Meredith said. "And if you think I'm going onstage with this asshole opposite me, without the proper rehearsal, think again."

"Are you the one that played Anne in *Anne of Green Gables* and had the nervous breakdown on opening night?" Amber said, letting her curiosity get the better of her diplomacy. "I heard about that." She turned to Shane. "You never told me that was her."

"The show closed the week after and we were all out of a job," Shane said. "Her fault."

"Wasn't there an understudy?" I said.

"You don't have understudies in summer stock," Shane said. "The company was in trouble anyway. Every actress in Toronto who ever played Anne was away somewhere doing it. The actress playing Diana took over the part but she was awful. So the show closed, and the company lost a bundle."

"Don't talk about me like I wasn't here," Meredith said. "That show closing wasn't my fault. The actor playing Gilbert sucked."

"I don't think so," Shane said.

"Not only did he suck onstage, he sucked offstage, too,"

Meredith said. "Most actors wait on tables between jobs, Shane. I guess the tips were better waiting on Johns, eh?"

Shane got the look in his eye that I'd seen once before, just before he threw Rico down the stairs at the party.

"Hey, you guys, that's enough!" I shouted, and stepped between them. "Whatever the hell happened the last time you worked together is history, got it? I don't think anyone in this room gives a good goddamn about the details. We've all got a past—big deal. Right now, we've all got a rehearsal. If anyone here can't do this gig, then for heaven's sake quit now so we can hire somebody who can."

There was a long, impossibly theatrical pause.

"It's going to mean a lot of overtime," Meredith said.

"They'll pay," I said.

"They'd better," Shane said. Truce, for now. We headed downstairs to unload the van.

Thirty

CAT: *It pays to be observant when there's danger close at hand /
The things that scare us most are things we just don't understand.*
 -The Glass Flute, Scene vii

The rest of that day, the cast of *The Glass Flute*
worked with the kind of demented, desperate energy usually
saved for the kind of opening night when the set's not
finished, half the costumes are missing and the lead actor
arrives drunk. Oddly enough, the morning storm had cleared
the air a good bit, and I actually caught Meredith and Shane
running lines together, staring into one other's eyes with the
intensity of championship chess players, each daring their
opponent to make a mistake.

As soon as Ruth arrived, we set up for a run. Rico, who had
come in with me that morning and was downstairs still
working with Kim and Sam, came up to the studio and told us
he'd ordered a couple of on-the-house pizzas from his uncle's
place, Amato's, across the river. The cast agreed to a half-hour
lunch break, provided that the company paid the Equity
lunch hour infringement. Juliet's premature preview was going
to cost the company a pretty penny, and we all agreed that that
was only fair. There was a "them and us" feeling in the studio—
the cast against the management, and rather sadly, against our
poor, unsuspecting preview audience, who could hardly help

the fact that the command performance was creating hardship for the entertainers. Heck, they'd probably have preferred to stay at home. I know I would.

We arranged to do three runs, the first with music, but no black hoods, working under the regular fluorescent overheads, so the cast could see what they were doing. The second, after a break, would be done with the UV lights on, to make the puppets glow, but still with no hoods, then the last would be a real dress rehearsal, hoods on, peripheral vision zero. The staff of Steamboat agreed to come and be a test audience for that one, and we figured we wouldn't get to it until after the dinner break, so Juliet would be able to see it, too.

I had agreed to be backstage for the preview, prompting (on book), in case anybody lost it so completely that they needed to be fed a line. Usually, stage managers are at the opposite end of the playing space from the actors, either in a booth or at a table at the back, calling lighting and sound cues (or running them) and taking notes. There were no lighting cues for *The Glass Flute*, because everything was done under UV light. Well, I guess there were two—"ON" and "OFF". Under normal circumstances, I would be running the show tapes from out front. Being backstage was weird, because I couldn't see very much of the action. Still, the actors were all suffering from chronic Yikes, so it was only fair that I was there sharing it with them. Fine tuning would come later, when we were on the road and everything had settled down.

At its proper pace, the show runs just under an hour. It's for kids, so there's no intermission, no chance for the young audience to lose the thread of the story. It's action-packed, colourful and exuberant, designed to hold onto the fragile thing that is a modern child's attention span. Juliet Keating knows her market. *The Glass Flute* fits very nicely into a school schedule, to be played in the first class period of the day, or the first one directly after lunch. This means, on tour, that you're on the road at seven in the morning, toting barges and lifting bales to get set up by showtime at nine-thirty. If you want to know what this is like, imagine how fine your voice sounds during your morning shower, then imagine that you're singing that same shower song in front of two hundred pint-sized critics, after having just rearranged your office furniture by yourself, dressed up in your best duds afterwards without benefit of a shower, climbed up on your desk under a harsh spotlight and struck a pose. There are reasons for calling this kind of theatre work "paying one's dues."

Sometimes, when a cast is under-rehearsed, a kind of magic sets in. It's born of adrenaline, mostly, a distillation of the actors' perception of what their roles are supposed to be, without enough time for the director's vision to have had a marked effect. It's scattered, but inspired. The first run had this quality. It truly sparkled.

The actors kept to the script most of the time, and if a line was lost, Ruth filled in with a bit of improvised music. If there had been anybody in the audience, they wouldn't have noticed anything amiss. After the final moment, we all burst into a spontaneous chorus of self-congratulatory whoops and hollers, which felt wonderful.

"That was fantastic, you guys," Ruth said. "You could take it on the road tomorrow."

"We're going to," Meredith said, but with good humour.

Shane ran a hand through his hair and then looked at his palm.

"Brad, in that last bit, just before your dragon spurts fire, can you get the big guy's head a little higher? I got a mouthful of smoke that time, and I swear a couple of sparks landed in my hair."

"Yeah, sorry," Brad said. "I think I pressed the button a little early." The trigger for the dragon flashpot was in the head of the puppet, and it was up to Brad to fire it. I knew it was going to be a problem. Brad wasn't terribly accurate when it came to cues.

"That's one cue you have to be sure you don't jump," I said. "It's distracting, eh?"

"Won't happen again," he said.

"Shane, don't worry about the flashpots," I said. "That stuff is designed to combust instantly. The sparks aren't fire sparks, they're glitter."

"Tell that to my hairdresser," he said.

"You'll be wearing your hood," I said. "All the costumes, drapes—the whole schmeer is treated with flame retardant."

"My head isn't," Shane said.

"We won't do the flashpots for the next run," I said. "We'll put them back in for the dress run tonight, okay?"

"Fine with me," Shane said. "Thanks."

"Scared of a little puff of smoke?" Meredith said.

"Frankly, Miss Equity Deputy, yes. Can't you write a risk clause into my contract?"

The diversion to duty worked like a charm. Meredith seemed to give the suggestion serious consideration.

"I suppose we could," she said. "I never thought of that. We should all have one of those. Who knows what could happen? I'll have to check the Green Book." She hurried away to get the Equity book from her purse.

"Thanks, Shane," I said, the sarcasm as thick as butter.

"No problem," he said, grinning. "It'll keep her occupied."

"Polly, the waist belt inside the serpent costume is a little snug," Amber said. "Could you loosen it for me?"

Shane looked at her belly with a small, smug expression on

his face. Of course. The measurements Amber's agent had sent with her contract had been taken, presumably, before she was pregnant. Although I assumed, when she'd told me, that she was only a little way along in the gestational process—early enough for her to be legally able to terminate the pregnancy—there's still an immediate thickening and tightening of the midriff. Amber caught Shane's look and returned it with one of her own, a very private one that embarrassed me a bit. With Jason out of the way, it appeared that the two had sort of claimed one another. I wondered if the young actress would really go through with an abortion.

"Bring it over here and I'll adjust it," I said. "The buckles just need easing off a bit, probably."

"Ruth, can we take a moment to go over the Axe Song?" Brad said to her. "It went a lot faster in that run than we rehearsed it."

"That was your tempo, not mine," Ruth said. "You trotted through that number like your pants were on fire."

"I know," Brad said. "Nervous. You were just keeping up, I guess."

"Damn right. I tried to slow you down and ended up a couple of bars behind you. Here, let's do it now."

The second run after lunch, with the UV lights on and the overhead fluorescents off, was chaotic. Although there was enough daylight in the space to allow the actors to see each other, and they were performing hoodless, the added element of UV-activated puppets and props was disorienting.

"You get sort of hypnotized by them," Amber said afterwards.

"Yeah, like you're supposed to look at the puppets when you're manipulating them, and when you look away, you can still see them," Brad said.

"I wonder if working under UV light is dangerous," Shane

said, looking at Meredith. "Are we all going to get headaches and blurred vision?"

Meredith thought for a minute. "I didn't have anything like that last time," she said, "but I think we should watch out for it. With the pyrotechnics and the UV light, we may have to have a rider attached to our contracts, Polly."

I glared at Shane, who winked at me. "You can take it up with Juliet after the run tonight, Meredith. You're all covered under the Equity insurance policy—that should be enough, unless you're talking about danger pay. I doubt she'll go for it."

"The Equity insurance, is that the thing that says you get, like $4,000 if you lose an arm, and $350 per eye, that sort of thing?" Amber said. "I thought that was sick when I saw it in my contract package."

"It's standard," I said. "I guess they keep the settlements low so you won't be maiming yourself on purpose to collect the cash."

"Like, I'm really going to poke my eye out so I can pay my rent this month," Amber said.

"Exactly."

For the dinner break, the cast decided to hit the Burger Barn downtown.

"Take the van, so none of you gets lost," I said, shifting instantly into mother-hen-mode. "We want to start the dress run dead on time."

"Aren't you coming?" Shane said.

"No, I've got to wire the flashpots and check the preset," I said.

"You want us to pick you up anything?"

The Burger Barn, originally a drive-in, had been a fixture in Sikwan since the fifties and had miraculously survived, in spite of a McDonald's franchise opening a few doors down. Its dressed-up hotdogs all had bizarre dog-names. A Lucky Lassie had American cheese on it, and the Schnauzer came with sauerkraut and was served on a kaiser. The burgers, in various forms, were named after heavy machinery. It enjoyed a kind of cult-status in town, having achieved a degree of nostalgic cool that no big-corporation advertising budget could ever manufacture. The current owners, a Portuguese family who had immigrated to Canada in the early seventies, didn't bother putting ads in the papers or on the radio. They just smiled happily, remembered their customers' names, flipped burgers on an immaculate grill, hired high school students (who stayed on for years) and raked in the bucks. Why mess with a good thing?

I ordered a Bulldozer (double patty with fried onions) and some onion rings. Normally, I don't eat fast food, but it had been a long day with no end in sight, and sometimes a good dose of saturated fat is just what you need.

"What happened to the health regimen?" I asked Meredith, as I gave her the van keys.

"Rules are made to be broken," she said. "Just ask Juliet."

"Point taken," I said, and we exchanged a reasonably friendly smile. Things were looking up.

Ten minutes later, as I was carefully wrapping thread around an electric match, I heard heavy footsteps on the stairs.

"Polly?" Becker said. "They said I'd find you up here. We have to talk."

Thirty-One

MOTHER: *When people get together in a group, they think as one / Join in, my son, but don't forget there's peril in the fun.*
-The Glass Flute, Scene i

"**We found another body,**" Becker said.

"Oh, please. I'm not going to fall for that one again."

"It's not a snowmobiler, Polly. It's a young male, thin, with dark hair, dressed in black."

"Oh, Lord. Jason?"

"We think so. His parents are on the way down. I thought you should know."

"Where did you find him?" My heart was beating much too hard, and I lost my grip on the pyro squib I was building. It flipped out of my hand and skittered across the table, dumping pyro powder everywhere. I resolved not to light a cigarette until I'd washed my hands.

"Just where you'd expect to find him if he went into the river up here. The current's pretty strong. He was wedged under a dock a couple of kilometres downstream. Got a call this morning."

"Did you get my e-mail?"

"That's why I'm here. You think he was blackmailing somebody? You said you could prove it."

"He was collecting dirty laundry. Blackmail? I don't

know—maybe. You're sure it's Jason?" I said.

"No, not completely. The face is disfigured. But we're sure enough to need to go over the details of last Sunday night again, and you said some weird things have happened around here since then."

"Your timing is terrible," I said. "We've been told that we're supposed to do a show for the Kosovar families in Laingford tomorrow. We've been rehearsing like crazy today, and there's a dress run in about half an hour. I don't suppose you can wait until it's over, can you? The cast is a little high-strung at the moment."

"That depends on what you can tell me now, Polly."

"And if I tell you the wrong thing, and you end up suspecting one of my cast members, you'll take him or her in for questioning, and the show's toast."

"You'd want to continue doing a puppet play with a murderer?"

"Becker, I've thought Jason was dead since Monday. You guys didn't. If someone tossed him into the workshop pool, and it's one of us, then we've been rehearsing with a murderer for a week already. One more day isn't going to make any difference."

"I've heard that 'the show must go on', but this is ridiculous," Becker said.

"Yup."

"Look, you mentioned something about a death ten years ago in Laingford. What's that about? If you want to make me go away, you have to give me something, Polly. Either that, or I'll just shut this whole thing down right now, interview everybody very, very slowly and—I believe the expression is—it's curtains for your play."

"All I'm asking is for you to wait a few hours. If you have

found Jason, then the news of his death is going to absolutely freak everybody out. They're all convinced, like you were, that he just had a tantrum and skipped off to Toronto. Amber's going to fall apart when she hears it."

"She wasn't too cut up about her boyfriend's leaving," Becker said. "I saw her and that blonde actor downtown yesterday, and they looked pretty chummy."

"Having a fiancé walk out on you is one thing, having him croak is another," I said.

"What if she helped him croak?" Becker said.

"Hardly. Amber Thackeray's a little mouse."

"Mice bite if they're cornered," Becker said.

"Look, I'll make a deal with you, Becker," I said. "The cast is due back any time now. We have a dress rehearsal of the show, and then we have to strike and load the set into the van, which will take us up to about ten o'clock. I have some stuff that might help you, or it might not, but I don't have the brain-space to talk about it right now. I'll meet you wherever you want at ten-thirty."

"Maybe you could find the 'brain-space' if you came up to the Laingford station with me," Becker said.

"That wouldn't be productive and you know it," I said. "You don't know that my information has any value whatsoever, but I have a choice to be cooperative or not. I'll be cooperative. But not right now."

"You are one huge pain in the ass, Polly Deacon," Becker said. "I'm trying to investigate a suspected homicide, and all you can think about is a stupid puppet play."

"It's not stupid," I said. "It's my job, and I don't get them very often, Officer. Anyway, you don't know it was a homicide. Earlier this week, you thought it was an accident, if it was a death at all. I'm the one who's been overreacting every time something strange happens around here, and my boss doesn't like it. If this dress rehearsal is canned because the cops suddenly decide that it wasn't my imagination after all, Juliet's going to think I was pestering you and playing Nancy Drew instead of working for her."

"Isn't that exactly what you've been doing?"

"Yes, but I'd rather she didn't have it confirmed. Come on, Becker. Be nice."

"Only if you tell me about the death in Laingford. Then I'll go away and check it out and meet you back here at ten-thirty. And if you tell Morrison that I made a deal with you, I'll deny it and then come search your place for drugs with a pack of German Shepherds."

"I hate it when you do that tough cop stuff. It doesn't suit you. Besides, you can't just burst in and search someone's house, Becker. It's unconstitutional."

"I can certainly search your place if I have reason to believe you have illegal substances in your possession."

"I gave it up, Becker."

He knew perfectly well I wasn't telling the truth on that one, but I couldn't help noticing the tiny flash of pleased surprise that skittered across his face when I said it. It was gone in a moment. "Look me in the eye and say that," he said.

"Okay, never mind. But I have a note from my doctor," I said.

"Your shrink, maybe," he said. "Now talk."

I heard the van arrive—the low, crunching rumble of the van's sliding side door open and shut. They were back with my 'Dozer burger and onion rings, and I still had the flashpots to prepare before the run.

"Okay, okay. Briefly, a drama teacher at Laingford High, I don't know his name, died about ten years ago. I don't have a firmer date than that. There was something funny about it that they didn't tell the students, and afterwards they called it 'The Incident.' No charges were ever laid." I wasn't going to tell him about Shane having been questioned. At least not at that point. He could find that out for himself.

"What does this have to do with Jason McMaster?" Becker asked. The actors were coming up the stairs.

"Jason was one of his students."

"So?"

"So, I don't know, Becker. Someone tampered with a puppet yesterday and left a photo behind that sort of connected the two."

"A photo? You've lost me."

"Look, I'll tell you later. We've got a dress rehearsal to do, and you promised you'd go away if I gave you something. That's all I know about the teacher's death, but if you can find out the details, then maybe some of the other stuff will make some sense."

Becker was, understandably, looking exasperated. He was in plainclothes for some reason (he was one snappy dresser) and assumed the classic Gentleman's Quarterly "perplexed model frowns at camera" pose. It was very annoying. I felt the urge to reach out a hand and smooth the frown lines away, which would have been entirely inappropriate, especially as my hands were covered in pyro powder and I'd have left a smudge. I'd been talking intensely with him for some minutes, and even though there was nothing left between us except some messy history, his one-on-one closeness made me feel decidedly warm.

The actors boiled into the room, laughing and goofing around. The Burger Barn will do that to people—turn them into giddy teenagers. It was nice to see them getting along so well. The Mother-hen microchip in my brain clucked approvingly. I didn't want Becker to ruin it.

"Hey Polly," Shane said. "They're naming a new hot dog after Amber's puppy—the Portia Portion." The puppy was, as usual, snuggled in Amber's arms like a teddy bear. It wore a smug expression and was licking its incredibly cute chops.

"They took a picture and everything," Amber said.

"I'll see you at ten-thirty," Becker said and left quickly. I let out a small sigh of relief, and on the in-breath caught the mouth-watering aroma of my 'Dozer burger, which Shane plopped down onto the table. They'd all taken their food to go and were busy unwrapping burgers and onion rings.

"Who was your friend?" Meredith asked. As usual, Becker had been unrecognizable out of uniform.

"An old buddy of mine," I said. It's a weird power that cops and priests and people who wear uniforms have. They enjoy a kind of double-personality, so that even people who know them quite well when they're suited up, think they're meeting someone new when they're in civvies. I first noticed this phenomenon at a charity ball in Laingford. I'd been engaged in a long conversation with an elegantly-dressed woman at the bar, feeling I knew her from somewhere, but not having the temerity to ask that goofy question: "Haven't we met before?" Turns out she was the checkout clerk at the Sav-Mor, where I've done my grocery shopping for the past three years. Without the orange polyester romper-thing they make them wear, she was a different person. Go figure.

I let my 'Dozer get cold and finished rigging the flashpots. By the time I got around to eating, we were at the ten-minute call, and our "'est audience" was settling down for the show.

The "calls" for a show are one of those stage management things that non-theatre people don't understand, and amateur companies don't take seriously, which is why little-theatre productions almost never start on time.

The idea is this: It's stage management's responsibility to make sure the show goes up, or starts precisely at the time appointed. To make this happen, you give calls to your actors and crew, and to your audience. In a big theatre, you do this by using the intercom system. Traditionally, the calls begin at the half-hour. "Half-hour, please," the stage manager or assistant says to the actors and technicians. Everybody involved with the performance of the show is expected to be in the theatre at least by the half-hour call.

The proper response for the stage manager's call is to say "Thank you." This tells the SM that you've heard and understood. This venerable tradition, which dates back into antiquity (since the advent of the wristwatch, anyway), precludes the necessity of rushing into the dressing room just before curtain and saying "Aaaagh! The Queen's just arrived and we have to start, like right away!! Have you got your costume on yet?? Aaaaagh!!!" and rushing out again, effectively paralyzing your average actor.

Calls are given at the half-hour, the fifteen, the ten and the five. Then there's "places, please", and when you get word that everyone's in place, you can call the opening cues. This sequence of events is one of the most supremely satisfying things that SMs do. Going up on time becomes a badge of honour, and you can usually tell a crummy SM by the lateness of the curtain. The audience gets calls, too. If you've been to a performance, have you ever noticed that discreet little bell that goes "bong, bong" and tells you to go to your seats? Ever notice that the lobby lights start flashing? It's the SM who makes that happen. Now you know. Tell your friends.

Our audience for the dress rehearsal consisted of Rico

Amato, Kim Lee and Sam Ruttles, who had abandoned their work on the AIDS benefit in order to venture upstairs for a little light entertainment, which they probably needed at that point. Tobin Boone was there with his wife, Rachelle, and their small son, Artie. Juliet arrived at the fifteen-minute call, half-corked, on the arm of Harvey Ogilvie.

"Sorry we're late," Juliet said. "It looks like you managed wonderfully without us, Polly dear. I'll make sure you're compenshated."

Fish Gundy and his family came—I'd called them that morning—and George, Susan and Eddie had come down from Laingford. They didn't bring the Neighbour from Hell, though it occurred to me afterwards that Gamble's two little grandkids would probably have enjoyed it. Still, a social worker I'm not. They'd probably see it at school anyway, provided they were lucky enough to attend school.

In order for a dress-preview to work, it's important to fill the house with as many well-wishers as possible. Performing in full costume with all the pieces in place is horribly flat when the seats are empty. When the actors know the audience is made up of friends, they receive an infusion of performance energy, but they're in a safe environment. To throw this under-rehearsed cast in front of an audience of strangers at Laingford High without a "for friends" preview first would be traumatic. Actors, if you haven't gathered this yet, are creatures of delicate temperament. They bruise easily.

Backstage, the actors prepared. A single, dim blue bulb burned in the space behind the playbox. Without the UV light to give them life, the puppets and props, each set carefully according to where and when they would be needed, appeared as dim, fantastical shapes. The actors were dressed in their black gear, but none had donned a hood yet.

Every performer develops his or her routine for the cliff's edge moment before a show. No matter whether the performance is *The Tempest* on Stratford's mainstage, *The Naughty Knickers Cabaret* on the deck at the Barmaid's Arms or *The Glass Flute* in the Steamboat Theatre rehearsal space in Sikwan, the pre-show focus is always there in one form or another. Amber, true to her theatre school training, was performing a routine of diaphragm-stretching breathing exercises, arms at her sides, huffing and puffing like a steam train. Brad was bent over at the waist, trying to touch his toes. Shane was pacing and muttering and Meredith was standing stock-still, her eyes shut, humming. Ruth, who would be providing live accompaniment, had elected to wait backstage, in a gesture of solidarity that I found touching. She stood at ease, smiling in the half-light. Ruth had performed Shepherd's Pie concerts to packed halls across the country for years, appeared on television and radio, recorded albums and was, essentially, a celebrity, in as much as a Canadian musician who hasn't sold out to the States is ever a celebrity. She probably had her pre-show moments too—everybody did—but hers, I guessed, were very internal.

"Places, please, everybody," I said, gently. They muttered thanks, and Ruth stepped out to her keyboard.

"Is Juliet here?" Brad said, and in response, her bark of laughter came wafting backstage.

"She's in a terrific mood and she loves you all," I said. "Don't worry, this should be fun. If you get lost, just jiggle the dolls and make like the Three Stooges." They all laughed. It's easy to make pre-show actors laugh. Tell them anything, but keep it upbeat, is my motto. They donned their hoods and immediately became clones of each other. I headed for the front.

"Wait, Polly." I think it was Meredith. "Come back for a

sec." The pressures of the day had somehow bonded us all. Don't know how or why that is, but all the petty jealousies and rivalries had been replaced, at least for the moment, by warm fuzzies. The four cast members were standing in a tight huddle, arms around each other's shoulders. The circle opened to admit me. We stood staring into the black centre of the circle for a moment and wordlessly began a tiny-step shuffle to the right, some sort of dance that bubbled up from nowhere. Someone started a soft hum, and then we were all doing it, shuffling and humming in a circle. It was the melody from the Axe Song. It only lasted for a moment or two, and it ended as organically as it had begun. No explanation, nothing planned, just one of those weird, spontaneous little things that make the observer think you're all completely wacko. I knew that the circle-hum-thing would become a mandatory pre-show ritual. Every cast has its lucky rabbit's foot. We had found ours.

I went out to the front, smiled at our assembled audience, flicked off the fluorescent overhead lights and cued Ruth to begin, then zipped backstage to prompt. The first performance of *The Glass Flute* began.

Thirty-Two

KEVIN: *I think it might be smart to find a place to have a rest / I'll stay awake in case we get an uninvited guest.*

PRINCESS: *You're sleepy too, I saw you yawn. I'll take a turn for you / We'll share the watch; protect ourselves like all real soldiers do.*

-The Glass Flute, Scene v

These are the things we learned from our dress rehearsal: Bradley Hoskins had the potential to shed about five pounds a show through sheer water loss, and he needed a stronger deodorant. By the time the final notes of *The Glass Flute* died away, the playbox smelled like a gym after a Grade Eight soccer game, and all the puppets that Brad had touched were damp.

Amber, when she messed up, had a backstage vocabulary which was truly spectacular. Something went wrong with the mouth mechanism of the serpent, she got flustered and lost a whole section of dialogue. Afterwards, she came offstage in full spate, using several words I've never heard before and adding to the Brad-thick air.

The black flags, used to make things "disappear" during the show, were almost invisible backstage. People kept tripping over them and couldn't find them when they were needed onstage. I started grabbing the flags whenever someone tossed one down (the action was too fast to place everything carefully—it was a matter of running backstage, dropping one puppet or prop, grabbing another and running on again). Whenever someone came back for a flag, I'd whisper "flag" and hand one over. But I wouldn't be able to do that on tour, because I'd be out front. I decided to make a kind of umbrella stand, paint it white, put it where it could be seen, and make sure that used flags got deposited there after every exit.

There were bits in the play that the audience found hilarious, which weren't supposed to be. The bittersweet farewell scene between Kevin and Mother in the first sequence, with soft, sad music playing in the background, made the children howl with laughter. It was very disconcerting, and it put Meredith in a towering rage that lasted most of the run.

As we had expected, Shane would have to be pulled back on his Axe-acting. Even watching from the wings, I could see that he was upstaging Brad's Woodsman quite shamelessly. While the audience loved it, it added a good three minutes onto the running time of the show, and it made Brad sweat more.

Generally speaking, though, the run went well. Our test audience enjoyed themselves and applauded heartily at the end when the cast came out, hoods in hand, for their curtain call. As per Steamboat tradition, we conducted a short question-and-answer session after the bows.

The children in the audience, Fish's twins, Tobin's son and Eddie (who was sixteen, but as curious as any of the younger ones) asked the usual kind of questions that the cast would have to answer every day for the next couple of months. The Q&A was an important part of the show, especially from Juliet's point of view, as teachers, principals and librarians loved any educational element which could justify the performance fee.

"How do you make the things glow?" would always be the first question asked, guaranteed. The trick in a Q&A was to answer as if the cast had never heard the question before, and to answer respectfully, without being flippant. After fifty times of being asked to explain UV light, the tendency would be to blow off the question and just say it's magic.

The cast took turns answering questions, and the adults threw in a couple as well, for practice.

I got to answer Rico Amato's "how did you make the fire?" question, but I think I got too technical. I was trying to explain pyrotechnical chemistry when Shane jumped in with: "Don't try this at home, kids." I didn't see what the problem was. Rico had seemed quite fascinated.

After the audience had dispersed and the cast had peeled off their wet costumes, we met for a quick debriefing before striking and loading the set.

"Thank you all for a marvellous job, darlings," Juliet said, sending a cloud of Chanel perfume and chablis-breath out over the gathered cast. "I know it's been unfair to put this added pressure on you, and I know your Equity rep is keeping careful track of your overtime, which we'll pay, of course. There'll be an added bonus on your first paycheque as well." Meredith assumed an expression of efficiency, and I suspected she'd had a word with Juliet in private. Good for her, I thought. "This performance tomorrow is very important," Juliet said. "It's our chance to give something back to the community and put some sunshine into the lives of those poor refugees, so it'll be worth it." There was a municipal election coming up. Maybe the chairman of the Steamboat board had his eye on the mayor's job.

"What about the flashpots?" I said. "I think we should cut them for tomorrow's show." Juliet glared at me.

"Why on earth would we want to do that?" she said. "They're the highlight of the show. The kids love them."

"The kids who'll be watching tomorrow aren't ordinary kids," I said. "They've had bombs dropped on them. I think the flashpots will scare them shitless and will probably frighten the adults as well."

"That's a good point," Shane said. "Sudden loud bang and fire, type of thing. We could have them running for the exits."

"This is theatre, Polly, not real life," Juliet said. "Just because tomorrow's audience doesn't speak much English, it doesn't mean they're stupid. I didn't know you were prejudiced."

"That's totally unfair," I said. "I'm not being prejudiced, I'm trying to be compassionate."

"You're underestimating your audience," Juliet said. "*The Glass Flute* is a magical experience that will take them out of themselves. The flashpots are part of the magic."

"Then, at least make sure they know about them before the show starts," I said.

"That would ruin the surprise," Juliet said. I couldn't understand why she was being so pig-headed. I let it go, but resolved to make sure myself that our Kosovar audience was told, before the show started, that there would be some pyrotechnics involved.

"I don't have any notes for you," Juliet said, which surprised the heck out of me. Usually, after a dress rehearsal, the director spends a good hour going through the careful notes she or he has made of the performance, pointing out slips-ups and making suggestions to tighten the performance. It's part of the job. Once the show's up and running, taking notes is the stage manager's responsibility, but I hadn't taken many, partly because I was too busy handing out black flags and following the script backstage so I could prompt if anyone got lost, and mostly because I hadn't been able to see the show from out front. The puppet manipulation and visual comedy bits could've been a total mess, and I wouldn't have known. Without regular notes throughout the performance run of a show, the staging can get sloppy. After a couple of weeks, actors tend to get bored and start to add things or "forget" to perform bits of business the director liked but they didn't. I've seen shows completely transformed after a month on tour. Not doing notes after a dress rehearsal was setting a dangerous precedent, but considering the mood Juliet was in, I didn't think it was wise to say so.

"I'll leave you all to get down to the nitty-gritty now," Juliet said. The chairman of the board was waiting by the door, tapping his foot. "I look forward to tomorrow's performance, and I'll come backstage before showtime, just to wish you well. Afterwards, I'll take you all out to lunch. Toodle-oo."

We watched her go.

"Sozzled," Shane muttered.

"We should probably give each other notes, then," Meredith said. "There were a couple of things I caught."

"Me, too," Amber said. When actors give each other notes, unless they know each other really well and have worked together for a long time, there's enormous potential for conflict. Criticism, no matter how constructive, is hard to take from a fellow actor.

"Let's do that tomorrow," I said. "We've put in a 12-hour day, and we won't have time to do another run before the performance at the school, so why don't we meet here at eleven? It's half an hour to Laingford, which'll give us an hour and a half to set up, and run bits if we feel we need to. The show's at one-thirty, so that gives us a bit of leeway."

"Oh, good. We can sleep in," Amber said.

"I won't sleep, I'm totally wired," Brad said.

"What about the costumes? Are you going to have time to do laundry before the show?" Meredith said. The wet, used blacks were steaming in a nasty little heap in the dressing room.

"I'll try to get them done first thing in the morning," I said. "The hoods, anyway. You may have to use your second set, though."

"If you leave them for more than a few hours, they're going to grow mould," Meredith said. She turned to Brad, and I just knew she was going to make a remark about deodorant, which wouldn't have gone down very well right then.

"Let's get this set struck and then we can all go home," I said quickly. It did the trick, and we got busy. Someone suggested that we celebrate by going to the Falls Motel Pub after the strike and load. Amazing how a powerful thirst can motivate you, even when you've put in a deadly-long rehearsal day. Ruth, Rico, Sam and Kim helped cart the stuff downstairs (we weren't going to bother sticking to the assigned "who carries what" list at that point) and the whole business took less than forty minutes.

I wasn't going to be able to join them at the pub, because I'd promised to meet Becker at ten-thirty. This fact made me feel sorry for myself. The first booze-up after a successful run is a sacred part of the theatrical bonding process. The actors wouldn't wait for the next day to give each other notes. They'd do it in a good-natured way, lubricated by a couple of Kuskawa Cream Ales. The performance would be dissected, amidst much hilarity. Problems and things that needed to be done would come up in conversation and Kim, Rico and Sam would be able to give insights on how the show went from out front.

My absence would allow a tiny wedge to be driven between

me and my cast. Call me paranoid if you will (okay, so you're right), but I've done too many tours not to know this is true. Things would be decided at the pub that I would only find out about later. I'd give a note the next day about the flag-thing, and someone would say "Oh, don't worry, we worked that out last night." Rico or Kim would mention the Axe-acting and Brad and Shane would negotiate between themselves what worked and what didn't. Meredith would probably take notes and hand them to me the next day, making me feel guilty and out of the loop. What would happen in the hour or so to come would be a kind of production/direction meeting by committee. I resented not being able to be there.

I'd kept the serpent puppet out of the pack in order to fix the mouth mechanism for the next day's show. It was only nine-thirty, so I had an hour to kill before Becker arrived. I tried hard not to play the martyr. Saying "I can't come to the pub because I still have work to do" would have pissed everybody off. I told Rico privately that I was staying behind, so he could bum a ride from Ruth, but I told everybody else that Susan, George and Eddie, who had seen the show, were waiting for me at home.

After they'd gone, Lug-nut and I puttered around the studio with a green garbage bag, cleaning up the fast food wrappers and discarded water bottles, the spoor of the rehearsing actor. Then we went into the dressing room and were assaulted at once by the stink of the costumes, curled like a moat monster in a pile in the middle of the room. Luggy growled deep in his throat and moved in carefully to investigate. He backed off after one close-up whiff, hackles raised. It wouldn't have surprised either of us if it had moved. As I bagged them, Luggy gave me his "You have got to be crazy" look and went out to the studio to see if there were any nice, pleasantly perfumed Portia-leavings to be checked on. Everything is relative. I left the garbage bag in the dressing room, ready to take it to the laundry the next morning, then carried the big serpent puppet out to the stairs.

The old waterfront building which houses Steamboat Theatre has quite a bit of history attached to it. In the thirties, when it was a working marina, the owners had run a notorious speakeasy in the upstairs room we now used as a rehearsal hall. There had been a lot of trouble there, in the old days, according to the History of Steamboat Theatre tourism pamphlet in the lobby. Legend had it that Al Capone himself had paid the place a visit during a secret vacation in Canadian cottage country. The booze had been kept in a tiny attic room above the rehearsal space, accessed by a metal ladder bolted into the wall above the main stairs. I was tempted to climb up there and check the attic to see if they'd left any bottles behind. I figured I could use a pre-Becker snort.

I fixed the puppet quickly with a bit of wire and duct tape. Then I locked the serpent in a storage cupboard, just in case the prankster was planning to drop in, and curled up on the couch in the lobby to wait for my date.

I was awakened from a light doze by the ear-thumping racket of Lug-nut in full bark by my side. The bag of laundry was making its way down the stairs, slowly and horribly, end over end, like a big, sluggish slinky.

Thirty-Three

DRAGON: *I'm hungry for something—I don't think it's food / Though I like to eat maidens and boys who are rude.*
-The Glass Flute, Scene ix

As luck would have it, Becker showed up at the lobby door, just as Luggy pounced on the laundry bag. Becker knocked politely while my dog summarily ripped open the green garbage bag with his bare paws and snarled at the sweaty cotton. Then he apparently started eating it, but I was too distracted to stop him.

I let Becker in, my heart thumping horribly, not because of the policeman, but because there was no doubt in my mind that someone had heaved the laundry bag down the stairs and that whoever it was, was still up there somewhere.

Lug-nut ignored Becker completely.

"What's with the dog?" Becker said, as I locked the door behind him, then had second thoughts and unlocked it again, in case we needed to make a quick escape.

"Thank God you're here. More weirdness. Someone just threw a bag of costumes down the stairs. We have to go up and see who it is," I said.

"Whoa there, hold on," Becker said. I was pulling on his arm. "Explain first. What costumes? What somebody?"

"I'm alone here," I said. "At least, I thought I was. I packed up the show laundry in that green garbage bag and left it in the dressing room. Then I flaked out here waiting for you. Luggy just went nuts barking, and I opened my eyes and the laundry bag was coming down the stairs by itself."

"You didn't leave it at the top of the stairs?"

"Nope. Dressing room. Miles away."

"Why would somebody throw a bag of laundry down the stairs?" Becker said, reasonably.

"I don't know, Becker. To scare me, maybe. There's been a lot of that, lately. Now c'mon."

He accompanied me on a tour of the studio. We didn't find anything, of course. The rehearsal hall, the bathroom, the dressing room—they were all empty, and I felt like an idiot.

"Been putting in long hours, Polly?" Becker said, gently.

"Some," I said, trying hard to remember whether or not I'd carried the laundry out to the stairs with the serpent puppet. I could have, I supposed.

"Have you eaten?"

"I had a 'Dozer around six," I said, gathering up the costumes that Luggy had scattered around the lobby. "The onion rings were cold. They're really gross when they're cold."

"Have you finished here?"

I tied the laundry bag up again. It was ripped in a couple of places, but its contents didn't deserve much better. "Yup." My nose hurt, and I felt dizzy and bewildered.

"Then I'm taking you to the Rock Cut for some food and you can tell me what you need to tell me and I'll tell you some things too," Becker said. "Jason McMaster's parents identified his body. It could have been an accident, but now I don't think so."

"It's about time," I said, thinking of the quiet intimacy of the Rock Cut Steak House, the fact that Jason was officially terminated, and the list of suspects, including, presumably, me.

"We could go to the Falls Motel Pub, where everybody is," I said. "You could arrest them all right there."

"No need," Becker said. "I sent Morrison over there a little while ago. Don't worry, you won't be missing anybody tomorrow. He's just going to ask some pointed questions. Get this thing cleared up."

"Who dunnit, Becker? Do you think you know?" I knew his record. He'd been wrong before. Did he still secretly think it was only an accident and was just humouring me? My stomach, which had admittedly been melting at the prospect of Rock Cut chicken wings, a beer or two and a pleasant chat with what appeared to be a mellow Becker, tightened.

"We don't know who dunnit," he said, "but we have a pretty good idea. Now why don't we lock up this place and I'll meet you out there at the Rock Cut?"

"Fine." I was planning to take a detour first. To the Falls Motel.

Things were rocking at the motel pub. The flashing electric sign over the crowded parking lot proclaimed that a local band, Baggy Chaps, was playing. The lead singer was a relative of Earlie Morrison's, and they played the kind of New Country stuff that sounds like all the rest until you listen to the lyrics. I probably drove faster than I'm supposed to. I didn't even notice the cruiser on my tail until I stepped out of the cab, telling Luggy to stay put.

"This isn't the Rock Cut," Becker said, right behind me. He was pissed off, I could tell.

"That's the next stop," I said. "You wouldn't have had time to have more than a sip of your beer before I got there, Becker."

Another cruiser was parked near the door. Morrison was getting out of it, and when he saw us, he looked pissed off too.

"I thought you were going to leave me to do this, Mark," Morrison said, when we got close enough. "You two think I can't handle it or something?"

"Of course you can handle it," Becker said. "Perhaps you'd like to explain to Ms. Deacon here that her presence isn't required in there."

Morrison made an annoyed little "tsk" sound. "Polly, there are times when we've got to do our jobs without you," he said. "You shouldn't be here. You'll just get upset."

"Who are you taking down, Morrison? Shane? Meredith? The technical director?"

Morrison glanced inquiringly at Becker.

"I haven't talked to her yet," Becker said.

"Well, take her away and talk to her then," Morrison growled. "I don't want her here." He gave me the kind of look you give a small, yippy dog who wants up. "Scram," he said.

To say I was hurt would be putting it mildly. Morrison had never spoken to me like that. He was my friend, for Pete's sake, and the honorary uncle of my aunt's ward, Eddie. We'd gotten drunk on scotch together, and Morrison had a marionette I'd made of Becker hanging in his bathroom. I looked up at him with what I imagine were kicked-puppy eyes, but he didn't flinch. What was he planning to do in there that I wasn't supposed to see? Beat his suspect to a pulp? Who was it?

"The only way you're going to know what's happening is if you get in your van and follow me to the Rock Cut," Becker said. "Either that or you can get in the cruiser and come with me to Laingford, where I'd be happy to talk to you about obstructing a police officer in the course of his duty."

"So this is like, date me or I'll arrest you?" I said.

"Any chance that we could have sat down like two adults and enjoyed a friendly conversation about this case is long-gone," Becker said. "A date this ain't. I'm just offering you a choice about the location of our interview."

"Cop shop or chop shop," I said. "I guess I pick the chop shop."

"Good choice," Becker said. "Now let's go. And if you try to elude me, I'll pull you over."

"I wish you'd stop threatening me," I said. "It's getting to be a habit with you, and it's not very attractive."

"I can't help it," Becker said. "You bring out the bully in me. I don't like it either." It was the most honest thing Mark Becker had ever said to me, and I mulled it over as I followed his police car all the way to the other side of town. I imagined him checking his rearview mirror every couple of seconds to make sure that my headlights were right there. I resisted the temptation to put my high beams on and leave them on.

So, I brought out the bully in Mark Becker, did I? How disturbing. People who bully, according to those popular social-worker studies, are individuals who need to have control over their environment and the people in it. Was Becker being pushy just with me, or did he treat everyone he knew that way? Had he tried to control his ex-wife? Is that why she left him? Did I bring out the bully in him because we shared some sort of complicated mutual attraction? The old "If we're going to be lovers, I need to be the one in charge" trip? The most disturbing thing about his last remark had been the way it made me feel.

I have always been an advocate of equal partnership—of a healthy, level, shared intimacy. I had thought for a very brief time the previous fall that there was potential to have that with Becker. All my relationships with men have started out like that, offering the perfect balance of partnership and pleasure, give and take. So far, though, the guys I've been involved with have, at some point, required more "give" than I've been prepared to cough up. Every time I've been on the point of dumping someone (I'm more often the dumper than the dumpee), I've examined my own behaviour and battled with the notion that I might, just possibly, be more demanding than the guy is. Why am I not able to make compromises with Bob, or Colin, or Albert, or whoever he is? Why am I unable to devote as much of my precious solitude as it takes to maintain a relationship? Am I a selfish person? In dump-land, I'm usually the one heaping garbage on my own head. The dumpee usually helps. It's not a good place to be.

I found myself appreciating the warning Becker had given me. If I brought out the bully in him, then I should stomp very heavily on the little fluttery, libidinous creature that appeared in my brain whenever he was around. I had a feeling that he brought out the bully in me, too. Not a partnership destined for success.

The Rock Cut Steak House, built on a cliff overlooking the town of Sikwan, is the place where businessmen take clients at lunchtime, and young executives takes their wives at night. The decor leans towards the baronial, dark beams overhead and red flocked wallpaper, candles flickering in glass goblets and heavy linen napery. The patio is more casual than the dining room, and that's where we sat. It was chilly and buggy, which is probably why nobody else chose to join us. We kept our jackets on.

Becker ordered a big plate of wings and a Blue, and I asked for an ashtray and a half pint of Kuskawa Cream. If I had to endure a sit-down session under duress on a chilly patio with Detective Constable Mark Becker, to whom I wasn't allowed to be attracted because I brought out the bully in him, then by heavens, I was going to smoke.

"Thanks for choosing to cooperate, Polly," Becker said, after the beer came. "What have you got to tell me?" I brought out my weird occurrences list and let him read it.

"So there are eight things you think are related here," he said. "Your transvestite friend gets pushed down the stairs, McMaster's vest is found in the pool tangled up in a bunch of audio cable—"

"Tied to it," I put in. "In a neat knot."

"Okay, the vest is knotted up in a bunch of audio cable. An actress accuses an actor of being a prostitute, another actress says she's pregnant, and somebody searches the pockets of the vest. Am I with you so far?"

"I don't know. You sound a little sceptical," I said.

"Uh-huh. Then somebody plays a couple of tricks with your puppets and leaves a scrap of a photo for you to find."

"And number nine, which we should write in, is that someone threw that bag of laundry down the stairs," I said. Okay, I know it sounded stupid, especially coming at the end of my long list of totally meaningless and mostly trivial incidents, but I said it anyway. Then I told him about Jason's notebook and the things that he had written in it about the people at Steamboat Theatre.

"What are your thoughts on this?" Becker said. He was treating me with a mock seriousness that I found hard to take. Stalling, I guess, while Morrison arrested somebody back at the motel pub—unless they were all over there signing the forms to have me committed to the North Bay Bin for the Barking Mad.

"First tell me what you found out about that death at Laingford High," I said.

"It happened in 1989," Becker said. "You're right. They do call it 'The Incident.' The teacher was a very friendly guy, mid-forties, very tight with his students. One of your cast members, Shane Pacey, was questioned about it, but then you knew that, didn't you?"

"He told me yesterday," I said.

"The investigation was inconclusive," Becker said. "The medical examination revealed that the teacher, who all the kids called 'Mr. A.', asphyxiated. He was found in his office with an audio cable tied around his neck. Nobody was ever charged with anything."

"Shane told me that part. He said the students were really freaked-out about it."

"Some were more freaked-out than others," Becker said. "The administration tried to keep the details quiet, but some kids knew more than they ever told. Jason McMaster was the boy who found the body."

"Poor kid. That must've been awful."

"The teacher wasn't just strangled, Polly. He was naked from the waist down and appeared to have been engaged in a sexual act just before he died."

"Oh, Lord."

"His name, in case you're wondering, was Amato. Tony Amato. He had a son, Rico."

Thirty-Four

CAT: *Hurt yourself, did you? Is that why you're crying? / The noise that you're making, you'd think you were dying.*
-The Glass Flute, Scene vi

It was a close fit. Rico Amato, my latest best friend, had the means, the motive and the opportunity for most of the weird stuff that had happened.

Rico had been at the theatre since the first day of rehearsal, and he knew the schedule, the ins and outs of the building and where things were kept. He could easily have defaced the daisy puppet while we were rehearsing. He could have been harbouring a smouldering anger at the person (if there had been one) who had strangled his dad, or at least at the situation that had robbed him of his father. I knew he had grown up in Laingford, moved away and then moved back. That was really all I knew. Rico didn't talk about his family very much.

Maybe Rico had arranged the whole seduction scene with Shane on Sunday night, to set the stage. Maybe he had somehow managed to go back to the theatre after I had dropped him off at his antique shop in Cedar Falls. Maybe he thought Jason, being the one to find his father's body, was responsible, too, so he killed Jason and tried to implicate Shane. A lot of maybes, though.

"It does make sense, Polly," Becker said, as I thought it

through out loud. "If McMaster and Pacey were somehow involved in Amato's death, it makes a sick kind of sense for his son to avenge it and clear his father's name. Nobody likes to have their Dad branded a pedophile, even if it is true. Pacey never spilled the beans about what was going on, but McMaster did. Seems this 'Mr. A.' was a bit of a kiddy diddler, and Jason and Shane were his favourite little friends. Pacey denied it."

Becker produced a folded paper from his jacket pocket. "Look," he said, "this is from the Laingford High School yearbook, 1989." It was a photocopy of an "In Memoriam" page. A school staff headshot of Rico's father was ringed in black, along with a poem written by one of his drama students, and a cast photo from *Hamlet: The Rock Musical.* Front and centre in the photo was "Mr. A.," with his arms around the shoulders of Jason McMaster and Shane Pacey. I pulled the scrap of paper I'd found in the puppet-mouth out of the back flap of my notebook. They matched, of course. Now that I knew the circumstances, the look in the eyes of the boys was no longer full of teenaged fun, the way it appeared in the torn-out scrap. Now, they both looked haunted. The problem is that the haunted look may easily have been in my imagination, or in Becker's. The power of suggestion is a dangerous thing. Look at any newspaper photo, cover the caption at the bottom with your hand and tell yourself that the photograph is of a criminal. Immediately, the eyes go shifty and the face takes on a sinister aspect. Just because a young Jason McMaster had told the police that Rico's dad had molested him, it didn't necessarily make it true.

"I guess Earlie's talking to Rico right now, is he?" I said. "How are you going to prove any of this?"

"We can't," Becker said. "All we can do is try to find out if

Amato went back to the theatre after you dropped him off that Sunday night. Some of the other incidents—the things you call 'weirdness' may or may not have been Amato's doing, but they're not crimes. One thing's for sure, though. We're not falling for the trick of being made to suspect Pacey."

"He'll be relieved," I said. "And Rico—he'll be free to go after you talk to him?"

"I imagine so," Becker said. "Unless he confesses."

"He's not likely to do that," I said. Privately, I knew he wouldn't confess, because he hadn't done it. But I wasn't planning to say so to Becker. It might bring out the bully in him. If Rico was safe for the time being, then I'd just have to work a bit harder, trying to figure out who really had killed Jason McMaster.

Becker paid our tab and stood up. I stood up, too, so I could look him in the eye.

"Morrison will have taken Amato aside, first," Becker said. "I told him not to break up the party, but talk to each person individually. You know, ask if anyone saw Amato back at the theatre after you left. All we need is one ID and we've got him."

"And if nobody did see him?"

"Then we take another tack," Becker said. "Or it may end up like the death of 'Mr. A.', death by misadventure. That would have a kind of poetic justice, now, wouldn't it?"

I did a double-take. "Did you just say poetic justice?" I said. He smiled. "Yup," he said. "You aren't the only artsy-fartsy around here, you know."

"After Morrison gets through questioning the people at Steamboat, I'll bet I'm the only friend Rico's got left, though," I said.

"That may be true," Becker said. He didn't sound particularly regretful.

"I don't suppose it would do any good at all to tell you I think you're barking up the wrong tree, would it?"

"Arf, arf," Becker said.

"What about Jason's notebook? The one I told you about that has all the dirty laundry notes in it about the Steamboat staff?"

"I think that Jason McMaster wasn't a very nice young man," Becker said, "but he didn't deserve to die for being a gossip, and I don't think that's why he died. I think he died because he said some nasty things, probably true, about a drama teacher who messed with him ten years ago."

"What do his parents think?" I said.

"They believe it was an accident, and we're not going to tell them anything different until we know for sure," he said. "And if I hear that you've been in touch with them during their time of grief, Polly Deacon, you're in deep shit."

"Not even a sympathy card?" I said.

"*Nada.* I mean it."

"You're bullying me again."

"Your fault," he said. Then, just to screw me up completely, he glanced around to make sure there was nobody watching, then he kissed me. What's worse, I kissed him back—a lot. There we were, on the patio of the Rock Cut Steak House, necking. Dammit, I'm an idiot.

Being the pushy, nosy friend that I am, I decided to drop in on Rico on my way home. I didn't really have the energy to talk to him, and I needed what little head-room I had left for the show the next day, but I suspected he'd be a little freaked out and would appreciate the support.

There was a light burning in the upstairs apartment over the Tiquery, so I left Luggy sleeping in the truck and knocked quietly on the door. The footsteps that I heard coming down the stairs were unsteady, and when Rico opened up, I could see why.

"Polly," Rico said. "S'nice to see you. Cops send you round to check up on me?" A thick wave of booze-breath enveloped me.

"Nobody sent me, Rico. I just wanted to make sure you were okay."

"Oh, I'm maaahvellous, dahling. Why wouldn't I be? That nice big policeman asked me all kinds of personal questions and practically accused me of murdering Jason. Very nice evening."

"You want to talk about it? Can I come in?"

Rico regarded me gravely, teetering a little bit. He was really very drunk. I'd never seen him like that. In spite of the fact that he made his own wine and tippled regularly, he was usually pretty controlled. "Well, you know, I don't think so," he said, after a moment. "I'm not very good company right now. I'm having a private party, you might say, and you're not invited."

"I had nothing to do with this, Rico," I said.

"Oh, I'm sure you didn't mean to," he said. "Keeping secrets in bed is never easy."

"What the hell is that supposed to mean?"

"It means be careful what you say to people who fraternize with policemen," he said. "And don't expect them to keep you in the loop, even if it means you're prime suspect number one. Thanks, Polly. I was going to come to the show tomorrow, you know, to provide moral support, but I find I've lost my taste for the theatre just at present. Goodnight, dear. Sleep tight." He closed the door in my face, and I stood there, stunned, listening to him make his way slowly back up the stairs. I couldn't believe it. Rico, my "best friend" Rico, believed that

I'd ratted him out to the cops. Not that ratting him out was possible, because there was nothing that I knew that would have put them on to him in the first place, was there? Feeling horribly snubbed and inexplicably guilty, I returned to the truck and headed home. Rico wouldn't be at the show tomorrow. I felt like it was my fault.

Luggy was fast asleep beside me. He hadn't stirred when I climbed back into the cab at the Steak House, and I figured he was exhausted. All that laundry scent, probably. I didn't want to disturb him.

When I got to George's, Susan's car was there. It was filled with boxes. The move had begun, then, and there was nothing I could do to stop it. I wished I felt more positive about it. After all, the two people I loved most in the world were embarking on an exciting journey together. I just couldn't shake the feeling that they'd bought passage on the Titanic.

"C'mon, Luggy. Let's go to bed," I said, opening the passenger door so he could jump down. He didn't even bat an eyelid. "Lug-nut?" Nothing.

Oh, I'm probably overreacting, as usual, I thought. I reached over and shook him and when I got no reaction, I slipped into immediate full-blown panic.

Thirty-Five

WOODSMAN: *He lives in that cave over there by that tree /*
Dragons hide 'till it's dark, which is when they can see.
-The Glass Flute, Scene ix

Susan later said I'd been incoherent.

"Now you know what it feels like when your child is hurt, and there's nothing you could have done to prevent it. Reminds me of when you collided with that tree on your toboggan," she said helpfully. We were sitting in the vet's office at midnight. Luggy was having his stomach pumped. I still have a scar from the toboggan episode. I just hoped my dog would get off equally as lightly.

The vet said that Luggy had ingested a narcotic of some sort, and a lot of it was absorbed into his system by the time we got him to the emergency animal clinic in Laingford. We had to carry him in. He was totally unconscious and I was crying so hard that Susan had to do the talking.

"I wouldn't be surprised if that evil man next door had put down rat poison for him," Susan said.

"Rat poison affects the canine in a rather permanent way," the vet said. "This is a sedative of some sort, but powerful. Did he get into your medicine cabinet?"

"He's been with me all day, and it can't have been the Neighbour from Hell," I said, between hiccups. "Luggy was already unconscious when I got to George's. I thought he was asleep in the van when I came out of the restaurant in Sikwan. He must have eaten whatever it was much earlier."

"You keep sleeping pills in your van, maybe?" the vet said. "Look, you'll have to wait out in the other room while we wash out his insides. It's not very pleasant."

"He'll be okay?"

"I expect so, but we have to work on him now," the vet said. It was Dr. Singh on call that night, a very young vet who handled his patients with a gentle firmness that was remarkable to watch. He specialized in farm animals, but occasionally put in time in the small animals emergency clinic. I'd seen him sew up a gash on Julian of Norwich's udder with such deftness she didn't even notice, just nibbled his hair and muttered goat nothings into his ear. Luggy was in good hands.

Out in the waiting room, Susan made the toboggan remark, which I think was supposed to make me feel better.

"I guess someone could have tossed a poisoned scrap of meat or something in the van window while I was in the Rock Cut," I said. "But why would they do that? How would they know I was there?"

"What were you doing at the Rock Cut? That's hardly a hang-out for actors," Susan said.

"I was being interviewed by Mark Becker," I said. "Don't ask." Susan drew breath for another remark, then thought better of it. She could hardly have ragged on about how bad policemen were after her testimony of the night before. However, her natural distrust of cops was still there, below the surface. If I told her about his conclusions concerning Rico, she'd start ranting, and though I might agree with her, I didn't have the energy for it.

"It's more likely that your dog got into something at the

theatre," Susan said. "Maybe he nibbled on some explosives."

"That stuff's kept locked up in a box, and anyway, it was in the van with the rest of the set," I said. "The only thing that wasn't packed away was the serpent puppet, which is still down in the workshop. That and the laundry." The laundry. The green garbage bag full of stinky costumes that had inexplicably rolled down the stairs by itself. I remembered Luggy attacking it while I let Becker into the theatre, and our subsequent search of the rehearsal hall upstairs for an intruder. The dog had ripped the bag apart, I thought, because of the compelling whiff of thespic sweat, but perhaps there had been something else in there. Something yummy, laced with a substance guaranteed to be bad for dogs. I was immediately certain of this, and with that certainty came extreme, red-rimmed anger. Someone had deliberately tried to hurt my dog. Whoever it was would pay, big time.

Dr. Singh emerged from the inner sanctum, looking cheerful. "Well, we got the stomach all cleaned out. You don't feed him table scraps, do you?"

"Never," I said. "It encourages begging."

"I thought not. Most of what was in there was high-grade kibble. But there was a chunk of raw meat in there, too, barely chewed. That's the saving factor. If he'd chewed it, we might have been in a bit of a pickle. I'll analyze it for you, but I think you can be fairly certain that someone slipped him a bit of doctored beef."

"I thought so," I said. "He'll be all right, then?"

"I'd like to keep him here overnight for observation," the vet said. "Call me tomorrow around noon. He should be alert by then."

"Can I see him?" Okay, I know this Dr. Kildare stuff is maudlin and perhaps overdramatic, but you have to understand that Lug-nut, whom I'd had for less than a year, was the love of my life. Only a dog, you say? I don't think so.

He was wired up to an IV drip, like a fuzzy extra on ER, and his tongue flopped out the side of his mouth in cartoon, dead-dog fashion.

"They all do that," Dr. Singh said. "Totally relaxed, that's all." I kissed Luggy's head and whispered something I'd rather not admit to into his ear.

"Attached to that dog, aren't you?" Susan said on the drive back. We'd taken her car, so I could hold Luggy in my lap on the way there. Susan's glove-compartment is full of unpaid speeding tickets, and she has more demerit points than a shopaholic has Air Miles. We made it to the vet's in about six minutes, but now she drove more circumspectly.

"Yeah, Susan. We're joined at the hip," I said. I told her about my suspicions concerning the laundry, and then filled her in on the Becker/Rico theory. As expected, she ranted. I waited until she'd run out of steam.

"At least they haven't arrested him," I said. "They've got no evidence to speak of, and you and I both know that there's no way Rico Amato would hurt anybody or anything. What I want to find out tomorrow is whether everybody at Steamboat went to the Falls Motel last night while I was waiting for Becker, or whether somebody stayed behind. I'll bet you it wasn't Rico."

"Of course it wasn't. That nice little man? Honestly, I don't know why we bother with policemen at all."

"Oh, they have their uses," I muttered. I was starting to fade. It was well after midnight now, and I had a show the next day. I said my goodnights and stumbled up the hill to my cabin. It was awfully lonely and quiet without Luggy. I locked my door, made sure the windows were shut and went to bed.

The fact that Laingford High School hadn't changed very much shouldn't come as a surprise to anyone who has had the misfortune to return to their alma mater after a fifteen-year gap. It was smaller than I remembered it, of course, and more depressing. The lockers were still painted the same old military green, and the hallways were still filled with surly teenagers in packs, leaning up against the walls and making comments about passers-by. The office (in which I'd spent next to no time, having been a "browner" with perfect attendance) still made me feel nervous, and the cafeteria (which my friends and I had avoided as enemy territory) still smelled of mashed potatoes and sour milk. In order to get our *Glass Flute* gear to the gym, which was on the third floor and didn't have any access doors, we had to carry everything up two flights of stairs and through a maze of hallways. A six-pack of Laingford High hockey team members had been dispatched to help us. They were very glad to do it, as the assignment effectively excused them from class, and so the load-in took less time than we'd expected. Because of this, we had over an hour to put everything together, which left the cast more time to fret than was healthy.

They had been told about Jason. Morrison had told them the night before, I suppose in order to justify the questions he had asked about Rico. Predictably, nobody had seen Rico at the theatre after I left with him on Sunday night. That left the field open in terms of who dunnit. The cast was subdued and not inclined to chatter about it. Amber was preoccupied. She had left her puppy at the motel with the daughter of the owner.

"I'm paying her prime babysitting rates," she said, "and she's going to give Portia a bath." Best of luck to her, I thought. Amber patted her little belly and smiled, rather sadly. "I guess I'll be keeping the baby," she said privately to me. I wondered if she were trying to imply that the baby was Jason's. Not that it was any of my business, but I had a feeling that when the child was born, it would be blonde and gorgeous, just like Shane Pacey. Amber's decision to keep the baby didn't surprise me. After a week of looking after an infant creature, even if it's just a puppy, the maternal juices are shaken, not stirred. Shane, Amber, Portia and the baby would make a lovely family. It occurred to me that Juliet might have encouraged Amber to get the puppy in order to set the stage for this decision. Maybe the director was a closet pro-lifer or something.

I had gone in early to get the show laundry done at the twenty-four-hour laundromat in Sikwan. None of the costumes appeared to have been chewed, which was a blessing, and when the cast arrived for their eleven o'clock call, I didn't bother telling them about the walking laundry bag incident of the night before. I received various versions of the Falls Motel Pub interrogation, and Shane wasn't speaking to me, so I guessed that Morrison hadn't been easy on him. He had dark circles under his eyes.

Meredith had asked pointedly where our canine companions were. Amber explained her puppysitting arrangements, and I just said that Luggy was taking a sick day.

"Oh, He's not well?" Meredith said. There was an evil little smile on her face.

"Just a touch of stomach trouble," I said, watching her carefully.

"Huh. Must have been something he ate," she said. "That's what happens when you let dogs loose in a theatre. They get into all sorts of things they shouldn't." I wanted to strangle her right there, but I controlled myself. I knew she hadn't liked the dogs being around, but I wouldn't have thought she'd actually stoop to poisoning Lug-nut just to have a dog-free show day.

I resolved to ask Brad later if Meredith had arrived late at the pub. I was almost certain she was my laundry ghost.

After the set was erected and the puppets and props pre-set, we still had tons of time to kill. Shane and Amber ran lines, Meredith and Brad worked on the Mother and Woodsman "happily-ever-after" scene, and I deked outside for a smoke.

I took the eerily familiar route through various basement hallways, past the machine and woodworking shops to the lower back entrance of the school, what we used to call "the north doors". When I had been at Laingford High, the north doors were the official student smoking area. Now, of course, students are prohibited by law from smoking on school property, but fifteen years ago, the administration was mature enough to recognize that teenagers will smoke no matter what the rules are. Allowing them to do it in an out-of-the-way place which was theirs kept the sight of adolescent vice away from the disapproving eyes of the local townspeople, and probably made them smoke less. Now, high school students smoke while walking to and from school. They light up as soon as they cross the school property border and are generally more public (and subsequently more defiant) about it. Back in the old days, teachers had been known to join the students occasionally for a pre-class puff. Now, if they're seen smoking at all anywhere near the school, they get hauled up before the teacher's council. Progress. Go figure.

Our audience was arriving. A couple of yellow school buses had arrived at the bottom of the hill behind the school, and a line of men, women and children was trudging up the path.

"They could at least have dropped them off at the front," I muttered to nobody in particular. Making them walk up the hill as the high school students were expected to do didn't seem quite fair. Especially since long, forced marches were supposed to have become a thing of the past for these people. When they got closer, I could see that there was a festive air about the procession, though. There were smiles and some laughter.

Leading the group was Laingford's mayor, Gord Staples. I was glad to see that he had obviously chosen to slum it on the bus with his guests, rather than to arrive in his Lincoln. He was a large man, and the short climb was making him sweat. His round, florid face was glistening, and he dabbed at it with a big white handkerchief. He was deep in conversation with a handsome, middle-aged man wearing a Nike t-shirt and a tweed jacket.

I expected that it would take some time to get the audience settled in the gym. In fact, if they were going to enter the school via the warren behind the north doors, it could take upwards of an hour to round them up. Instead of stepping on my half-finished smoke and scurrying up to warn the actors that showtime was approaching, I elected to stay put.

Staples didn't recognize me. He frowned as I held the door open for him. "Shouldn't you be in class?" he said. I took it as a compliment.

As the group swept past me into the building, I noticed one or two of the Kosovars glancing briefly and longingly at my cigarette. Long ago, the Red Cross used to include cigarettes with the packages they sent prisoners of war, along with chocolate and wool socks. The military supplied "gaspers" to soldiers on the front lines; it was considered part of the survival gear. Since tobacco is considered Public Health Enemy Number One these days, it seemed highly unlikely that our Balkan guests were getting free smokes. We had supplied them with infinite wardrobes (I'd heard that literally tons of second-hand clothing had been donated to the refugee relief effort) and adequate food (I'd seen the donation boxes at the local Lo-Mart), but I had no idea whether they were being given any Canadian cash for sundries. Even if they were, I'd bet they'd feel horribly guilty spending it on cigarettes.

One member of the audience-group hesitated at the door after the others had gone in, looking at me inquiringly. I had no idea know how to say "hello" in Albanian, so I smiled and proffered my smokes. He was about my age, I think, but a much older man dwelled behind his eyes. He took a cigarette from the package and carefully lit it with my disposable Bic, cupping the flame against a wind that wasn't there.

"Thank you," he said.

"I hope you'll like our play," I said. I spoke slowly, in that cautious, too-loud speech one can't help using after one has been told that the person to whom we are speaking may have trouble understanding.

"You are from the theatre?" he said. "I thought so. I want to ask you something." I immediately felt like a dink for assuming that his English was limited to "thank you".

He told me his name was Ari, and that he had come to Canada with his wife and daughter and his younger brother.

"My brother worked in a theatre in Belgrade," Ari said. "We heard there was a theatre in the next town, and Negjib, my brother, was excited. He thought he could get work there. It is bad for us not to work."

"I'll bet it's frustrating," I said. "Well, you never know. There could be something for him. Tell him to come by."

"That is what I am asking you," Ari said. "He went to visit your theatre six days ago. He has not come back. Have you seen him?"

Thirty-Six

DRAGON: *It comes upon me suddenly, this need to belch forth flame / I've tried to stop, but instinct wins, and barbecue's my game.*
-The Glass Flute, Scene ix

"Did you call the police?" I said. The man's eyes widened, and he shook his head

"We are afraid," he said. "The police—not a good word for us." He didn't need to elaborate. I'd read about the police in Kosovo, and how some of them treated ethnic Albanians. Their distrust of our force would be heart-deep, no matter how compassionately the matter was handled.

"Have you told anybody? The mayor?"

"We hoped he would return. Negjib is young, he likes to go by himself sometimes and play tricks on us. My brother is an unusual person. He is maybe exploring."

"There are a lot of deep woods out here," I said. "Exploring in bug season may not be a very good idea."

"He did say he wanted to visit your theatre. He knew it was in the next town. Are you sure you have not seen him?"

"I'll ask the rest of the cast and crew. We should go up, anyway. I have a show to do." On the way I explained to Ari about the pyrotechnics in the show and suggested he pass the word around before the lights went out. "They're pretty and not too loud," I said, "but they might frighten some people if they were unexpected."

"Thank you for telling me. I will ask Uvo to make an announcement." Uvo must be the guy the mayor had been talking to.

Backstage, the cast was in a predictable state of hyper nervousness.

"Where have you been?" Ruth asked. "Brad's freaking out, and Meredith and Shane are ready to kill each other."

"Why?"

"One of Brad's costumes is missing, he says. Shane said it didn't matter, because he only needs one per show—unless he was planning to sweat so much that he'd need the second one after the first number. Brad wasn't amused, and Meredith called Shane an unprofessional jerk."

"That's mild, for her." I went over to the cast and apologized for my absence, explaining that I'd been out warning our audience about the flashpots. I didn't tell them that some of our audience appeared to speak English after all. Why contribute to the pressure?

"Polly, my backup costume is missing," Brad said.

"I know. Ruth told me. I expect it's a laundry mix-up. We'll find it. Don't worry. As long as you're covered for this performance." I didn't try to placate Shane and Meredith, because the tension back there was thick enough to chew on, and I guessed that any remark from me would precipitate a blow-up.

"Ten minutes, please," I said, and received a chorus of grunts from the cast. Out front, a man, presumably the one called Uvo, stood and spoke briefly to the audience in their language. His speech was beautiful to listen to, a kind of dark maroon, liquid cascade of words, remarkably vowel-free, like the pronouncements of some noble and ancient bird. There was a mild sensation from the gathered Kosovars and a murmur afterwards.

"That would be the flashpot warning, I gather," Ruth said. "Hope we don't lose anybody."

"Better safe than sorry. Five minutes, please."

"I'd better go out front," Ruth said. "Have a good show, you guys. Break a nail."

Juliet came back to wish us luck. "This is an important moment for Steamboat Theatre," she said. "It's a chance to cross borders and share our culture. Maybe we'll get a European tour out of it."

"You want us to go to Yugoslavia?" Shane said. "Thanks a lot."

"Maybe not now, but you know what I mean," Juliet said. "It's called networking, dear. Have a good one." Off she went, and Shane shook his head as she disappeared behind the side curtain.

"Our employer is insane," he said. "How 'bout it, guys? Shall we extend the tour and take a detour to the Balkans? We could set up in a bomb crater and do theatre in the round."

"You're one sick puppy," Brad said.

"Two minutes, please. Have a good show, you guys, and don't worry. It'll be great," I said.

"Wait! Group hug," Amber said.

Once again, we did our weird, circle-shuffle thing. It calmed us all. Rituals, however fresh, will do that quite handily. I'd decided to watch from out front for the opening sequence before slipping backstage to prompt. The first public benefit performance of *The Glass Flute* was about to begin.

I held the lights until the mayor finished his introductory speech. Staples was known to be long-winded and a little pompous. Perhaps that's one of the things they teach you in mayor-school. He introduced Juliet and the chairman of the board and various other dignitaries. He welcomed the Kosovar audience and cracked a couple of little jokes that received no response at all, so either Kosovar humour was a little different from Gord Staples's, or Ari and Uvo were the only ones who spoke English.

The opening sequence of the *Flute* is quite lovely. After the lights went out, (which produced a couple of small whimpers from one or two children in the audience), Ruth played a bewitching lullaby. The UV lights were switched on in darkness when there was nothing on stage, so you didn't notice them out front. Then the moon appeared, a huge, cheery, comical face, bright blue. It got a gasp and giggles from the children. I love it when something I've designed gets a good response. I suppressed a grin and settled down to watch the scene and take notes while I could. As the music changed, the moon was jostled, then bumped from the sky by an equally comical, large orange sun. Blades of grass poked up from the black velvet ground and whispered to each other, flowers bloomed from nowhere and entwined and a couple of cheeky birds did a dance across the sky. It was a morning scene that would translate into any language, any culture. Pure, innocent magic.

Using a series of progressively larger cardboard cutouts of Kevin and Mother's house, which appeared, then disappeared behind black flags, the audience was treated to a puppetry-version of a close-up zoom. The outdoors scenery was whisked away, and we were inside Mother's bedroom. The first dialogue scene started, and I slipped backstage.

"Great opening," I whispered to a hooded figure, who emerged from the playbox and deposited a black flag in the flag stand. The figure nodded, grabbed a fluorescent butterfly and went back on. Amber, then. She'd make the butterfly flit around the bedroom and eventually land on Mother's head.

Another hooded actor came out carrying the Mother puppet in the bed. Meredith. I took the pieces from her (they're awkward) and received a muttered thanks.

The scene went smoothly and we were on to the next. Someone came off with the bedroom window piece, saying "Shit, shit, shit" under his breath. Brad. The window sill had come apart, and he'd had to hold it together onstage. He dumped the prop and grabbed the Woodsman puppet and went back on.

Shane came back, carrying the Kevin puppet. He had a sixty-second break before Kevin's next entrance, and he took the opportunity to lift the front of his hood and take a swig from his water bottle. The water bottles, white plastic sports jugs with each actor's initial painted in huge black letters on the sides so they could be seen backstage when you were wearing a hood, were their own responsibility. They were filled and set on a small table at the back of the stage. Shane sputtered after he drank.

"Jesus!" he gasped, then rushed back onstage. As he passed me, I caught a distinct whiff of gin. Gin? At one-thirty in the afternoon during a performance? I checked the bottle marked "S". Gin it was. If Shane had planted it himself, Meredith wasn't far wrong when she called him an unprofessional jerk. Drinking before or during a show was absolutely and utterly taboo. I hid the bottle and fumed inwardly.

Some time later, when all four cast members were on stage doing the Princess/Kevin/Woodsman/Cat scene, I detected a movement out of the corner of my eye. I looked over towards the side curtain and saw a small figure standing there in the dim blue backstage light. A child, with its hand in its mouth. I moved quickly over to it.

"No, sweetheart. Go back. Not allowed." Closer, I guessed

it was a little girl, of about eight or nine, with huge dark eyes and a solemn expression. She answered in something that wasn't English.

"I know you don't understand, but you shouldn't be here," I said, trying to guide her back through the stage door she had obviously slipped through. Why wasn't she being supervised?

She balked and repeated what she had said before, a little louder.

"I'm sorry. I don't understand," I said. Then an adult appeared. It was Ari.

"I'm sorry," he whispered and admonished the girl gently.

"It doesn't matter. But it's not safe back here. Maybe she wants a bathroom."

"I will take her," Ari said.

"Negjib," the girl said, distinctly. Ari replied in the negative and led her away, speaking softly to her. I imagined that her uncle Negjib, Ari's brother who worked in the theatre back in Belgrade, had probably taken her backstage a time or two. That would explain how she figured out how to get back there. Perhaps she was stage-struck already. Neat.

A hooded figure came offstage, and then another. Back and forth, the actors executed their moves. The show behind the scenes was as intricate and involved as the one the audience saw. There were times when the pace was so fast, the flurry of activity so complicated, that it looked as though there were six or seven actors instead of four.

The first flashpot went off without a hitch. It was the small one that heralded the dropping of the serpent out of the tree in front of Kevin. There was a gasp from the audience, but no screams or crying. It was an admiring gasp, and I thanked Providence for giving me the chance to warn the audience. I also wondered if Juliet had been right, and I was underestimating the fortitude of our guests.

The second flashpot went well too. That's the one that the cat uses, to perform a magic trick. Lots of glitter, not a lot of bang.

It was in the Dragon scene that things started to go wrong. Shane was late for his first entrance and Brad, playing the Dragon, got flustered. Ruth did a vamp on the keyboard, stalling for time. Amber, who was working the Princess puppet, came offstage in a flap, hissing "Where's Shane, dammit?" Shane appeared from behind the wings on the other side, staggering a bit.

"Feeling sick," he muttered behind his hood. "Threw up over there." He blundered onstage and the scene went on. Shane's voice was slurred, and he wasn't picking up his cues.

"I thought I smelled booze on him," Amber said bitterly. "I'll kill him. He's allergic to anything stronger than beer, and he knows it." She shook the Princess puppet as if it were her fellow actor and stormed back onstage.

I figured the puke, wherever Shane had left it, could wait until after the show. Maybe I'd suggest he clean it up himself. I whispered a puke alert to the hooded actor on the other side.

Shane was late again on his second entrance. He was supposed to go off stage left and grab Kevin's knapsack, then come back on, produce the flute and play a tune that would vanquish the Dragon, who would blow a final fiery blast and expire. I heard Ruth vamping with the music again, and heard Amber doing a creditable job of ad-libbing as the Princess, telling the Dragon that Kevin would be back any second. He wasn't. I could also hear that Brad was panicking. His roars were getting high-pitched.

Then the Dragon flashpot exploded. I could see the glare from backstage—it lit up the entire area—a great, blinding orange flash, accompanied by a noise that was far, far too loud. Then the screaming started.

Thirty-Seven

DRAGON: *The legends about me? They're all of them true /
I'm grumpy and mean when there's nothing to do.*
  -The Glass Flute, Scene ix

Hell happened for a little while. Brad, Meredith
and Amber came roaring backstage, all of them shouting.
Brad's costume was smoking. The force of the mass exodus
knocked the whole structure off-balance, and it fell with a
creaking thump, tangling everybody in black velvet. Brad
ripped off his hood (thank God everything was flame-
proofed—he'd have been shish-kebab otherwise) and trampled
on it, and we patted him down. Amber was emitting little,
repetitive shrieks until Meredith, who had also ripped off her
hood, grabbed her and hugged her hard to make her stop.

With the playbox in a state of collapse, we had a clear view
of the audience. Someone had pulled the fire alarm and the
clang was deafening. Out in the hallways, the thunder of
evacuating students could be heard. Several peeked in the
doors before being shooed away. Most of the Kosovar guests
had fled, someone had turned on the lights in the auditorium,
and Juliet and Tobin were making for the stage.

I grabbed a nearby extinguisher and aimed a cascade of
white foamy stuff over the mass of black velvet curtains, some
of which were smouldering. Ruth was onstage already.

"Where's Shane?" she asked.

We found him, half buried under the stage left curtains. He was lying on his belly, legs splayed awkwardly, the Kevin puppet still clutched in his hand. An audio cable was tied tightly round his neck, and he wasn't breathing.

Ruth flipped him over, cut the cord with her Swiss Army knife and started CPR. Brad jumped in with artificial respiration, and I called 911 on my cellphone.

"How much powder did you put in that damn flashpot?" Tobin said. "Someone could have been seriously injured." I glanced significantly towards the floor, where Ruth and Brad were hard at work on Shane. They didn't seem to be getting anywhere.

"The show was going so well," Juliet said. "Now it's all ruined."

"Is Shane going to be all right?" Amber said.

"Meredith, you didn't by chance substitute gin for the water in Shane's bottle, did you?" I said. "As a joke, I mean?"

"Why the hell would I want to do that?" Meredith said. "I'm not an idiot."

"He's allergic to alcohol," Amber said.

"He had a beer last night," Meredith pointed out.

"Anything more than beer and he gets really sick," Amber said. "He wouldn't drink gin on purpose."

"It wasn't gin that throttled him with an audio cable," I said.

In spite of the fire alarm, some of the Kosovar audience members had come back into the auditorium and were milling around in groups, watching the stage area but haunting the rear exit. Many of the children appeared to be crying.

The mayor came up to the apron of the stage and told us that he'd ordered the school buses to pick them up at the front of the school as soon as possible.

"This has been traumatic," Staples said severely. "We have to get them out of here." Juliet hopped down to talk to him. I gathered this accident wasn't going to do Steamboat Theatre much good, PR-wise. When the ambulance, fire department and police arrived, the Kosovars became very still and wary, like deer caught in the headlights, then most of them melted away. Someone finally turned off the alarm. The silence was deadly.

The ambulance people weren't able to revive Shane either, though they commended Ruth and Brad on their prompt action.

"He died some time ago," one of the paramedics said. "You guys didn't have a chance." Charming, I thought. Someone covered Shane with a blanket while Amber sobbed in Meredith's arms. Brad's left hand had been burned by the explosion and was tended to while Becker and Morrison (of course it would be them) asked questions. The firefighters, who had stormed in, wearing heavy gear and helmets, assessed the wet mass of curtains and foam and declared it safe, then tromped out again.

"Was Mr. Amato attending the performance?" Becker asked.

"No. He told me last night that your accusations had put him off theatre," I said. "He was drinking a little. I doubt he's anywhere now but in bed."

"Did you notice anyone backstage who shouldn't have been there?"

"Only one of the audience members. A child. She came back during the show, but her father came and took her back out front."

"Do you know who it was?"

"You don't think Shane was strangled by a Balkan baby, do you?"

"She may have seen something." I gave him Ari's name, then immediately regretted it as Rico's words of the night before came floating back to me: "Be careful what you say to people who fraternize with policemen." Still, I'd read enough whodunnits to know that withholding evidence never protects the people you're trying to help. I just hoped it would be Morrison and not Becker asking the questions. Maybe Ari would summon the courage to tell them about his brother's disappearance the week before.

"Wait," I said aloud. "The week before—that's when the weirdness started."

"Huh?" Becker said. I told him briefly about Ari's brother, Negjib, who had disappeared around the time that Jason had drowned at the Theatre. Not that I was happy suggesting that the horrors of the past week could be blamed on some poor youngster from Belgrade, but it was too much of a coincidence for there not to have been a connection.

"Where would I find this Harry character?" Becker said.

"Ari. No 'H'. He's one of our Kosovar refugees and he's afraid of the police. If you talk to him, try to be nice, okay?"

"Don't tell me how to do my job, Polly," Becker said.

"If Rico wasn't here, that lets him off, doesn't it?" I said.

"Look, right now, we've got another death connected with your theatre company, and as far as I'm concerned you're all under suspicion," Becker said. The ambulance guys were taking Shane away on a stretcher and we all stood forlornly, not knowing what to do. Brad heard Becker's remark.

"It couldn't have been any of us. We were all onstage," he said.

"Go over the sequence again for me," Becker said. We explained as best we could. With the playbox in a heap on the stage floor, it was difficult to describe what it had been like back there—how dark it was and how busy we all were. If

Shane was waiting in the wings stage left for his entrance, anyone could have come up behind him and strangled him, then slipped away. I told Becker as much.

"How long between Pacey's last time on stage and the explosion?" Becker said.

"Not more than a minute or two," I said.

"That's not a very big window of opportunity," he said. "The strangler must have had to know your show pretty well." I agreed. "And everybody was on stage for that two minutes except you, Polly?"

"Brad was doing the Dragon, Amber was the Princess and Meredith…" What had Meredith been doing? I couldn't remember.

"I was waiting with a black flag to make the flute disappear," Meredith said. "I was in the box, too."

That was weird, I thought. The flute disappearing was supposed to come after the Dragon fire. She hadn't needed to be in the box at all. Brad, Amber and I all looked at her.

"You were early," Amber said.

"I was nervous," Meredith said. Becker, who had been taking notes, was scribbling furiously.

"I'll need to take statements from everybody," he said. "At the station, I think."

"You're taking us all in?" Brad said. His voice cracked like a teenager's.

"Excuse me, officer. Can I interrupt for a moment?" Juliet was standing at the front of the stage, looking up. Becker went over to her. We closed ranks as if we were about to do our circle ritual.

"I didn't do it," Meredith hissed.

"We know you didn't," Brad said, but he didn't sound sure.

"Who did, then?" Amber said. "And what about the gin?"

"I saved the bottle. It's under the table in the cardboard box. I should give it to Becker, I guess."

"Your fingerprints will be all over it," Meredith said. The fact that one of us had just been murdered didn't seem to have registered with any of us yet. The energy-level within our circle was peaking, as if we were still in the middle of the show.

Becker came back. "The school needs the stage," he said. "You'll have to clear out your stuff."

"What? No yellow 'Police Line Do Not Cross' tape? No forensics?" I said.

"We don't work like that," Becker said. "There's nothing we can do here that we can't do at headquarters."

"I can't believe this. You've got the scene right here," I said.

"I'll make a sketch while you pack up," Becker said. "We can reconstruct it all later."

"What big, important thing is happening that the school needs the stage?" I said.

"Basketball tournament. Starts at three. Lots of teams coming in."

"Oh, gosh. We can't inconvenience the athletes, now, can we?"

"The mayor's son is on the Laingford High team," Becker said and walked away. My jaw hit my chest and stayed there for a moment. In small towns, sporting events rule, I guess.

It was the saddest strike and load-out I've ever experienced. Every little job that Shane used to do had to be done by somebody else. I tried to give the water bottle to Becker, but he wouldn't take it, he just made a note in his little book.

"Don't you want to analyze it?" I said. "Maybe there's poison in there, too."

"Pacey was strangled, not poisoned," Becker said. I stashed the half-full bottle in my paperwork box. My show report, I thought, was going to be a doozy.

Detaching the soggy curtains from the collapsed playbox and folding them was a big pain. We didn't find any clues hidden in the folds, though. Meredith and Brad stuffed them into their hockey bags as best they could and placed them at the foot of the stage, ready to haul back down to the van.

Under the table at the back of the stage, where the water bottles had been, I found the pyro box where I'd left it after setting the flashpots. The lock was gone, and most of the canisters were empty. Whoever had tampered with the Dragon flashpot had loaded it up in order to do damage, or at least to create a diversion. The question was, how did they know Brad would panic and trigger it early? Or was that just blind luck? I showed it to Tobin, who was standing against the stage right wall, his arms crossed, glowering at nothing.

"I told you to lock it every time," he said.

"I did, Tobin. It was a flimsy lock."

"Either that or someone else had a key."

"When would anyone have had time to doctor the flashpot after you did preset?"

I told him I'd gone out for a smoke and watched the audience arrive.

"You should have stayed with the set," he said.

"I could hardly have known what was coming," I said.

"You screwed up, Polly. If you'd been there, nobody could have messed with the flashpot or put booze into Shane's bottle."

"How did you know about the booze?" I said. He hadn't been in on our circle discussion of Shane's alcohol allergy.

"Amber told me," he said.

"When?"

"Just now. Look, Polly, don't try to shift the blame. Remember the old SM's answer to everything…'I'm sorry, it was my fault, it'll never happen again.' You could say that about now."

"I don't think it would help. And thanks for your support, Tobin." I walked away from him, fighting back the angry tears that were gathering at the base of my throat.

The load-out went quickly, because our hockey team reappeared. They were dying for details, and I heard several cast members filling the boys in as we carried the equipment down the stairs.

"Oh yeah? Shane Pacey, eh? I heard about him. He was a fag, right?" one of the boys said.

"Yeah," another boy said. "I heard he was screwing that drama teacher that died. Him and that other drama pussy. You know, the one that went crazy and had to go to North Bay?" I stopped listening. Ugly stuff. Obviously, the Incident lived on in the mythology of the school.

Becker showed up as we were packing away the last of the stuff. Kind of like when someone in your family grabs a dishtowel, just as you're polishing the last of the cutlery. We were all there, the cast, Juliet, Tobin, Ruth and me. We'd sent the homophobic hockey players back to math class. There we stood at the back door of the van, looking at each other, not saying much. Less than two hours before, we'd been high on pre-show jitters. Now one of us—well, two, I guess—were dead, and the show was doomed. The worst of it was that I knew darn well we were all in mourning, not so much for Jason and Shane, but for a good gig. *The Glass Flute* was toast. No matter who ended up being nailed for Shane's messy demise, and for Jason's drowning, the fact was that we were all out of a job. The fact that one of us was a murderer wasn't nearly as horrible.

"Well," Juliet said.

"Yeah," Tobin said.

"This is awful," Amber said.

"Tell me about it," Meredith said.

Brad grunted.

"I'm going to need to take statements," Becker said. "Shane Pacey's parents will have to be notified as well. Anyone know where they are?"

"They're both deceased," Juliet said. "I think he has an uncle in Toronto, though. I could check his file."

"Do that," Becker said. "But first, you will all have to come to the station, where we'll interview each of you separately."

"I want my lawyer present," Meredith said.

"Me, too," Brad said.

"And me," Amber said, but I think she was just joining in. I'd never had a lawyer in my life, so I didn't say anything.

"I'm not charging anybody," Becker said. "I just want to get the details down."

"You could have done that back up there at the scene of the crime, if you hadn't been so eager to make way for the mayor's son's basketball game," I said.

Becker exhaled, slowly.

"Where's Morrison?" I asked.

"Interviewing that Kosovo guy and his kid," Becker said. "Look, folks. This doesn't need to be this bad. Just come on in to HQ and we'll talk, okay?"

We piled into the van and spent the rest of the afternoon drinking bad police coffee and hanging out in the policeman's version of the greenroom as Becker talked to us one by one. He took me last.

"So, Polly Deacon. Here we go again," he said. He looked tired.

"Are you any closer to figuring this out?" I said.

"I think so. I've got a lot of background, now. And the rest of your crew were very helpful. Now explain how this show works again." I did so, going over and over the Sunday night party, the rehearsal period and the first and last performance of *The Glass Flute* with a fine-toothed Mark Becker comb. It certainly didn't add up to Rico any more. It didn't add up to anybody, actually.

Finally, Becker closed his notebook, shut off the tape recorder and told me I was free to go.

"So…what? You going to make an arrest?" I said.

"Probably. Maybe tomorrow. A few details to iron out. Go home and get some rest, Polly."

"Who, Mark?"

"Can't say. But I have to tell you that all those weird things that happened at the theatre do make sense, once you've got the big picture." I think he was talking through his hat. He had no more idea than I did.

"I can't go home yet," I said. "I have to pick up Luggy from the vet and unload the set." I'd told him about the Lug-nut poisoning incident. He hadn't even written it down. Insignificant, apparently.

"You have to unload it yourself?"

"Something tells me that the cast won't be in the mood. Tobin will help, I expect."

"Look, I'll finish up here and come down when I'm done," he said. "Don't go lifting that stuff by yourself."

"That's not in your job description, is it?"

"Nope. But I'd like to help. If you don't mind."

"Mind? Of course not. I'll see you there."

It was a nice note on which to end a really lousy day. I was probably smiling when I came out of there, but there was nobody to see it. The cast had bailed.

Thirty-Eight

KEVIN: *I'm not scared of fire and smoke / I'll play my flute and make you choke.*
-The Glass Flute, Scene ix

A lone young policewoman sat in the greenroom where Becker had sent her, perhaps to make sure that we didn't cook up stories amongst ourselves. Her name was Marie, and she had taken her job quite seriously, politely but firmly breaking up any conversations we tried to have by sidling over and standing there with a notebook.

"The other people said to say they'd all got a ride in your director's car," Marie said as I stood looking forlornly around the empty room.

"Did they say where they were going?" Marie shook her head. Home, probably, to pack up their gear, call their agents and get ready to leave Kuskawa forever. After the week from hell, it was unlikely that Brad, Meredith or Amber would want to do another show here. That is, if they were available to do one. One of them could very well have been destined for an extended run in a drama therapy group at a correctional institution, depending on whether or not Becker figured out who dunnit.

I knew Tobin had come in his own car and was probably back at the theatre. Either that or they were all back at the

Falls Motel Pub, drowning their sorrows. Would it matter that they'd all be wondering if one of them dunnit? Probably not. Actors are resilient.

The first thing I did was go to the Laingford Animal Hospital to get Luggy. Dr. Singh wasn't there, but the receptionist was glad to see me.

"Your dog's fine, now," she said. "He's been whining for you all day. We tried to phone you, but there was no answer." I had given them my cell phone number. I was surprised I hadn't heard it. I pulled out the infernal thing and checked it.

"The battery's dead," I said. "Sorry. It's been a difficult day. I should have checked in." I guess the 911 call that afternoon had drained the last of my cellular's energy. I knew how it felt.

There are few things quite as rewarding as the celebratory love-dance your dog does when he sees you after a separation. The back end whips back and forth in a puppy samba, the tail leaps about with a mind of its own, knocking things over, the eyes gleam and the mouth (at least in Luggy's case) drools and grins. We shared an exuberant few minutes on the floor of the vet's office, watched over by a benevolent receptionist.

"I never get tired of seeing that," she said. Then she immediately dampened my enthusiasm by handing me a bill for the emergency stomach pumping and an overnight stay. Good thing I had a week's pay coming. Yikes. The sooner Canada establishes medicare for pets, the better.

We headed for Sikwan and the theatre, Luggy sitting up in the passenger seat (he likes to wear a seat-belt), alert and full of Lugginess.

"When we get there," I said, "no eating anything you haven't run by me, first, okay?" Or, in Luggy-speak, "Blah, blah blah, etc." He pretended to understand, though. It's what I love about him.

Both Ruth's and Tobin's cars were in the parking lot, and there were some lights on in the Steamboat building. When there's an after-hours load-in to be done, you really get to know who your friends are.

"Sorry we left you there at the cop-shop," Ruth said, after I'd backed the van up to the door. "It's not the nicest place to hang out, and we didn't know how long you'd be. Marie, that policewoman, said Detective Becker considered you his star witness, whatever that was supposed to mean."

"Not a heck of a lot," I said. "Thanks for coming back here, though. If we'd been thinking straight, we would have loaded your equipment into your car back at the school. I guess we won't be needing it now."

"You never know. Juliet's talking about finding someone to replace Shane and continuing the tour," Tobin said.

"You're kidding. What do the others say?"

"I think they're too numb to consider it, at this point. And it depends on whether the police decide that one of us killed Shane and Jason. We may be looking for more than one replacement."

"Maybe three," I said. "You may want a stage manager who doesn't screw up and cause explosions and murders."

"Sorry about that," Tobin said. "Out of line, I know. I was just so mad."

"Yeah. Me, too. Let's talk about this later." At least he had apologized, not very gracefully, but it was probably all I was going to get. Besides, he had been right. If I hadn't given in to my nicotine addiction and left the stage for a smoke, we'd probably be having a first-night party instead of a wake.

"Where are the others?" I said.

"Falls Pub. I tried to get them to help with the load-out, but Juliet said she wanted to talk to them, and she was buying."

"I knew it. Sounds like conscription to me," I said. "Still, she can be persuasive."

It took us a fair bit of time to unload the equipment into the lobby, to be dealt with in the morning. Ruth's stuff, the keyboard, speakers and amp, all went into her Subaru.

"These cables are ours, aren't they?" Tobin said. "Aren't these the backups and replacements Polly got in town?"

"I guess so. Take 'em," Ruth said, wearily. I thought they were hers, actually, but neither of us had the energy to argue. Easier to buy more.

"Are you going to the pub?" I asked her.

"You kidding? After today, all I want is a hot bath and bed. Tell Juliet that if the show's still happening, I'll make the tapes for her, but I don't think I'm up for any more live performances."

"Will do," I said. Considering Ruth's celebrity status and all, she had been remarkably low-key about everything. I appreciated it, but I could see that she was sick of the whole business. Stuff like that doesn't happen when you have a top-notch road manager—the kind that Shepherd's Pie hires. It only happens when shows are run by vice-riddled dilettantes like me. She drove off, and Tobin and I headed back into the building.

Luggy balked at the door and refused to come in.

"Whatever happened to getting back on the horse after it's thrown you?" I said to him. He just sat there, looking at me and whining. "No laundry this time, Luggy. I promise." He still wouldn't budge. I relented and put him in the cab of the van, feeling sick and guilty. I wanted to keep him with me and watch him every moment. If he was flaked out again when I came back, I'd have to shoot myself.

"I'll just take these cables up to the sound storage room and then I'm out of here," Tobin said, heading for the stairs. "You going for a drink?"

"I don't think so," I said. "I have to take Luggy home."

I carried the pyro box down to the workshop. I was planning to stash it at the back of the paint cupboard for the time being, then try to convince Becker to have it checked for fingerprints. Ditto for Shane's water-bottle, which I also carried downstairs, wrapped in a towel so I didn't smudge the prints.

It was cool and pleasant down there. The water lapped gently at the sides of the pool, and someone, probably Tobin, had tidied up the worktables. There it all was, ready for the next show. In the middle of the worktable was an envelope with my name on it. From Juliet, I figured. Severance pay, perhaps. Quick work. I opened it, but there wasn't any money inside, just a typed letter on Steamboat Theatre letterhead.

"Dear Polly Deacon," it began. (Jeez, Juliet. If you're going to fire me, you could at least do it to my face, I thought, then read on.)

> Dear Polly Deacon:
> You don't know what it's like to be an outcast. You don't know what it's like to have someone you admire betray you. I know that by now you will know what happened at your old school back in 1985. But what you found out isn't the whole story.
> All I wanted to do was work in theatre. My Dad said it would turn me into a homosexual. It didn't do that. What it did do was hand me over to a monster. Mr. Amato was a great teacher. He was very friendly, and he had a couple of students that he'd invite into his office to hang out. I was

one of them. He gave us booze and cigarettes and stuff, and he was a lot of fun. By the time things got strange, it was too late to back out.

One of his students was really into S&M, and there were a couple of parties in his office that would make your hair stand on end. When he died, it was an accident, but it was his fault. He had it coming. It wasn't his death that ruined my life, it was what happened afterwards. There's more, but I want to tell you face to face.

That was it. No signature, no indication of who had written this sad, bewildering letter to me. I sat back and considered my options. To my left, over behind the blank wall next to the pool, came a sound like the scrabbling of mice...or rats. Mice I was cool with, but rats had a bad reputation, especially dock rats. I lifted my feet up and stared at the wall, expecting a four-pound, red-eyed bruiser to appear and come for me like a rodent-extra from a Stephen King movie. Slowly and quietly, the wall opened, revealing a door I'd never known existed.

Jason McMaster stepped out into the workshop.

Thirty-Nine

MOTHER: *Tell me all, my brave and clever boy / Your courage is a mother's pride and joy.*
-The Glass Flute, Scene x

I admit that I believe in ghosts, especially unshriven spirits that hang around in the places where they died, looking for absolution, or at least a convenient human out of whom to scare the poo. I was too frightened to scream.

"I thought you were supposed to be this shit-hot detective," Jason said. "You didn't get any of it, did you?" I just stared at him. He seemed to be pretty solid. No flickering. No banshee wailing. This must be a living, breathing person then, I thought. Relief flooded through me, and when I spoke, I was surprised to hear how calm I sounded.

"I was getting there, Jason. I was doing your job at the same time, and besides, I'm no detective. I'm just a backwoods puppet-maker."

"You were doing okay. I watched you."

"How? You got a camera set up somewhere?" Jason opened the secret door a little further and shined his Maglite in to reveal a narrow set of stairs leading up. The last time I'd seen the Maglite was in the pocket of his drowned vest in Juliet's office. I guess he'd rescued it.

"I discovered this passage on my second day here," he said.

"I think they used it to smuggle booze up to the attic from the boats that brought it in. It's really cool up there. There are spyholes all over the place."

"You've been up there the whole time?"

Jason nodded, grinning like a kid who's pulled off a particularly successful magic trick.

"Your parents think you're dead, you know. How could you do that to them?" I said.

"Oh, they don't care. They haven't for years. Not since the Incident."

"If you're standing here alive, then who did the cops drag out of the river and make your parents identify?"

"That's the thing of it," Jason said. "This guy shows up on Sunday afternoon, the spitting image of me, I swear. Some foreign dude who was looking for work. I told him to come back that night. That's what gave me the idea."

"You killed him to fake your own death, you mean."

"Yup. It wasn't hard. I took him by surprise." Jason's eyes, even in that dim light, showed the kind of blank pleasantness of someone who has no conscience. It was like he was talking about brushing his teeth or wiring a lighting cable—just a task that he had completed.

"So how come you faked your death?" I said, trying to match his tone to show him that I was just as blasé about the whole thing, just as unconcerned and not a bit frightened. My legs were tucked under me (the rat-thing) on one of the two big easy chairs we keep down in the shop for catnaps. Jason came across and curled up in the other one. Storytime.

"Lots of reasons," he said. He was carrying an audio cable, which he draped casually on the arm of the chair. I guess I could have made a dash for it, but I wasn't sure he was out to harm me, and I really wanted to know what had happened.

"After the Incident, I told the police and my parents about what Mr. A. used to do with us. Shane Pacey and a couple of the other guys said I was making it up. It was Shane who came up with the strangulation-thing. We'd take turns jacking off while someone else tightened the rope. If you're choking and coming at the same time, it's amazing. Mr. A. really liked it, but I told him it was dangerous. I think Shane was the one holding the rope when Mr. A. died. I told the police that, but it didn't help. Nobody believed me. It was obvious that Mr. A. was a sicko, they said, but they didn't believe any student could be involved. Afterwards, Shane and the others left school, but my parents made me stay. Everybody knew, and it was like I was a leper or something."

"That must have been a nightmare," I said.

"It was. I thought it would blow over, and I went for counselling and everything, but nobody would leave it alone. I got suicidal and tried to off myself. That's when my parents sent me to the North Bay facility."

"How was that?"

"Up there, they believed me, which was good. I did anger-management and lots of therapy stuff. They eventually said I was cured, and I went back home and then to Theatre School."

"You still wanted to work in theatre after all that?"

"Not much, really. I did it to piss off my Dad. It worked. He believed that the whole thing had turned me into a fag."

"Does he still think that?"

Jason chuckled. "My Dad thinks I'm dead, remember?"

"I mean, before."

"Yeah, he did. When I told him Amber and me were getting married, he couldn't believe it—that I even had a girlfriend. He told me to prove it, like I was going to bring her up here and fuck her in front of them or something."

"But you did agree to introduce them," I said.

"Yeah, that would have been good," he said, a little wistfully. "But as soon as I heard Shane was coming up to do the show, I knew it would fall apart. I was right, wasn't I? She's never gotten over him, eh? No matter how hard I tried, I was just kind of a fill-in."

I felt like a shrink or something. There we were, having this nice cosy chat on the comfy chairs at Steamboat, Jason telling me his life story. I was suddenly afraid that I would say the wrong thing, ask the wrong kind of question. He sounded so hopeless.

"So you went to Theatre School to piss off your Dad…"

"And to get away from Laingford. And wouldn't ya know it, when I got to Theatre School, there was Shane Pacey. Star actor. Got away scot free while I went nuts. God, I hated him, and it was obvious I couldn't get away from him."

"But you ended up with his girlfriend."

"Yeah. That felt great. After he dumped that other girl, he wanted Amber back, but I wouldn't let him have her. She was mine, but only for a while. A fill-in, like I said. You saw how quick she went back to him after I was dead. That was one of the reasons I set this whole thing up. To see what would happen. If I was going to marry her and be normal for once, I wanted to make sure it would work. If I could prove to my Dad I wasn't a fag, I'd inherit a whole bunch of money and we could start a theatre company together or something. But she had to really care about me. Turns out she didn't. I suspected that already. Shane was always around, even after we all graduated. I was always real careful to use protection with Amber, so I guessed her being pregnant wasn't me."

"So you faked your death and killed someone you didn't know, to test your girlfriend?"

"Sort of. Mostly I wanted Shane to go through what I went through. I figured he'd be the number one suspect, but then the body didn't show up and you all thought I just ran away. That burned me, Polly. So I started leaving clues. Talk about slow! Not only the police, but you, too, Polly Deacon. Miss hot-shit detective. Duhh."

"So how come you're telling me this, Jason?" I said.

"There were a lot of sick people up in North Bay," he said. "One guy had killed his Dad, eh? He said they caught him because he couldn't stand people not knowing how smart he was to get away with it. So he told his Mom."

"Well, you certainly fooled us," I said.

"Yeah, but I failed, as usual," Jason said. "Shane didn't suffer at all, even when I left puppets hanging around with audio cables around their necks. Pacey may be pretty, but he's stupid."

"Oh, he suffered, Jason."

"Well, he did today, anyway."

"You killed him at the school, I guess."

"That was me. Fooled you again, eh? I just blended in with the students and sneaked backstage. I put gin and some pills in his water bottle while he was necking with Amber on the track and field mats. They didn't even see me. Did your dog live, by the way?"

"Yes, Jason. He's okay."

"Oh. Guess the pills don't work on dogs, then. I wanted to test them. Worked slower than I thought, I guess. He sure went for the meat, though, eh?"

"He sure did."

"Anyway, I knew from the Mr. A. sessions that the gin would make Shane sick. When he was sick enough, I snuck up and throttled him. It was great. I don't know if he came or not, though. You think he did?"

"I doubt it."

There was a pause as we both contemplated the last moments of Shane's life—me with growing horror, and Jason, I think, with fondness. He was gazing off into the middle distance, a smile playing at the corners of his lips.

"Nice explosion, by the way," I said, to cover up the pounding of my heart.

"Thanks. One of my best. There are some things I'm good at. I like pyro."

We sat there quietly, just the two of us in the dim light of the workshop. I don't think I could have walked if I tried. And oddly, in spite of Jason's horrible story and sociopathic lack of remorse, I felt sorry for him. Not so sorry that I wouldn't have welcomed some backup, though. Tobin should have checked in by now, I thought.

"What do you want to do now, Jason? You want to go back to North Bay?"

"No way. The food sucks and they'd make me do anger management again. I'm too fucked-up, Polly. They'd keep me there forever."

"Your options are limited, you know."

"There's only one option, really, after everything that's happened. So, I was kind of hoping you'd help me on that."

"What do you mean?" To say I was feeling uneasy would be really inaccurate. Quickly, Jason formed a noose in the audio cable he had brought with him. I tensed for a battle. He was planning to strangle me, too, but it wouldn't be easy. I outweighed him by a good thirty pounds.

No battle. He slipped the noose around his own neck and unzipped his trousers.

"Oh, Jesus, Jason," I said, standing up.

"It's easy," he said. "You just pull on the end of the cable here and I'll do the rest. You don't even need to watch if you don't want to, just make sure you pull real tight and hang on. I won't struggle. It'll be something I've done right, you see?" He started rubbing himself.

"I can't do that," I said. "Stop it, right now."

He was crying.

"You can't stop, once you start," he sobbed. "That's what Mr. A. always said. You can't stop once you join the club." He was pulling on the cable himself now, masturbating madly. I made a dive for him and he leaped up and ran to the pool, his trousers around his ankles. At the same moment, the secret door burst open and Tobin ran into the room.

"Tobin, help me!" I shouted, meaning "help me save this kid," but Tobin dashed between me and Jason and spread his arms like a line-backer, to protect me.

"Not me—him!" I said, but Jason toppled backwards into the pool, didn't even try to save himself, and sank like a rock.

At which point, detective constable Mark Becker entered the scene, slouching casually down the stairs.

"You guys finished unloading yet?" he said. "Anything I can do?"

Epilogue

WOODSMAN: *My life as a woodsman was lonely, you see,*
MOTHER: *But there's three of us now,*
KEVIN: *Like a family, you'll see.*
-The Glass Flute, Scene x

Jason's body was found later that night. The OPP sent a diver down (they didn't blow it off this time, seeing as Becker had been right there), and they found him right away. His half-dressed state and the cable around his neck confirmed my story, but Becker didn't think it was as sad as I did. He was just annoyed that he had missed Jason's confession. At least Tobin had witnessed Jason's last hurrah, and I gave a pretty clear account of the whole thing.

Tobin said that someone had locked him in the sound storage cupboard upstairs. As he was wandering around in the dark trying to find the door (so he could kick it down), he heard footsteps overhead. When he got out, he climbed up the ladder to the attic room, saw the sleeping bag and fast-food boxes and thought it was a vagrant camping out. The entrance to the secret passageway was open and he followed it down to the workshop, carrying a beer bottle as a weapon.

The dead guy they had thought was Jason was, of course, young Negjib Ademi, Ari Ademi's brother. Morrison showed up at the theatre moments after Becker did. Ari had shown him a snapshot of Negjib, and Ari's daughter, Saba, had insisted that she saw Uncle Negjib in the auditorium of the high school, slipping through the backstage door. That's why she had come backstage, to find him. Earlie put the pieces together pretty quickly after that. They were actually further ahead in their investigation (at least Earlie Morrison was) than I gave them credit for.

Jason's parents were no more upset identifying the real body than they had been the first time, according to Morrison.

"Dr. McMaster's a pretty cold guy," he said.

Even with a total of three dead people, the whole mess still ended up being labelled "The Steamboat Incident". I suppose this was because of its connection to the original Incident, and the fact that the murderer wasn't around to face the music. The police still did all the necessary paperwork, and the deaths made the papers, but they were never connected.

The photo that the local newspaper reporter took of Shane, Amber and the puppy did end up on the front page, in full colour, with a discreet little article saying Shane had died of an allergic reaction to alcohol, which, in fact, was true. The audio cable had made him choke on his own vomit, but it hadn't cut off his airway. Jason had still effectively murdered him, but it might have turned out differently if Jason hadn't had the chance to fill the water bottle with gin and pills. I blame myself for that.

The Ademis buried Negjib in a private ceremony which was covered by a total media blackout. The Kosovars had traded one regime for another, I guess.

Jason's death wasn't reported at all. Up here in Kuskawa, suicides never are.

The Glass Flute never did go on tour. In spite of the fact that Juliet plied Amber, Meredith and Brad with drinks, sympathy and the offer of ridiculously high salaries, none of them was up to it. Instead, Juliet called in a bunch of favours and had a remount of *The Happy Little Computer* up and running in less than two weeks, so she didn't lose much money. She didn't offer me the stage manager's position, and I returned the cellphone and laptop.

Meredith got a last-minute gig understudying the role of Anne in *Anne of Green Gables* at a summer festival in Thunder Bay. (Ironic, considering her disastrous Anne in Gananoque, but perhaps that mark against her career died with Shane.)

Brad went back to Toronto and waited on tables for the rest of the summer. I haven't heard how he's doing, but I saw him playing a villain on *Nikita* a while ago.

Amber also went back to Toronto. As her pregnancy, which she decided not to abort, progressed, she got lots of work doing diaper and life insurance commercials. Eventually, she bought a condo and found a nice ad executive to settle down with. She didn't want to keep Portia, so she gave the puppy to me before she left town. Lug-nut now has a buddy, and he's teaching her everything he knows, which is basically how to be a dog. I renamed her Rosencrantz (Rosie for short) because I figured if she was going to be stuck with a Shakespearean name, she might as well have one that wasn't goody-goody.

I made up with Rico, or he made up with me, whichever way you want to look at it. It turned out that he had no clue at all about the original Incident, which is why he was so pissed off at me, because he thought I did, and was keeping it from him. He told me his parents had split up when he was a child and it hadn't been pretty. Visits were rare and heavily supervised, and when his father died, he remembered feeling very little except relief. Whatever it was that made Tony Amato molest young men, it appeared that Rico's Mom had her suspicions about it. When Morrison questioned Rico, he said he wasn't surprised to find out how his biological father had died. That was all he had to say on the subject, and I understood that for me, anyway, that door was shut.

Aunt Susan and Eddie are now firmly established at George's place, and my work as a farm hand seems to be drying up. Eddie is helping out a lot, and Susan has bought a computer and some farming account programs. Her store's still up for sale, and Theresa Morton's running it single-handedly now. She told me she wants to buy it and turn it into a bistro.

The shack belonging to the Neighbour from Hell burned down one night in late August. Old Man Gamble had spent the day loading stuff onto his beat-up pickup truck, and it was pretty obvious he torched it before he left. The parents of the boys never showed up, as far as we could tell, and I think the kids are still in foster care. Probably just as well.

I'm back to making puppets again. Becker and I are getting along better, now that the Steamboat Incident is over. We've been out for Tim Horton's a couple of times, and we've done a careful dance around the possibility of spending an evening in each other's company. It hasn't happened yet, though.

Last week, I was commissioned to design a mascot for a big grocery store chain that's setting up in Laingford. The money's amazing, and the job includes research, focus groups (whatever they are), designing and building a mascot costume (including the head) and training the poor sap who gets to wear it. It sounds like fun and if I'm hanging out in a grocery store, I'm not likely to stumble across any more dead bodies, except the ones nicely butchered, wrapped in cellophane and sold by the kilo.

In case you were wondering, my nose finally healed. It now has a stupid little bump in the middle. Earlie Morrison says I look like a lady wrestler he once had a crush on.

At least my dogs still love me.

photo by Laura Bombier

H. Mel Malton **was** born in Oxford, England, but was raised in Bracebridge, Ontario. After studying at the Ontario College of Art, Ryerson Polytechnic and Acadia University, she toured North America for ten years in the professional theatre business. Mel worked for a number of years as reporter/photographer for a community newspaper in Huntsville, in the Muskoka region of Ontario. She lives in a log cabin on ten acres of swampland and shares her life with two dogs, Karma and Ego. Her first Polly Deacon novel, *Down in the Dumps*, was nominated for a 1999 Arthur Ellis Award for Best First Novel by the Crime Writers of Canada.

Also available in the
RendezVous Crime
series:

Down in the Dumps
by H. Mel Malton

In the first Polly Deacon Mystery, Polly's rural life is violently interrupted when she finds her best friend Francy's abusive husband lying dead in the local dump with a hole in his chest. Exasperated with the ineptitude of the police and determined to shield Francy from suspicion, Polly digs deep into the seamy underside of their small town to uncover the truth.

ISBN 0-929141-66-0—paperback—$10.95 CDN—$8.95 U.S

SPEAK ILL OF THE DEAD
by Mary Jane Maffini

When a vicious fashion guru is crucified in a downtown hotel room, it doesn't really come as a surprise to anyone. Crusty young lawyer Camilla MacPhee's best friend Robin is the police's prime suspect, but she won't talk to anyone. Camilla quickly realizes that she'd better find out who did it fast, because the murderer is leaving a trail of victims, and Camilla has a feeling she'll be next.

ISBN 0-929141-65-2—paperback—$11.95 CDN—$9.95 U.S.